Lost in Heaven

Gary Livengood

Lost in Heaven

An unbeliever's journey
through heaven

Gary Livengood

RIVER BIRCH PRESS

Mesa, Arizona

ISBN 978-1-956365-61-0 (print)
ISBN 978-1-956365-62-7 (e-book)

For Worldwide Distribution
Printed in the U.S.A.

River Birch Press
P.O. Box 7341, Mesa, AZ 85216

*To my wife, Carol, who has shown a divine level of kindness,
love, and patience to me for many years in all my odd pursuits
and interests. Only the most divinely inspired love
could account for her faithfulness to me.
Carol, your faith and love are unsurpassed.*

CONTENTS

PREFACE

I have always wanted to be an author. Reading great sci-fi in my youth and then Tolkien and Lewis, among other great novelists of many persuasions in my college years, only whetted my appetite. But as I widened my worldview and observed those around me, in the workplace, in graduate school at a secular university, in the proverbial "marketplace of employment and ideas," and in numerous media and culturally relevant means of communication, it became more and more clear to me that if I were to write, it must be something of significance.

I had to write something that mattered and addressed, on the deepest level, what my small mind could conceive as the purpose of human existence. That is the great question that every human must face, every human must answer, and every human does answer in one way or another. Sadly most of humanity gets the answer wrong in the end, at least if the precepts and prescriptions of the living God are to be trusted. And I believe they are trustworthy.

The pages herein tell the tale of a man who rejected his childhood faith. (Calvinists and Arminians can argue that out on their own time.) The story indirectly reflects the lives of many people I have known, some of them very close friends. It is written with an urgency and an awareness that, although the story is undoubtedly speculative as to the nature and specific conditions of heaven, it is nonetheless based on the absolute certainty that life does indeed have meaning and purpose. It is by divine design, and there is a God to whom we must answer some day.

The truth that God has shown humanity unfathomable love, patience, grace, and mercy is beyond question. This story endeavors to clarify that via the kindness, compassion, and endless longsuffering shown to the agnostic roaming heaven. Although I do not believe such skeptics will ever roam the realm of heaven, it is nonetheless true that the living God gives common grace to all, incomprehensibly beyond what we should realistically hope. In that regard, I don't believe the essence of this story is in the least outrageous. In fact. I think it may open eyes to a new degree in the appreciation of God.

In Ephesians 1, Paul tells us about God's riches, glory, surpassing greatness, rule, authority, power, dominion, eternity, lordship, and fullness in filling all in all. It's almost as if when Paul opens the spigot in this passage, it becomes a firehose blasting out the majesty and glory of God, so much so that Paul himself could barely shut it off. I sincerely hope that this book has a similar flavor to it in seeing God in new depths of His awesomeness, splendor, and wonder.

And speaking of the great apostle, Paul tells us in his greatest epistle that God is virtually shouting at us throughout the passing of our lives. The Lord reveals Himself through many means regarding His presence, His desires, His calling, and our culpability. Through no necessity or obligation whatsoever, the Lord God declares Himself to us in many portions and in many ways. In fact, that idea may very well be the most fundamental component of this story.

That leads to the second matter at hand, which is disturbing. In the story's antihero, we see the depth of darkness in the human heart's denial and unbelief. God surrounds him with evidence in extraordinary ways, as He has done for all members of the human race. Yet truly, "The heart is more deceitful than all else and is desperately sick; who can understand it?" The culture, the world, the enemy of your soul, wants you to believe that humans are basically good, and God has no real substantial case again us. Nothing could be further from the truth.

I would like to make one comment regarding the character of Melchizedek. Plenty of uncertainty exists about this mysterious Bible character. My description of him may depart far from what commentators and theologians assert, which is my literary license for the sake of the story! I make no claim to any special knowledge of Melchizedek, whomever he may be. He simply serves a redemptive purpose in the story.

Gary Livengood
December 2023

1

Descent into Darkness

I felt as if my body were evaporating . . . vanishing like steam drifting off a boiling pot. Not that I was hot. If anything, I was perhaps cold, but that does not describe the sensation. It was more like . . . becoming empty.

Then I experienced a period of feeling stretched, as if whatever there was of my body was being pulled apart or lengthened. Yet no feeling of pain was attached to this process. It felt as if I were becoming very long.

I was in absolute darkness. I could see nothing, or perhaps my eyes were simply gone. This lasted for a while, although this sensation isn't easily described either. It was impossible to guess the passage of time; it did not have a linear sense. Perhaps there was no time. Maybe it was like being thrust into eternity.

Initially, even though I had fallen seemingly a long way, there was no clear sense of movement. Yet activity of some nature must have happened. I certainly ended up in a place totally unlike that which I left. This was not at all like the accounts I had read of the tunnel that supposedly leads into the afterlife, although I had considered myself an expert on that subject.

Before long, I regained a sense of physical awareness despite my eerie lack of physique. I found myself "standing" on what I took as a rock floor. The floor was not a smooth-cut, polished surface but rough, sharp-edged, cold, and unforgiving in the utter blackness. I spoke once, the only sound I had heard since the beginning of the fall, and the emptiness had an echoing quality. I may have been standing in the black darkness on the pit's floor. I remained standing, but my weight was not like that on Earth. There was no gravity, or my body, what there was of it, had some alternative essence. At moments, perhaps I was floating, but that is somewhat unclear.

Eventually, I began to move and felt what might have been air flowing over me. Without any sense of acceleration, I started soaring headfirst, so it seemed as if I were going up, at a tremendous rate, the air rapidly slipping by. The blackness continued, so the motion of the air was the only realization of movement. Time became real again, as though I had departed from some ethereal state and returned to a linear perception of reality. Perhaps the movement catalyzed this.

For many minutes and perhaps as much as a few hours, I sped what appeared to be upwards. I do not know if the idea of direction had any meaning. If a direction existed in this unearthly expanse, I might have been plummeting downward. But leading with my head as I was and with no sense of gravity, it seemed I was going upwards. For a while, I feared coming to a sudden halt by slamming headfirst into a ceiling of rock or some other hard substance since I could not see anything above me. As this did not happen, I finally overcame the fear of not coming to a halt. When would this dark ascent end?

Over time, the temperature grew uncomfortably hot. This was not due to any energy expenditure on my part; I was neither tired nor hungry, but the environment was changing. Streaks of a reddish light started passing by me, or rather I passed by them, on a vertical plane. These were intermittent, perhaps every ten to fifteen seconds. It was impossible to tell how close or far the lights were from me. They were so faint, so tantalizing, that I thought perhaps my eyes were playing optical tricks on me. I suddenly realized how desperately I longed for light in this black darkness.

The heat continued to increase, and I began to fear the possibility of physical harm. I could not recall any summer day on Earth approaching anywhere near this heat level. Perhaps I was perspiring, but my ascending speed was so great that I could not tell. Despite all the rapid air movement around my body, I was beginning to experience severe pain. I wondered if my skin was turning red from the heat, the first inkling of being cooked, like a lobster thrust alive into the boiling water.

The streaks of red light now appeared more regularly, but focusing on them was impossible. They flew by, or rather I passed by, so quickly that they looked like nothing more than a flash, a meteor tearing through the night sky and gone in a few seconds. And it grew hotter. I was now in agony. I screamed from the searing heat. To my amazement, I believe someone or something shouted an agonized response! It was over so quickly that I barely knew it had happened, yet whoever had shrieked was also clearly in pain, no doubt from the torturous furnace. I am not certain even to this day, and don't think me insane, but I suspect that the tormented cry I heard was from one of the red sparks of light I rocketed past. It also seemed that the voice I heard crying out echoed from behind me as though I was flying through a vast, dark enclosed chamber like a long narrow vertical tunnel.

But the heat . . . Surely my skin must be peeling off my skeleton. I was being cremated alive. I was like a rocket entering the atmosphere with the fiery red-hot buildup of flame blazing across my body, scorching me beyond recognition. I wondered what I would look like if I were to survive.

Then, without warning, I flew into some kind of dense substance with a jelled liquid feel. It was smooth and slightly wet against my body. The sensation itself was not a particularly pleasant one, and in other circumstances, I might have been repulsed at the memory of things on Earth that were slimy or greasy. Here, however, only one thing mattered, and in it, I rejoiced; the heat was gone. Blessed relief! Incredibly, my body felt intact. I felt instant relief and no residual pain from the heat. I pondered momentarily how this could be possible, but the thought quickly dissipated.

I enjoyed the release of fear and pain only long enough to realize that I could not breathe! I had not had a chance to take a deep breath but was unexpectedly thrust into this odd mixture. I would soon suffocate. I could not hold my breath long, and it did not appear that breathing was an option owing to the density of the substance that encased my body. No air was available, wrapped as I was in this cocoon. For an instant, it occurred to me that, although it seemed that earlier my body had strangely dissipated into nothingness, since I had felt the air and now this odd substance against my body, had seen flashes of light, and was aware of my sudden inability to breath must mean that in some sense my physical body had fully returned to me. Then, just as abruptly as I had entered the jelled mass, I was free and again flying headfirst in the darkness. I breathed deeply.

I never saw the flashes of light again.

But now I recognized that it was not as dark as it had been in the black pit. I could not see where I had flown from, but I could tell quickly that this new space was wide open. In fact, on the far distant horizon, I saw a narrow column of light ascending up and up, forever it seemed, until it passed beyond the perception of my sight. The column of light was not pure white but a blended effect of white, rose, and blue. Indeed, many colors merged into something like a rainbow, but there was no bend to this symphony of color. It stretched straight up in the midnight sky and appeared to go on forever.

The horizon out of which this wondrous column of light grew appeared to be much farther away than the horizon on Earth. In fact, given the distance, I am not certain how I saw it as clearly as I did. The scale was much more expansive than that of an earthly horizon.

Still, despite the distant light, it was a night sky from horizon to horizon. As I was staring intently at the column of light, I immediately stopped. There was no deceleration or sense of jerking to a halt, just an instantaneous stop. There I simply floated in the night sky some unknown distance above what I assumed to be the ground.

The distance below, although likely impossible to calculate with much accuracy given the seeming immensity of the surroundings—not to mention my complete alienation from the environment—looked to be many miles. Above me, much like any clear evening in our world, stars were in the sky, although their appearance was distinctly different than in our world. They looked larger, closer, brighter, with a shimmering quality. And there seemed to be an immense pattern, on a cosmic scale, to their arrangement, although its complexity defied definition and description.

The ground far below me did not look like an earthly terrain. There were no lights, no cities, towns, or villages, no roads, and no neatly squared fields with crops. It had a thoroughly unwelcoming look of desolation and emptiness. The light from the distant column ever so slightly illuminated the ground below me. And was it possible, the boundless array of stars overhead also added a dim luminescence to the land?

Nonetheless, the entire scene had the definite look of the night. The abject barrenness of the land far below me gave the night scene a fearful and lonely cast. No sun was lighting the ground or even a moon casting its wan reflection on that planet.

As for me, I simply hung there in the night sky. A sense of timelessness came over me once again. I do not know how long I floated there, perhaps minutes or hours. The very words lose their meaning, and the question of *how long* seems senseless.

At some point, I began to search for the place below me where I must have come up through the ground. There must have been some location where the jelly-like substance was visible. Since all the rest of the soil appeared so featureless, at least from my vantage point, it seemed reasonable that it might be possible to identify my point of origin. Yet, I never saw it. It did not seem likely that it was so small a fissure that it was invisible from my height, but no hint of its location was on the ground. The only alternative was that I did not come up through the ground. That was not much of an answer and gave me no comfort.

I returned my gaze to the column of light. It probably took up no more than one percent of the whole horizon, but it was so striking, so opposite in comparison to everything else, that it demanded my attention. Then I blinked several times. Were my eyes deceiving me? In the far distance of the column, a slight change of brightness had occurred for an instant. Then a thrill of fright ran through me. Something that had come out of the Column was flying toward me at a tremendous speed.

I had experimented too long in things about which I knew too little. That is, I now realize I knew too little, far too little, about those matters. In the beginning, I thought I was informed. And even along the way, I believed I knew enough to control the events I anticipated might transpire.

On the other hand, I am not sure initially that I thought anything would ever happen at all. The skeptic in me, the learned materialist, doubted much of what I had read in religious writings, especially The Book. Indeed some, maybe even most, of my motivation was to disprove something.

In retrospect, I am not sure how I planned to disprove anything. Not being able to reach what was perhaps an impossible destination is hardly proof that what is beyond the arrival point does not exist! We are blinded to the spiritual realm. That was true to a degree I had never dreamed of, but I eventually discovered how deep and dark our blindness is. Seeing dimly as through a glass is an understatement for every human, even perhaps for the one who said it. And I believe he saw the most clearly of all of us that ever lived.

Ultimately, I am certain, no matter how I may try to paint the intellectual canvas, that my purposes came out of rebellion. Rebellion against my childhood training, rebellion against my parents, but mostly, rebellion against God. Deep down, I desperately wanted to prove I answered to no one. I am like a mountain; I am self-sufficient; I am an independent being.

How dull were those silly classes on Sunday morning, those ridiculous stories like the one about a fish swallowing a man. I knew better than such fallacious nonsense, and some of the preachers even agreed with me! The minister at my parents' church believed it all, but plenty did not!

And why did my parents insist I find better friends than John and Bill? I liked being intellectually challenged, although my parents saw their ideas in an entirely different light. "The same old depraved and youthful arrogance dressed up in new clothes," my father once said. Somehow my parents intuitively knew that those friends fed my defiance against authority.

Nonetheless, despite my skepticism that anything or anybody was really out there, I was intrigued. I must have vaguely believed something about the afterlife. My parents had tried endlessly to indoctrinate me into this belief. I heard so many accounts of after-death experiences, which included lights, tunnels, warmth, and peace.

I knew there must be some reasonable basis causing the similarities of these stories from all over the world. Even people who were blind from birth had described post-death scenes exactly like the sighted. It did occur to me early on that it might be the shared race consciousness of primal fears, instincts, and the wish-fulfillment fantasy. Later I realized what malarkey these doctrines were—the stuff of modern man playing the same dangerous hide-and-seek that I was playing, at least at the beginning. In losing this game of hide-and-seek, however, the consequences were of eternal significance.

But the same vexing problem still stared me in the face: how to measure, explore, and research the experience on my own. That was the challenge. Of course, dying was hardly the answer! There had to be another way to enter the spiritual realm, if there was a spiritual realm to enter. And, if there was no spiritual realm, then I would have been right all along. And I was off the hook, in a manner of speaking.

That is where my search began in earnest—how to experience the afterlife and enter that realm, if it existed, without that frightful toll being exacted. To cheat death, as it were. To go there and come back again. In my initial smugness, I even considered that name for my dissertation, one that might carry some scholarly literary merit and lend credence to my efforts: *There and Back Again, A Holiday in the Afterlife.*

I read countless books and articles and searched endless resources to find a path to the Other Side—or to prove there was no Other Side. At times I thought myself insane for searching out such a ridiculous journey, but then some new hint of possibility would surface in an obscure article or book, and I would be aroused anew to keep on the trail. I perused The Graduate Library, the Philosophy Research Library, the Religious Studies Center, went to ancient churches, read books on ancient civilizations, history books, devilish books of spells and rituals, and went anywhere else I thought might have pertinent information.

Some of these places frightened me. In the security of academia, however, along with the others hiding from life, I was soon known by sight in the libraries. Then I was on a first-name basis with the librarians. In two of the libraries, I was dubbed with appropriate titles. The people in the Religious Studies center, certainly the most befuddled and modernly directionless people I have ever known, began jokingly referring to me as Dante. In the Graduate Library, I was renamed Faust. Not surprisingly, those in the philosophy department could not come to any definite conclusion regarding a nickname, unless "what now?" might serve such a purpose. I don't think they liked me.

Surprisingly, my research discovered many bizarre accounts

of journeys to the Other Side. I tried to hold to my materialist values—perhaps a statement of the ultimate oxymoron—but I found that increasingly difficult. Unfortunately, these "journeys" I read about were usually preceded by death! I wanted no part of that, and, in fact, I wonder if perhaps that fear was a more significant catalyst for the whole investigation than I ever cared to consciously admit.

I also read many accounts of occult activities, séances, and "visitations," which fell into two basic categories. The first type was usually attended with ludicrous attempts to lure some spirit (human or otherwise) to come and chat or to convince the familiar to frighten some enemy of the party participants. On the whole, this type of activity was relatively mild.

The second type of occult activity was dangerous, not to mention often illegal, to the point of life-threatening. I'll not reveal any details of the sometimes horrifying and twisted accounts. I have searched them out and read much. Sometimes, I spoke with those who engaged in these redoubtable gatherings. I now think it highly probable in these instances that there were spiritual visitations on some occasions. These always ended in terror and violence, and often even those involved in the summoning seemed shocked and petrified at the events surrounding the visitation. Needless to say, I did not want to repeatedly pursue that direction!

Other possibilities included divinely granted visions and dreams. This did not seem too terribly likely to happen to me. It appeared that a certain degree of religious devotion was required before God was willing to grant such an experience. And I was not too sure that He, if He was even there, was pleased with my investigation. I now know, with frightening clarity, the masculine quality of the Deity. Still, I was so modern at the time that I attempted to consider a potential deity as genderless or multi-gendered.

So, after much research, inquiry, and analysis, I was left with only two alternatives in my efforts to visit the Other Side. One was to physically die. This approach did not hold any interest or viability for me, to say the least!

That left me with only one option.

I shall not give the actual names of people or places that led me to successfully navigate the nexus between this world and the next. Those who are going to the area of life, real life, do not need such information. They know that they shall go there according to His time. Those going to the place of death, the home of utter and final separation from every vestige of goodness, would not benefit from this knowledge. They are already in the first stage of their arrival. And even if someone came back from the dead to warn them, they would not believe their report. They cannot imagine the death they shall finally find! The separation from Goodness is forever beyond human imagination in the most hideous reality.

Some, incredibly, have imagined hell to be a grand party with guiltless indulgence, laughter, and endless satiation of their desires. Some imagine hell to include a hierarchy of rule over others, as if lawlessness and personified evil can support order, organization, and society. Some imagine hell as a blessed relief from the haunting and pursuit of Goodness! Yet they have no knowledge, understanding, or the slightest concept of the endless mercies and delights spread abroad by simply His common grace.

Of these matters of His goodness spread abroad simply by living, hell has no knowledge. This became painfully and horribly clear to me much later on. Those who refuse to see the multiplied blessings of common grace believe the world to be an accident, void ultimately of meaning and purpose. Yet it is common grace that makes this world, this age, a place to be lived in with a measure of joy, happiness, and peace—even, to a degree, for those who reject Him. At length, I found out about this stark and stunning reality. The price was steep indeed.

But, to continue, I sought out a place that I had learned of, located on the East Coast (not far from the university where I was teaching), where a long history of unusual phenomena of a spiritual nature had occurred. Occult activities and exorcism battles had been common, especially at the times in which spiritual awakening was at a fevered pitch.

The descriptions I read of these events were sometimes breathtaking, sometimes frightening: humans howling like wolves, contorting themselves into impossible shapes, foaming at the mouth, uttering unintelligible guttural sounds, throwing themselves into fire, committing sick obscenities, doing incredible feats of physical strength and endurance, abusing themselves beyond belief, and even telling the future with apparently some limited degree of success.

At the same time, righteous and brave men also did astounding acts. (Oddly, there was not a single instance of a woman directly taking up the battle against the forces of evil.) Demons were cast out, people who were supernaturally empowered and possessed were overcome with a single word, screaming lunatics were silenced, the mentally deranged became cogent and rational, and animals suddenly ran off in unexplained terror, never to be seen again.

Generally, this is the last place anyone would ever want to seek out, but by this time, I was addicted. Despite my early revulsion and even loathing, when it began to dawn on me that something authentic was going on in these matters, I was drawn to the darkness—especially the darkness—rather than the side of goodness.

But the Hound of Heaven was at work even then.

In human nature, the very thing that at first horrifies and repulses can also hold a strange and seductive lure. Witness the horror of human deformity. It frightens and draws simultaneously—the more bizarre, the more irresistible! Who cannot help but look? And if not a stare, at least a sly backward glance to see the strange sight. Witness further a tortured conscience regarding some hidden pleasure. The tempted person dreads the very wrongness, the repulsiveness of the allure dancing before his eyes. He knows and fears the wrong and understands well the danger of surrender.

But this is merely the beginning. Each moment of yielding fuels the remedy to the fear, twisting the soul inside out until what was repugnant becomes a secret desire. Then from secret desire comes the admittance of self to the deliciousness of the obsession. From there comes the irrational self-delusion of the goodness of the addiction and the God-given right to indulge! There I was, no longer able to resist, despite all rational arguments that this was dangerous, foolish, perverse, and even alien, as Jude suggests.

I had convinced myself that what I was doing was good, was deserved, and even important despite my recollections of those simpletons, those poor buffoons, who told me so long ago that these things were not to be dabbled with and to not consult with mediums. Those naïve, religiously crutched plebeians could never understand the significance and preponderance of my work. As a materialist, I served humanity by uncovering the falseness of religiosity!

Yes, I had overcome the repulsion. The allure had captured me. Besides, this was research. This was in the name of education—the advancement of knowledge! What higher and holier pursuit could any man strive for? Everything is excused for that calling, the highest of all purposes. Kinsey proved that!

To my initial surprise, but later a sardonic acceptance and private embarrassment that I had ever wondered at this, the prime nexus point was just outside the campus at a major university. Incredibly, funding was available for this research under the auspices of what else but the religious studies department. No one ever audited the progress of the research. This is the unaccountable loophole on which university researchers depend. Nor did administrators ask any questions about what was going on or why. It was our holy pursuit.

The nexus initially had the look of a séance. People chanted antediluvian mantras from some ancient Babylonian mystery religion. Certain symbols were painted on the floors, walls, and even the room's ceiling. The small building, stuffed in a neighborhood of somewhat broken-down old homes housing college students, had the shape of a pyramid. It was a downright moronic-looking structure. If its objective was to keep people away, it worked. If its intent was to not draw attention to its devotees, it didn't.

Interestingly, something about pyramids sends people of a mystical bent into paroxysms of occultic lunacy. Say the word *pyramid* in certain circles, and eyes glaze over, lips begin to twitch, and someone is sure to start chanting, "Marduk . . . Marduk . . ." It is quite the show.

In any case, there was chanting, fire, incense burning, and our delightful special discovery, the Talisman of the Thurrim. This seemed to be a central figure in the whole service, and I was assured, "This was the real thing, delivered from Tel Aviv." The Keeper of the Talisman of the Thurrim had been guarding it closely for some years. However, there didn't seem to be reports of any attempts to steal this supposedly valuable item.

The origins of the Talisman were too incredible to believe. Much of it was tied up with mystical-sounding derivations of overly supernatural Old Testament jargon. Not that I don't believe in the supernatural or the Old Testament. In any case, I do now! Yet sometimes legitimate events that transcend the human experience become their own *raison d'etre*, which is far beyond what their Author desired. Witness Nehushtan.

Near the end of the proceedings, there were some horrors that I cannot describe. There is no appropriate place to recount some things. I have since repented of this agony, and I am not inclined to replay certain torturous events perpetrated on innocent victims, albeit not humans—not yet. Violence to life is an inevitable outgrowth of service to the enemy of the human soul. No matter how it starts, how innocent, or even good it may be twisted to appear initially, the end is violence.

The testimony to human blindness, aided by the lies of that old dragon, screams out by the murder of the innocent for the pleasure, enjoyment, and convenience of the guilty. It starts with animals, but that is not his main interest. He revels in the success of his violence against God's creation of life, of which the devil cannot even manage a poor counterfeit. He is no inventor; he is a savage destroyer, and the more innocent the victim, the more delight he takes in the destruction. The more twisted and perverse the lie by which the "Anointed Cherub" veils the mind, the more satisfied he is with the outcome. By these things, he thinks, in his darkness, to thwart the plans of the Almighty.

During the ritual service I now found myself abiding in, the most significant factor to me was an item called the Walpurgis Door. The door led to nothing, as it seemed, but was lying on the floor in the middle of the room amidst many signs and drawings of a horrific nature. The door was quite old, having been brought from Boston some generations before to its present location. But its history did not begin in Boston. It began, so I was told, in medieval England.

Further information about its history was not forthcoming. Considering its age, it was in surprisingly good condition, made of wood and inlaid with silver. There were numerous inscriptions in a language unknown to me on the front of the door. I never saw the back side.

In retrospect, I see what a fool I was and perhaps how I had been used. I had ingratiated myself with this community of occultists ("scientists") and made my desires known for several months. Inexplicably it never occurred to me that no one in this group had ever actually tried the door on their own! What did this mean? Were they afraid of it? Was I a guinea pig? Did they, deep down, even believe in their own religion, or was much of this just an excuse for the dark pleasures they engaged in during their rituals? The witch of Engedi was shocked when her incantation worked!

After much chanting, blood, the anesthetizing of their conscience by illegal pharmaceuticals, and the bending and contorting of their bodies into strange shapes, I was directed to the center of the room where the ominous and foreboding door lay.

I stepped into the painted circle on the floor, the door at my feet. My mind was flooded with the stimulation of the strange surroundings, the bizarre behavior, and the drugged atmosphere of the room. The noise of loud, crashing, riotous music had now been replaced with a narcotic seductive Eastern-sounding melody. With the sweet smell of incense, the rising mantra of voices, and the veiled darkness lit only by fire and dim red lighting, fear rose within me. The room seemed blurred and hazy.

I was standing now by the door. What to do now? I waited. Perspiration began to soak me, and my trepidation escalated. In a moment, I would flee in fear. I was an idiot for ever seeking this out! For an instant, the slightest shard of clear thought and child-borne spiritual insight leaped through the darkness and the long-lost years to my seven-fold infested mind, screaming, "Flee, flee!"

"I can't do this! I can't do this!" I shouted.

Then I heard a howling scream from behind. I looked around and saw a person, as one possessed, lurching, stumbling, lunging forward toward me with a blood-curdling cry and saliva pouring from its mouth, its hair a jumbled mass of sweat, its eyes red and reflecting the now dim death-like hue of the room. I could not tell, was this a man or a woman? That face was so tortured and twisted into a horrible bent form. Where had this thing come from?

A shiver of terror ran through me. This was out of control. Fool! Fool! This was too real now. My heart raced and pounded in my ears, and my brain reeled in abject horror. I stepped back from the monstrous form approaching me and onto The Door.

It fell open, downward somehow into the solid floor, and I fell headlong into some dark place. And I saw the red hue of the room shrinking above me into the distance, with a hideous mangled face peering down into the darkness.

Then the door slammed shut. I was alone. Falling, as if forever, in darkness, in absolute silence, and my body seemed to be evaporating . . .

2

Odegeo

Something was flying toward me at a tremendous speed out of the distant column of light. At first, it appeared as no more than a point of light in the dark night. After several minutes, perhaps, the point of light became a glow. From a distance, it offered no menace. Even as it neared, it had a warmth, a pleasantness, a welcoming quality. I remembered my childhood Sunday School lessons, and now I wished I had listened because I had a distant recollection of seeing what was approaching.

Incredible as it seemed, I knew that this was an angel. And as it approached quite close, the radiance became piercing and no longer had that sweetness. Instead, it seemed as if I were naked before the light—not as unclothed but as revealed. I did not know it, but countless similar occasions would be ahead. I felt shame before this angel, a sense I had barely recognized at first. It had been so long.

The angel faced me now with no wings. The shining quality was still present, blinding me with dazzling brilliance. Then the angel spoke. "Yes. I will."

Immediately the light dimmed, and my discomfort diminished. No one was around, but clearly, it had not spoken to me.

"It" would not do. I vaguely remember hearing that angels don't have a gender, don't get married, or something along those lines, but this angel was definitely masculine. Masculine to a degree I had never seen before, indeed the very definition of masculinity. By comparison, every man I had ever known now seemed effete. Masculinity suddenly seemed an absolute, not a freely defined, environmentally shaped ebb and flow of culture as I had been taught. This masculinity was something born of a substance sturdier than the Earth itself.

I do not know if I looked terrified, but I was. I did not even make a manly pretense. In my earthly days, I would have covered my fear with my maleness, a show of strength, tough talk, or perhaps even an aggressive gesture at the source of anxiety. That was useless here. I knew that somehow this being would see through any false pretense. And I also suspected, if I were foolish enough to resort to some idiotic display of humanness and audacity that had gotten me here to begin with, that somewhere a lightning bolt with my name on it just might be standing by for me. Arrogance, the rebel attitude, and the haughtiness of my unbelief could all wait. I knew I would be undone in this angel's blink of an eye.

I was desperate for answers, but I spoke respectfully or, more to the point, fearfully.

"Sir, please, I don't know what's happened to me." My voice was trembling. "Where am I? Am I going to die?" These words and many others like them spewed from my mouth rapidly, so great was my confusion and fear. "What's going on here? What is this place? Please, sir, please can you tell me? I admit I'm scared to death."

The angel spoke evenly but powerfully. This was not a serene austere angel of a Renaissance painting.

"I was sent to you because of prayers."

"I haven't been praying!" I found my honesty frightening

and appalling at the same time. That was certainly not the answer I tried or even intended to give. I wanted to lie, but it seemed to be taken away from me. Nonetheless, I was relieved that I was even able to answer at all.

"That much is clear. Not yours."

"I'm sorry?" I said. I did not understand his response. "Hopefully it is not too late for being sorry."

I groped for words. It was clear that we were not communicating. Before I could explain, the angel said, "I understand now. I will say it in this way: I was sent, not because of your prayers but the prayers of others."

"Someone is praying for me? Is that what you are saying, sir?"

The angel's face at this moment had an intense but unemotional quality. Now a look of surprise, even astonishment, came over his face. "Do you not know?" he asked.

"I don't know anything," I said. And I believed at that moment that I really did not know anything. Nothing. My entire pitiful self-indulgent life flashed before me with a shock of recognition as empty, useless, pointless, ridiculous, and now, most poignantly, *godless*. (It wasn't much, but it was a beginning.)

The angel waited patiently.

The fear, strangeness, and alienness of it all suddenly came together in my mind, and I began to weep. I cried long and hard with great wrenching sobs. I would experience many more times of deep and incessant weeping during my journey.

Here I was, in the most bizarre situation that any human had ever known, and I was reduced to tears. Where was I? Who was the Being beside me? How could any of this transpire? What would become of me? Could I get back to Earth? Was there any hope that I could undo things?

And above all else, even amid the inhuman strangeness of this place, like tidal waves pounding the shore, the truth kept pummeling my mind. I intuitively now understood that I had been wrong all along, thoroughly, completely, profoundly, and utterly wrong. All those people (and now the phrase "good people" crept into my mind) at which I had sneered, laughed derisively, held in disdain, and treated contemptuously, scornfully, and with wanton arrogance—they had been right all along, and I had been wrong! In fact, it occurred to me that not only had I been wrong, but I had been dead wrong about the only issue in all of human existence that genuinely mattered!

During my self-examination and weeping, which was a considerable process, the angel waited. He was silent and, it seemed, had complete patience and peace, as if knowing that my introspection was leading me along a path of discovery. When I gained control of my emotions and wits, the angel spoke again.

"Your questions may be answered along the way, but you are here for a purpose. This calling was not . . . accidental." The angel almost seemed to stumble on the word *accidental*. It was as though he did not entirely understand if that was the correct word for the situation, or perhaps he did not know its meaning.

I was suddenly electrified when the significance of the angel's remark hit me. He referred to this as a "calling," not an accident, but a planned event! "If I may, sir, is there some name by which you wish to be called?"

"Yes. You may call me Odegeo."

"Odegeo, sir, you said this was a calling? Does that mean that I am not guilty?"

"You have been anticipated and foreknown. Heaven's calling does not remove your own action in His purpose, but His purposes are so complete that He can redeem even what you intended against Him. He is not thwarted or lessened by your rebellion, nor is your evil any part of His original purpose, but His sovereignty overwhelms all things to bring about His good.

"Am I then to think that He wanted me to—"

"No. That is the very matter to which I have just spoken!" The angel seemed to raise his voice a notch. Do not confuse your action with His reaction. He saw your purpose through eternity, but He did not ordain your action. Yet in His eternal counsels, these deeds become part of His work and glory must come to Him. All things for Him move from love and holiness. All His intentions are for good; indeed, He cannot act in any other way. And do not forget the prayers."

"He is . . . limited then? I mean, He is not totally . . . able to do whatever He wants?"

The angel gave what can only be called a look of amazed pity. "He is free. Only He is truly free. His freedom derives from His sovereignty, which is total and unchallenged. I perceive that what you refer to as freedom to act in a certain way is only the same darkness that was bent on the destruction of your race in Eden. The lie has never changed."

Here the angel appeared almost angry, and the color of his radiance darkened. Then quickly his countenance changed to a deep, profound look of something like sadness, but not exactly like human sorrow. This sadness was deep with comprehension yet without any desperation or hopelessness.

I remember a close friend of mine in college, a man like me of no faith, who had planned to marry. His fiancé was struck dead only weeks before the wedding in a frightful winter auto crash. On my friend's face was utter despair, a crushing hopelessness, an absolute empty sadness that I vowed to avoid in my life at any cost. The angel's sadness did not have that quality; however, I knew he understood humanity's loss in that sadness.

The angel continued. "The freedom to act in any way inconsistent with His nature is no freedom. It is the opposite of freedom. It is bondage and death. It is death in a degree to which you have yet no conception."

It struck me like a slap in the face that Odegeo had just told me that this death was something I did not yet understand, implying that perhaps I just might be required to come to a face-to-face confrontation with this death! Clearly, I was now at the mercy of this angel. I was thoroughly under his management to do whatever He saw fit.

Oddly, the realization that I was at His mercy, briefly brought me a flood of relief. Still, whatever ignorant thoughts I had once maintained regarding this insane venture I had embarked on, that I might be coming and going as I please, that I might be having a grand holiday in the afterlife had all horribly fallen in on me. *It had not been my game at all.* Then suddenly, the fear of seeing death in a way I could not imagine returned to me.

I ventured to ask, my voice trembling, "Odegeo, sir, I see that you said I don't *yet* understand this idea of death. Does that 'yet' mean that something may happen to . . . help me understand what it really is?"

"You shall see. You shall behold the wages for which humanity has worked. You shall behold the darkness, but before that you shall also behold Goodness, not in its wholeness for that would destroy you, but you shall see the blessedness of His realm, and perhaps you will escape the final destiny of your fallen race."

For the second but not the last time, I wept.

After some time, I recovered my composure. I began to take stock of my situation. In the initial stunning presence of this spiritual power before me, I had forgotten the incredible surroundings. Here I was, still strangely suspended miles above the dark and ominous planet below. By what means I was upheld, I did not know. Why I did not plummet helplessly into the planet's surface due to what must have been a tremendous gravitational pull was a mystery to me. This planet somehow appeared much more extensive than Earth. Indeed, how my very life was sustained at that moment was a mystery. I was breathing, but it seemed unlikely that this planet supported an Earth-like oxygen atmosphere.

We were a reasonable distance above the planet's surface, which on Earth would no doubt have meant a scarcity of oxygen. And, of course, that further implied that it must be bitterly cold at this altitude. The planet was not turning, although this was difficult to tell. It did not seem to be turning below us unless we were in perfect harmony with its rotation.

However, I did observe that the stars appeared to remain in the exact location, although I still had no awareness of the passage of time. It could have been minutes or hours since the angel had found me. This possibly indicated that this world was not in motion, but my knowledge of astronomy was so scant that I did not know for sure what this meant.

I had the eerie suspicion that this whole world was waiting for something. Just waiting and waiting. Further, the planet was unchanged in its relationship to the Column of Light. Something about that Column seemed deep, permanent, and foundational. It was as if the Column was a measuring stick, unmoving in a transient universe. The planet depended somehow on the Column. The Column did not move; therefore, the planet did not move.

Again the angel appeared to be patiently waiting. Whether for me to attempt to acclimate myself to the alien surroundings or whether awaiting some further instructions from an unseen authority, I do not know.

Presently Odegeo spoke. "We must go."

I am unsure if staying or going was more scary, but I had no choice. Without any apparent effort or sense of acceleration, we began to move. The angel did not touch me; we simply moved together as if being in his presence was enough to suffice. What alarmed me was not the movement or even the certainty that we were moving at a speed that I had never before experienced, but the direction of the movement was disconcerting. The angel was bearing down directly on the great column of light in the distance from which he had come.

As we approached the Column, the beauty of the pillar of light began to be revealed. The Column now took up my entire field of vision, and its size consumed my view. On its surface, a delicate intertwining of streaming and moving colors were in endless patterns of indescribable but delightful shapes and sizes. Some of the light designs appeared to run up and down the length of the Column for many miles. Others twisted around the Column out of my sight and re-emerged in fantastic shapes and configurations. The patterns seemed to vibrate at some times, and at other times, the figures shifted entirely into new and beautiful lines of vivid, flowing color.

Then they were weaving in and out, moving back and forth, and in the wonder of this marvel, the lattice-like combinations took on a three-dimensional appearance.

"What does this mean?" I asked in delighted wonder.

"It represents Him." Odegeo answered.

I stumbled for words. "How… how can it, how does it…"

"Everything comes into His purpose. This Column of Light, as you comprehend it to be, begins the movement, the shapes, the patterns, in ever new and unexpected ways, but He forms and designs them into things of beauty and purpose, never repeating themselves. The Column perceives the movements of the creation and interprets them in these lights and colors, but He shapes the paradigm and gives it meaning, makes it comprehensible."

"Wait a minute, sir…" I stammered again for words, for the revelation from Odegeo had stunned me. "Are you saying that this Column of Light is… a… living thing? And that what we are seeing is actually… somehow… reflecting actual events?"

"It lives, but in a way that you perhaps cannot conceive."

"Is it intelligent?"

Odegeo paused at the question, again as if listening to a voice I could not hear. Then he spoke. "It is a living instrument of His creation; it declares His glory. You did not know that?"

"I didn't… How could I know? I have never been here; I have never seen such a wonder!"

"The heavens declare!" For the first time, Odegeo had spoken in an animated tone. A depth of excitement seemed to rise within him, and the light of his being burst forth. He suddenly began to sing, but I cannot remember what he sang. It was not in any earthly language nor in any earthly tonality. I had never heard such music, but it was both somber and glorious, mysterious and declarative. If this is the music of heaven, the song alone will heal every hurt, every pain, every disappointment, every shred of despair, every broken dream, and every broken heart. I wept for time untold at the song and the Column and the glory and grace, the undeserved mercy, lavished on me, the son of rebellion in my pursuit of darkness.

Then somehow, the song of Odegeo took on its own life and was formed into an elusive and delicate substance, like a gossamer wing of rainbow colors, now leaping, now darting through the dazzling interstices of the Living light. Like a shimmering veil stretching out above us, the song was taken into the Living Column and intertwined with the light and glory. The beauty and the song became part of the pattern and were woven into the paradigm of His design.

After a while, I realized that the song had ended, and the angel was allowing me to gaze in astonishment at this overwhelming beauty. I do not know how long I stayed there. It could have been days by human standards. I was utterly and endlessly transfixed by the awesome display of light, the indescribable color, and the mysterious and magnificent complexities. And I knew that there was meaning in this beauty. It was not random or accidental. It was purposeful, and it meant something.

"It is ever changing, never ending yet never repeating. It is like Him."

For some time, I continued to stare at the Column and pondered the meaning of the angel's words. At last I spoke, not turning my eyes away from the Column, seeking understanding. "You mean . . . He is always changing? I thought He was always the same or something like that."

"He is said to be immutable in human terms, but that it not the best way to describe Him."

"Then He is not immutable? I mean, He is changeable after all?"

The angel hesitated, searching for the words to explain the eternal to the temporal, the immortal to the mortal. In what must have been eons of time for a celestial mind of the magnitude of Odegeo, he formed a response. I knew he was not confused about the truth of the answer, nor was he questioning the reality of immutability, but how to elucidate such profundities to one such as me: foolish, blind, ignorant, and faithless.

Finally he spoke. "He does not change. He cannot change, for He is perfect, eternal, and infinite in every expression of His nature. There is no change in Him, for change could only move to imperfection, in which case, He could not have been God. Yet He is never the same.

"He is always new, for He is not aged, and He does not age. He is outside of time. He is above time. That is how He can exist without beginning and without end. Time exists in Him, not outside of Him. Otherwise, time would be His master, which cannot be. Time is a small thing to Him, like a shard of crystal that captures the light for an instant and shines out a ray of brilliance for a moment, but it quickly passes. One day He will bring time itself to an end. It will have been like a grain of sand on an everlasting shore. He does not move through time as you do. His existence is not linear as is yours. He encompasses all things. All things exist together, simultaneously, and in perfect order for Him."

My mind reeled at this revelation; however, I never turned away from the Column.

The angel spoke again. "All the things of heaven, that is,

those things untouched, unspoiled by sin, reflect Him. They must. Such is His sovereignty."

"This Column . . . it is alive," I stammered. "It is . . . astonishing, it is . . . indescribable."

"It is a great creation, but you shall see greater yet, for He is eternal and infinite."

"I can't believe that. I can't . . ." I said.

"Such has been your existence."

I realized that Odegeo had made a remark that in other locales would have been interpreted as sarcasm. It was simply the stark acknowledgment of my life's predicament, unbelief.

"It is just that it is utterly beyond my experience, my comprehension."

"We must go," the angel said suddenly.

"I am in your hands, sir," I said with some sadness. "However, I hate to leave this sight."

"We are not leaving the Column," he said. "We are entering it."

3

The Column

As we approached the Column of Light, I swallowed hard. It amazed me, yet I approached it with apprehension. Brighter and brighter, it shone in my eyes, yet not painfully so. My vision seemed expanded, able to take in more than human physiology would typically allow. The brilliance of the light and shapes dancing upon its surface were close now.

I reached out to touch the surface but felt a warmth and a tingling in my fingers that climbed up my arm. And, although it was only a fleeting instant of perception, it looked as if the fabulous designs on its surface began to run up my arm, dancing across my skin!

Then we were inside the surface. There was nothing solid or hard about it. Odegeo and I seemed to float right into the Column. The only visual sensation was an instant of darkness, like a blink. My body, however, underwent a thrill of almost electric stimulation, not enough to hurt, but a definite wave of energy.

I am not sure how thick, if that is even the right word, the outer "wall" might have been. It only took a few seconds to pass through. It was difficult to tell the size of the inside. It seemed huge, yet there was no way to appreciate the scale initially. Later I realized that the Column is of different sizes in different places and is massive in its inner concourse.

There was no sign of the weaving and intersecting patterns on the inside. The inner wall seemed solid; however, I had little time to analyze its appearance. No floor was visible, but we immediately began to ascend, leaving behind the dark and dead world below. This time, instead of abject darkness, there was light. And although, for the most part, the ascent at the beginning was quiet, the sound of something faintly musical occasionally seemed to echo down the Column.

Despite the beauty and wonder of my surroundings, uneasiness was growing upon me. After some time, though that word had become nebulous, I ventured to ask my guide a question. "Sir, may I ask where we are going?"

As I turned to look at this angel, expecting his response, I noticed that a change had come over him. The brightness of his presence had not left him, but it appeared to be taking on a golden hue! Even more surprising was the look on his face. Previously he seemed spiritual, but now Odegeo seemed almost human, or at least the most human I had seen in him. He clearly had a look of joyful anticipation, a look of knowing gladness as any human might have when expecting something extraordinary.

It flashed through my mind that perhaps the expression on his face was really more intrinsically heavenly than human and that maybe our human faces are the anomaly as we bear the brunt of life and the toll exacted by what I now understand to be rebellion. I also noticed that he was looking upward. I had the distinct impression that I was in the presence of someone heading toward a sweet homecoming after a long time away. Indeed, as it turned out, that was the case.

Then, as if startled out of a dream, Odegeo came to my question. "Yes, we are going to heaven, as you would call it. I have been away." He seemed to be musing over this, remembering sweetly the pleasures and peace that he had deeply missed.

I had not expected such sentiments from an angel, yet I understood them perfectly. His frame of mind overwhelmed me so that I was momentarily swept back to a place in my life where I had been happy, peaceful, and totally free of worry.

My childhood summers were especially idyllic: happy, secure, and bright, with seemingly infinite days of play with my brothers. Lying in the warm grass, looking up at an endless royal blue sky, and believing my life would always be blissful, full of love and joy. At night I would sit in the living room with my family, enjoying pure and innocent fun and entertainment. The windows and doors would be opened to the cooling night air, and the huge exhaust fan my father put up every summer to pull in the night air would drone in the background, the humming of security as I now understand. My mother would cut the ripe, juicy watermelon, and we three boys would bury our faces in that delicious and cold heavenly delight.

Lying in bed at night, I could hear the gentle wind in the trees or feel the thrill of a summer storm as the lightning flashed and the thunder crashed. Or hear the washing of summer rain on the street, the popping against the roof, and even those sultry, humid July nights when the whir of that fan could not draw a breath of relief over my body in the sweltering Midwest heat—sleep came reluctantly on *those* nights.

The occasional car lumbered down our quiet road with lights ever so briefly dashing across the walls of our bedroom when it caught just the right angle from the street, and again the night air flowed over my body as it streamed through the house. That fan! Who would have thought that such a contraption could come to have such meaning!

I remember having a sense of family, security, peace, comfort, and even purpose. Why and how had I abandoned such a life? What went wrong? Was there no hope of returning? I wanted to go back so badly and live it again, to see the symbols of home again, to hear the sounds of home again, to smell the smells of home again. This was where I differed from Odegeo. He had left his heaven, but he was coming back. He *could* come back.

I could not.

His heaven was a reality. Mine was now a lost memory to which I could never return, a nostalgia, a sentimentality.

I suddenly snapped out of my reverie, finally realizing the force of what Odegeo had said. Heaven! We were going to heaven! Was I going to see heaven, what every human dreams of and fantasizes about? I knew I had no business entering that realm! Was it possible I would be allowed in? Or perhaps I would be separated from my guide. Although I could hardly say I knew Odegeo, I already felt such a solid link to him that the thought of separation unnerved me. In this utterly alien universe (perhaps *I* was the true alien), Odegeo was my link to reality, maybe even sanity! Without him, I would be completely unable to understand my existence here, my purpose here, and what was happening around me.

Nonetheless, I was both thrilled and terrified at the prospect of heaven. And the uneasiness in both my mind and soul grew. I was in turmoil. I knew who was in heaven and what was my standing likely before Him.

Then, far above me, I saw a large widening area. It was the end of the Column and the beginning of heaven. I knew that heaven, whatever it may be, was near and that I would soon be in a Presence that may not be altogether pleased with me, maybe not pleased at all.

I had thought at one time that when I would stand before Him, if that was even necessary, I would simply recount all my good deeds, all my service to humanity, and remind Him that I was as good as—no, better than my neighbor! I could point to my neighbor Mr. Henderson and assure the Almighty that I was indeed a better person than him!

And that might even be true on some level, but as I would find out, it meant nothing in the face of absolute eternal unbounded perfection. Of course, for most of my adult life, I had rejected the necessity of accounting to a supreme being, but that idea had suddenly been forced out of my mind.

I did not want, at this moment, to be pondering my moral inadequacy nor the preposterous idea of the goodness of the next guy, yet I suddenly seemed unable to shut my rebellion out of my mind. I had done this so successfully for so many years that when it flooded in, I was shocked and stunned at my own depravity. I wanted to feel the joy and thrill of happiness that Odegeo was experiencing. Yet, I was more and more overcome with the agony of my sin. I had been adept at calling it by other names. I had redefined it. I had modernized it. I had even occasionally pretended that it was good and healthy!

Now I was just barely beginning to know my life's abject guilt and shame. Long-buried words from some forgotten story boiled up, now screaming through my mind, "Unclean! Unclean!" Now the words applied to me, and I knew vaguely that the story from which they came was out of my childhood, one of the many old stories from that Book that I had relegated to the realm of the irrelevant.

We came to the top of the Column where the opening was and were delivered gently to the ground surrounding it. We stepped out of the circumference of the column and onto the land of heaven. Now, at last, I was able to walk. The ground was solid, though not hard. It had a blue cast, perhaps reflecting the perfect blue sky above. I do not know how long it had been since I had walked, and I wish I could have enjoyed the experience, but I was still overwhelmed by the deepening understanding and knowledge of my sin.

I now admitted that word into my mind. There was nowhere to hide in this world; no excuse would be acceptable, no blame could be cast anywhere, no cry of unfair treatment, no whining lies about some past slight or plea of victimization. I realized that a moment of bluntness, of abject honesty, of bleak, searing, naked admission about my failures before Him was coming. I did not know when this moment would arrive, but I knew its inevitable approach.

Odegeo pointed to a far distant glow of light toward the horizon, fanning out to illuminate much of the sky in that region. As I focused, I saw the light had a gleaming bright golden color with dazzling whirling sparkles like diamonds occasionally flashing above it, similar to lightning at times and then more like intricate fireworks. These were interspersed with the appearance of gigantic cosmic-sized wheels rising up and turning, twisting, and rotating in and out between each other and through each other in the sky in the most vividly intense electric blue arcs of radiance and energy. Sometimes they throbbed or pulsated and sometimes leapt out in wild fiery dances in a riot of labyrinthine patterns.

At times this ultra-blue radiance reflected in the golden sky so that the sky's hue subtly changed to a brilliant golden blue. Words cannot capture this color; it is beyond human sight. I have never seen this epitome of color anywhere else, but it must surely be the most heavenly hue, the perfection of color.

The perspective was impossible. These sky scenes must have been on a tremendous scale to be seen from this distance. I did not know how far the golden place was (nor did it matter at that moment, whereas on Earth, there would have been much concern about distance and time). Perhaps it was hundreds of miles across, with all manner of terrain along the way—mountainous areas, valleys, woods, waters of rivers and lakes, and areas of vast green grasslands.

"It is the City of God," Odegeo said with great reverence and longing.

I intuitively knew what awaited me there. Despite my fear of a particularly terrifying judgment, there was also a deep desire. Never have I known such a contradiction in my soul: chilling dread and profound longing touching the very purpose of my existence. Both assailed me feverishly at the same time. The whole pitch of heaven was purity and goodness, and here was I, an unclean thing, undone, a man who had purposefully rejected, denied, and even blasphemed in defiance against Him!

Yet now I longed to come before that Throne for absolution and propitiation. Oh, wretched man that I am! I quaked in fear and cried in longing! Memories flooded my mind, recollections of lies and compromises, cheating and blaming, lusting and using, hatred and jealousy, profanities and vulgarities, anger and deceit, coveting and greed. I remember hurting those who loved me and betraying those who cared for me. I recalled laughing at devotion and sneering at sacraments. I relived seasons of applauding the darkness and striving to invent new ways to experience evil. Again, I collapsed, for what seemed like hours, into a quaking, quivering, sobbing, pathetic thing.

But somewhere in the deepest recesses of memory, during my greatest agony of regret, I also recalled the golden light of an old church in my youth, those ancient-looking ceiling lights with their softly diffused light, not bright, but warmly inviting.

I remembered those classrooms with the painted cinder block walls, the flannel graphs with the stories of a great fish, a huge boat, and a slain giant.

I remembered the long sermons (I always wondered if the adults really were listening as much as they seemed), the songs from an old green book, the ringing of the piano, and the organ as the people sang.

I remembered the squirming, the waiting, and the certainty that we would be sitting in that seat (a "pew," I think they called it) forever, but also the security of my parents, a pencil, and a sheet of paper on which to draw.

I remembered the choir in the front and their robes (I thought them silly), their songs that I could never understand, and an occasional cantata (just a very long song, to my mind).

I remembered those windows, the many colors, curving lines, symbols, and figures in the glass.

I remembered those Sunday lunches, playing with friends, and eating with families.

I remembered those Wednesday nights, the peaceful sanctity of loving teachers, running and laughing through the church, hoping and pleading to stay just a little bit longer with my friends, then dashing madly across the parking lot in a race with my brothers for the car.

What sweetness it all was! Lost sweetness. What sadness now pierced me with those radiant memories. Such happiness, warmth, peace, and security. Even those things I did not grasp or comprehend at the time, I remembered now with crystal clarity, calling to me through the years, miles, and darkness. Memory beckoned me to come back. Still, I feared that the sweetness of those days had slipped away forever, the precious crystalline memories broken into irretrievable shards like the heart of the one who had swept from his soul the very essence of goodness and thus passed out of time's reach into the harsh reality of lostness.

What happened to me? What had I become? Again, I asked those questions. *Why did I leave it all behind for vanity, futility, and darkness?*

Odegeo, seeing my misery and waiting patiently, eventually comforted me with the simple, most wondrous and undeserving words: "Grace to you, friend."

I wept again at his words, but this time the dawn of something sweet was in my tears. Grace to me, to *me* of all people! I realized that *He waited for me*. He waited. How is it that He waited for me? How sublime, ridiculous, and astonishing that He waited for me!

It was time to go.

4

Arrival

We began to walk toward the far distant City. Here the sky above us stretched up endlessly. It looked infinite in depth and height and sparkled in a bright blue hue. It was somehow much higher than the sky in my world and was glorious! There may have even been a faint hint of a few clouds, so far up that they were barely discernable. Just a few were barely straddling a tiny part of the cosmic heavens; what did they call them on Earth, cirrus? Yes, the cirrus clouds, the highest of all I believe. They were feathery white, scraping the ceiling of this blue glory, except that these clouds now began moving in opposite directions. If that was the wind in the upper stratosphere blowing the clouds around as on Earth, it was a strange wind!

Perhaps they were not clouds after all. I never found out for sure, but the brilliant golden blue of the vast heavens radiated joy to my soul and spoke to me of something immense, deep, and limitless. Something long asleep was beginning to awaken in my heart.

But on Earth, the journey to the City would have been a daunting task and may have easily occupied days or even weeks and required carrying supplies. However, no thought of such labor or concern for preparation was required here.

My physical body had been strangely altered somehow during my transportation out of the Red Hue Room through that cosmic darkness and out of the dark planet from which I had ascended. My physical body was now back, but certainly not back to normal. My physical conditioning on Earth had been none-too-great, especially through my college years, as I had begun experimenting with the typical temptations, allowing for some loss of body tone and stamina. Yet here, I soon had nearly unlimited endurance; even though tiredness would come, I could still go forward without great muscular pain or exhaustion. Even in weariness, refreshment and energy came quickly.

My skin began to develop a rich golden tone I had never had on Earth. My hair grew rapidly and seemed to enjoy a healthy radiance I had never seen before. A nagging ankle injury from my high school days completely disappeared. My muscles hardened and eventually honed to an almost rippling effect. I began to look masculine, maybe as I was originally intended to be!

Perhaps it was simply the absolute purity of heaven that invaded my being: the air, water, plants, fruit hanging pristinely and plumply on the trees, and just being with Odegeo. Everything was pure in its essence except me.

We walked. I remembered the visions of the future that men had dreamed of on Earth: flying cars, all manner of airplanes and rockets, highways in the sky, and magical transporting machines. Heaven had no need or want of such devices.

Walking was filled with delight here. I had not enjoyed walking in years. Sometimes we ran, not to hurry, but just for the sheer joy of it! I remembered as a child just running to run. Odegeo now almost seemed childlike as he filled himself with the pleasure of heaven and being. Sometimes he would laugh, and the sound was music to my ears.

The sound of laughter in my earthly life now seemed hollow and pitiful; not really laughter at all, but a warped and dissonant smirking derision usually at the expense of another human. It was always all done out of cynicism and sarcasm (I was so knowing and superior), or even worse, the too-loud and peer-forced snickering at some perversity or degradation of human function.

But this was laughter from the soul. This was cleansing. And in it was the thinnest of lines from the most wholesome and joyous weeping. Indeed, I repeatedly fell straight from uproarious laughter to purifying rapturous tears within an instant. It was not from sorrow, but from fullness; not from darkness, but from the light; not from remorse and regret, but from hope and promise. My soul was moving past the plane of mere existence into a speechless, blessed realm, where joy and tears conjoin in the same exuberance of presence in the eternal moment.

The distance we traversed must have been many miles. There appeared to be no nighttime in this heavenly land, although Odegeo said once that heaven is not without night but so close to the Throne it cannot exist. Farther areas of the original heaven allow for darkness, but it does not result from cosmological movement. I did not know what Odegeo meant by original heaven and its darkness, but eventually, I would find out.

Despite the lack of nighttime, we did sleep numerous times. This slumber was not the result of exhaustion but more like a sweet and holy narcotic. For me at least, the sleep in heaven was deep and pure. And each time I awoke, I felt more real, alive, and solid, as if I were becoming what I was supposed to be by the original design.

I also noticed that Odegeo was becoming more aware of

and at ease with my humanness. That is, he better understood the essence of a human being. I began to sense that he had known humanity long ago but had been separated from human interaction and had simply forgotten what we were like. When he first met me, suspended in that night sky, he had seemed uneasy and uncertain toward me, not appearing to understand me. Now, however, he seemed quite free and, in some sense, relaxed in my presence. I did not feel the freedom to ask him about his history, at least not yet. I wondered, if my suspicion about his separation from humans was correct, where had he been, what had he been doing for decades? Or centuries? Or millennia? What had kept him apart from the human race?

But the journey from the column to the city! Such richness of life and living things! Through every glade and woods, over every creek and rushing river, climbing a mountain or careening headlong down steep valleys was wild and often thrilling. It was a degree of life I had never known and not dreamed possible.

The greenness of the life, the blueness of the waters, and the crispness of the air were all electrifying. And the animals! Some I thought I recognized (indescribably beautiful snakes with legs that could walk upright!) and other animals that were completely unearthly. I had not seen or heard of these in any biology studies. These animals were intelligent, and it seemed at times as if they could speak to me. My guide clearly knew the language of these beasts, although such a word seemed unworthy of them, and he appeared to communicate with them. Several obviously greeted him with great delight as in the meeting of old friends long parted.

And Odegeo was not an angel out of a Raphael painting! This was not a serene, expressionless, ambivalent incorporeality born out of the disconnected art of human history. No, this angel was alive with the thrill of this place, the rush of the fullness of life unknown on our hard-baked, sad little planet where the excitement was often concocted, arranged, or contrived. Odegeo was clearly home.

So wondrous, so complete was this time of travel that I was often able to put out of my mind the meeting that must surely await me. Occasionally it would come back to me that we were heading for the City. This would leave me temporarily uneasy and even fearful. Those moments did not last long. Still, when the distant City would intermittently come into view through the trees, above the hills, or across an expanse of water, I knew an inevitable appointment was pending.

After much travel and what must have been many days, we stood together at the top of a cliff, on a lush glade of the most vibrant, verdant tall grass imaginable. We were high up, several thousand feet at least, at the edge of a majestic forest of tall, stately trees in full leaf, from which we had just emerged. It was silent in this place, the silence of complete peace, contentment, and fullness. It called me back yet again to remembrances of my childhood, in those mysterious earthly moments when eternity reaches out to humanity with a whisper of what awaits, the deepness of unknown and indefinable desire for goodness fulfilled. I had felt those longings and known that there was a place, somewhere, where the dream came true. Eternity was in my heart.

But here, it was real and permanent. Ahead we looked out over a landscape below us of thousands upon thousands of multi-hued green trees, a spectrum of every green color ever invented, blanketing for still many miles ahead the undulating hills rolling through the mountains. The slightest cool breeze caressed and refreshed my face. The light of the heavens of heaven, that brilliance of blue in the sky, sometimes almost piercingly so (yet there was no sun) was basking and bathing every inch of the glorious scene with the brightness of the most perfect day ever dreamt of on Earth. I could not take it all in.

The beauty smote me in a place of desperate longing. The peace and joy were too much, too large for simple human comprehension. I flashed back to a summer day in my early college years when I knew my life was headed in the wrong direction, yet I could still sense the divine. I looked out at majestic trees in the distance blowing gracefully in the wind, framed by a June-blue sky, clouds wafting distantly, ethereally, timelessly, miles above me, which were untouchable and indifferent to me. The summer sun flooded the world with light, warmth, and goodness. An enormous longing came over me that nearly broke my heart. I yearned for beauty, wholeness, and something to fill my heart and soul forever.

Heaven is, perhaps, an ever-increasing ability to grasp the infinitude of God. This would be an eternal pursuit of the Eternal One. The purity, perfection, and purpose of it all struck me again in a season of laughter and weeping.

Still off in the distance but much closer now was the place of the lightning and an occasional view of wheels in the heavens that I had seen when we first entered. I almost avoided looking at it now for two reasons. First, I knew that this was the place of the Throne, and I would have business to attend to there—business that terrified me. But also, the scene in the sky above that City was so mesmerizing that to look upon it was nearly addictive. It was a dangerous beauty that was almost impossible to turn away from.

Farther off now, I saw a new wonder. An endless flat, shimmering area seemed to stretch far beyond the City's shape. It looked like a massive river that would appear lengthwise from a great distance and height. I could not recall any mention of the lakes or rivers in heaven from the long-lost Bible stories, not that it would carry much accuracy for me. Whatever the shimmering place might be, it could wait. The majesty of this present view was glorious.

I asked Odegeo about this place we had been traveling through. "This is not what I would have expected to see in heaven! It's amazing, it's . . . it's beyond my imagination, but I never thought of such a place here!"

"What is it about this that you did not expect?" he asked.

"The trees, animals, rivers, and mountains like on Earth. Not the same as Earth but the same design."

"Did you not know?"

"Know what?" I asked.

"This is Eden."

I was stunned at this revelation, and I noticed that he did not hesitate to call it Eden! Odegeo seemed to know little of some places or things about Earth and had even hesitated to form an answer or statement, almost as if he were listening to some unknown voice in his mind. Eden, however, was no stranger to him.

"Eden?" I said. "You mean that stuff about a garden? You mean that was not a legend?"

"By legend you mean a story about something that is not real?"

"Well, yes," I said, feeling sudden embarrassment like an untrained novice about to admit to yet another area of ignorance.

"Eden was and is real. The earthly place, where I served for a season, though a place of wonder and glory, was a shadow of this Eden. Yet, the Eden of your world was to have grown and become all that this Eden is and perhaps more." Odegeo spoke here with excitement. "His plan was perfect, astonishing, and beyond the grasp of even the greatest of our host." Then suddenly, he hesitated and spoke quietly, reflectively, almost as if I were not with him. "I was there in Eden. Mine was the flaming sword." Odegeo paused, then said softly, "If only . . ."

Odegeo hesitated. He was not at a loss for words, but he seemed almost wistful about what could have been but was lost. At that moment I did not understand what he meant about the flaming sword, but I knew what he was thinking about in the wistfulness of his, "If only. . ." Even my dim memories from The Book could recall that story. The serpent, the woman, the apple . . .

"But, surely, sir," I said, "He can remake it or redo it all, or something. I mean, He *is* God and all. Couldn't He just go back in time and change everything to make it right? To make it how He wanted it?"

"Time is not a question for Him. It all exists as a now for Him without forward or backward. He could go back, as you describe it in your frame, but He will not. And He would not change His plan or purpose for eternity. What was lost is lost forever. He is more pleased to redeem than to remake. It is an even greater glory. Remaking is part of redeeming, but the essence is different. He does not desire to remake or restart to perfect.

"So great is His desire to love and be loved for who He is, that even He will not violate that freedom that He gave. To remake for the purpose of establishing a fettered will is not His way. What your race has chosen was not hidden from

Him. He knew it would be such, yet He is ever-redeeming. And in this you see in Him a love and grace which even the angels did not know. His desire to redeem amazed all of us, but much more wondrous to us was His means of redemption."

"But, sir," I asked, "if hell is real and forever, why would He have created the world and allowed such a disaster?"

"Did you think that because of the failure in Eden, not His failure but yours, that He must be bound to give up, try again, or make the most of a bad situation? Do you not know that the Scriptures record that He pronounced it as "good" and even "very good?" What He has pronounced as very good cannot be undone and cannot be improved upon! (Here Odegeo seemed almost agitated.) Because it was His plan, it was perfect, and there was no better way. If He were mortal or limited, then it would have been a failure on His part. But He sees all outcomes all ways with all possibilities, and still He counseled it as so."

"But, sir, isn't that a little bit of the ends justifying the means? It didn't work out quite right so we just say, well, that must have been what was meant to happen anyway?"

"Did you not hear me? Understand this: He sees every possibility. He sees every contingency, every outcome of every free choice that was not made. Did you think that what you call omniscience might simply mean He knows everything that has happened and will happen? No, friend. He knows every possible outcome of every possible choice that could have been made by every creature that has ever and will ever live. Time, choice, contingencies, and destinies are beyond the finite. Our attempt to contain such knowledge must always end finally in either some measure of doubt due to our own limitation or the free acknowledgment of our own inability."

I pondered two of Odegeo's statements. First, I was surprised even he was overwhelmed by God's eternity and infinitely faceted workings. Second and far more significant was the vast and overpowering idea that God knows *every possibility of every possibility.* If I understood this correctly, it was easily the most mind-boggling consideration ever to enter my puny brain. In fact, the attempt to grasp such an idea was to admit to the utter failure of its apprehension. I finally came to no other conclusion but absolute awe.

"Why did He do it?" I asked, but now not from doubt or angry and shallow human sentiment, but from something far beyond amazement, reeling at the comprehension of the magnitude of God's Being.

"We have longed to look into this, to comprehend His love and how it determines His sovereignty and the freedom He offers. Where do they begin and end? Where do they agree, where are their paths intertwined, and where are they divided? Where does a single act part the flow of history, and how does He know and permit the liberty of the act performed apart from Himself yet ordain its existence from the foundation of the universe? He intertwines the perilous and uncoerced freedom of His creation with the inexorable and irresistible accomplishing of His will. These counsels are inscrutable and unknowable. To consider such things is to think about what is closest to discovering the depths, breadth, and height of who He is.

"However, you must not go beyond the gaze of the Scriptures in your meditations. Some in your world have imagined too much and ascribed things to Him that are not worthy of Him, although on the surface they seemed noble. It is perilous to wonder outside the realm of truth. When you ponder the things of the Almighty, as is noble to do, you must be careful to stay within the bounds of His attributes and nature. Otherwise, you will ultimately create God in your image. Such has been the pattern of man."

Then Odegeo added, in a most surprising segue, "How is it that Eden, the garden of God on your Earth, could be thought of as not real?"

That question had no easy answer! Certainly, it would only provide more embarrassment for me and the whole human race. How could we not believe in the most real place I had ever been? I decided to avoid Odegeo's question and hastened to a different subject.

"Does it rain here, sir? I mean, all this life and growth must require lots of rain, yet there are no rain clouds."

"Rain is that water that comes from the sky in your world."

I was not sure if Odegeo was asking me or telling me, but I answered, "Yes, that is how our plants, trees, and crops are watered."

"It is not so here, although I have heard of a place where the water falls from the heavens. I have never seen it."

This was another revelation to me. There were places in heaven that he had never seen? It had not occurred to me that heaven was, well, large like that, and Odegeo had not explored every corner of this realm. I knew enough to understand that he must be centuries, even millennia, old. So, how is it that there was still something unseen in heaven?

I ventured a question. "Sir, have you not seen all of heaven? Surely, you must be old as we count age on Earth. How is it that there are places you have never seen? Are you not allowed to go to some places?"

"You have asked questions with answers that are not easily understood." Odegeo hesitated here much as he had earlier when attempting to describe the unchangeableness of God to my simple mind. "But your first question was regarding the rain in the garden. A mist comes up from the waters in this heaven and covers the land, waters, and plants. It is a deep and dense mist. The mist has watered the land twice since we arrived, but you were sleeping both times. You will see and experience the mist much more once we leave Eden. It happens often in heaven.

"I recall that such was the original design in your world. I remember the cool and refreshing dew that covered the Earth and watered all life there. The water was then filled with fresh energy that brought renewal and joy. This was lost when your world was deluged, and it is now but a memory in your world. Many such things were lost."

I replied, "I think I know what you mean about the rain. That feeling after a shower. It is . . . elusive, but alive and almost electric. It never lasts long enough."

"That is always the way when sin has entered. Yet, those moments call to you of heaven and eternity—a soul's distant understanding and longing for the delights that were lost. He has set this in your hearts.

"But as to your other questions, no, I have not seen all of heaven. That is not possible. I do not mean that creation is eternal nor without end. It is a very physical thing—limited and small beside Him. It cannot be as He is. Heaven, however, is not within the universe. It is forever because He is forever. It is without end because He is without end. We are in the Son, and He is forever. He is not in time or any physical dimension, but it is all in Him. Have you not read the Ephesians?"

I tried to grasp some of what Odegeo was saying. I knew for certain, however, what Ephesians was. That much I remembered. Memorizing that list of books in some children's class at church was so long ago and so far away, a different life and a different person. Still, I remembered that name, but I had no idea what was written there. It held profound answers I had never seen or bothered to find.

Then a thought occurred to me. "Sir, if this is Eden, why are there no people here?"

"The Redeemed live in the land ahead, the Heavenly Realm, past the City of God. Eden is not the place for the Redeemed to live. It might have been, but what transpired in your world also affects heaven's life. This is by His permission alone. It reveals His great love for humanity. It hints at the dominion He gives to man and the extent to which He will go to bring His creation into a dynamic union with Him and His purposes.

If Eden on Earth was lost, then Eden in heaven is lost as well, lost to humanity. And even the Heavenly Realm for which we are heading is not the final dwelling place for the Redeemed. On that day, when He arises from His Throne, this land shall be no more."

Then Odegeo looked me straight in the face, and with a profoundly sober and ominous tone, said, "Do not be caught unprepared on that Day. When He arises from His Throne and walks through the land, He will gather up the Redeemed, and they shall return with Him. For those not of the Redeemed, *it will be too late*. The Son will have arisen. The night will have ended."

I struggled for a response. I knew not what to say, but I knew that the arising of the Son was an event for which I was not ready. From this time on, the thought was never far from my mind. It lurked uneasily like the fear a father holds whose son is engaged on a foreign battlefield. I worried that the rising of the Son from His Throne was a moment that could catch me ill-prepared. And the moment of that rising and gathering that Odegeo had referred to would bring an instant, and as I was beginning to understand, eternal fear, full of desperate regret and consuming despair.

But Odegeo suddenly continued. "Blow a trumpet in Zion, sound an alarm on My holy mountain! Let all the inhabitants of the land tremble, for the day of the Lord is coming. Surely it is near, a day of darkness and gloom, a day of clouds and thick darkness. As the dawn spreads over the mountains, so there is a great and mighty people; there has never been anything like it, nor will there be again after it to the years of many generations. A fire consumes before them and behind them a flame burns. The land is like the garden of Eden before them, but a desolate wilderness behind them, and nothing at all escapes them."

I wasn't entirely sure what Odegeo was saying, although I had a small idea. I had heard such references in church and recalled sermons having something to do with the end. Of course, I had long since dismissed the fanaticism of such religious extremists. But now, this matter frightened me greatly, and in reality, it always had. Perhaps that is why I kept it distant. I asked, "When will that happen?"

"I do not know. No one knows but the Father."

"But wouldn't the warning of His return and knowing the time help people come to Him? Wouldn't that be a good and fair thing?"

"Endless warnings have been given. You have heard many yourself, yet you have resisted. You speak of fairness and goodness, yet you have lived apart from both. Your idea of these matters is thoroughly temporal and does not recognize the fullness of His nature. You deny the reality of justice, holiness, righteousness, and the consequential necessity of wrath. You speak from a place of blindness. Yours is the same reasoning the enemy uses."

I was surprised at Odegeo's passion. He seemed as close to irritated or possibly offended as I had seen. "I'm sorry, sir. I just wondered about the chance that a warning or a miracle might help people turn to God."

"It was the same in the days of Noah. No one believed the report of the prophet. It was the same on the days He walked the Earth. They did not even deny the reality of His miracles, but their wicked hearts would still not receive Him! And those who love Him would love Him no matter when He arises. And those who do not love Him will refuse to see the signs and would not turn although they knew the day of His coming. Not even if someone would return from the dead. Such has been the pattern throughout the centuries of your world. When He put on flesh, He wondered with amazed sorrow at the unbelief of His own people."

I could not argue with Odegeo. Even the little I knew of spiritual matters revealed the truth of what he said. I had even had friends who had made the same remarks Odegeo was speaking about: "If I could just see one miracle, I would believe!" Given the historical record of people turning to God or not turning to God amid unusual events, what Odegeo said made perfect sense. Those who believed saw those events as miracles, the supernatural influencing the natural world in an extraordinary way. Those who did not believe, despite their claims of a potential epiphany at the possibility of witnessing a miracle, when push came to shove, simply dismissed the supposed miracle using a naturalistic explanation, no matter how weak or irrational the reason may have been.

Odegeo interrupted my reveries. "We must move on. The City of God awaits."

I took one last gaze at the wondrous scene ahead. We were about to descend into the forests that extended from the mountaintop to the place where the lightning filled the sky. It was breathtaking, but what lay beyond was even more remarkable, and yet, a place I feared.

5

The City of God

Eventually we come out of the Heavenly Eden. We had come many miles, perhaps hundreds, through the wonderful country's forests, glades, lakes, and rivers.

Now, before us was the City of God. It was raised up, far above the level plane we were on that extended out from this part of Eden. However, the City was not made of concrete, brick, steel, or glass. In fact, no buildings were there at all. There was, however, much stone.

We traversed an area that was a grassy field that appeared to stretch along the edge of the Heavenly Eden in both directions as far as I could see. The grassy plain through which we walked toward the City was no more than a mile wide. The grass was a deep, lush green, and very soft and cool. Contrary to all the wildness and uninhibited nature of the Heavenly Eden, this grassy plain was perfectly manicured. At the end of the grass, the stonework began.

Great sheets of what appeared to be granite were laid with divine precision into the ground. No seam was visible between the slabs. In fact, I do not know if the slabs had been laid at all; that was just my earthly reference point. Perhaps this had been created in this design with gigantic singular granite masses laid perfectly flush in the ground.

The rock was shot through with marvelous streaks of varying color, and much of it had a sparkling appearance, as if children's sparkers from an Independence Day celebration had been captured aglow, and living points of brilliance were sealed alive in the stone. It gave a dazzling gleam.

The granite plaza went on for perhaps several miles (and seemed to extend the whole length of the grassy plain as far as I could see) with regular breaks every hundred yards or so in a gigantic checkerboard square pattern. The breaks were each an oasis twice the size of the granite squares. Each oasis was unique but filled with lovely gardens and trees of all sizes and shapes.

Here no living thing perished, and all the plants were in their most vivid peak of bloom and flower. Many trellises, some the height of trees, covered each oasis. Grasses, vines, and beautiful flowers beyond description abounded in a cacophony of color and size. I would not see such astonishing garden beauty again till the far end of the Heavenly Realm.

Fountains and high water sprays saturated parts of each oasis with a glowing mist. It would have been the perfect cool, tingling refreshment to run through on a hot summer day. Rainbows constantly flickered in and out of sight, hanging momentarily in the air as we passed at just the right angle. I marveled at them since no sun was in the sky, only the pervasive azure brightness.

Trees also grew in each oasis. Some were of extraordinary size and spread and appeared ancient yet at the peak of health. Indeed, many of the granite areas were shaded with a dappled effect due to these massive trees. The shade of course was another issue. The tremendous sunless brightness caused shadows, but not like on Earth.

Along the stone way, arches and colonnades began to

appear. The closer we came to the City, the more numerous and impressive these arches became. They too were of a granite appearance with colors of mahogany, carnelian, onyx, and many deep and rich hues swirled and mixed together as if from the living rock of the foundation of the universe itself! Higher, nobler, and grander the arches and colonnades became. I had the feeling that there was some symmetry to the elegant design of these outer courts of the City, but it was undecipherable.

Despite the incredible beauty of the grass, flowers, trees, fountains, stones, and arches, the dizzying lightning over the City held my attention. I had seen this wonder when we first came out of the Column days or weeks earlier. It had often been obscured as we wondered through Eden, but now it was revealed in its fullness.

The City was ahead. We came to a series of stairways leading up to the City itself. Each stairway was hundreds of feet wide and grand, as the steps leading to a great earthly palace or an historic building from which heads of government ruled. And there were many steps on each stairway, perhaps as many as a hundred. Each time a new level was reached, there would be a wide concourse of more walks intermingled with oasis areas. Each new level seemed grander and more opulent than the previous one.

By the time we reached the seventh and final level, we were on the plain of the City of God. I turned back to look from where we had come and was amazed at the climb we had accomplished. The flat, turf-covered land from which we had ascended seemed a thousand feet below us. The grassland and the forest from which we had issued were miles back. Now great columns, archways, and colonnades of beautiful stone surrounded the city. Again, I sensed there was some pattern to their design, but I could not grasp it from the place where I stood.

And as we climbed the many stairs, we began to see angels coming and going. More and more of them appeared the closer we approached the top of the stairs and even more so as we approached the City. Angels were nothing like the ancient paintings that I remembered. Those effeminate, pasty, sometimes babyish messengers from heaven hardly provoked the type of fear and awe that I recalled from the angelic appearances in The Book! It seemed that those angelic manifestations usually resulted in fainting, fear, judgments, and stern commands.

In fact, angel stories were among the few clear memories I had from Sunday School. Those Sunday morning classes were always taught by what seemed to me to be elderly women who all wore the same dress, had the same gray hair piled up on their heads, and always managed to pull out too few crayons and too few colors to adequately draw the story about the little children coming to Him. But the angel stories always caught my attention! Even then, perhaps I was drawn to something of a spiritual nature, yet somehow not to the One Spirit.

These heavenly spirits, these angels, were clearly spirit beings, not flesh and blood. Of course, I had realized this having spent much time with Odegeo. But several things surprised me about the angels. First and foremost was the variety, although every angel I saw was decidedly masculine. I never saw a feminine nor an effeminate angel, and although I saw no sexual distinctions, clearly, the power and strength in the angelic being represented masculinity. There were many sizes of angels. I don't know if size was a function of power.

All the angels were taller than me. Odegeo was not the largest by any means, although he was easily seven feet high.

Some were much taller than him. And, as I was to find out soon enough, some angels were gigantic in stature. There were no obese, weak, ill, injured, or exhausted angels. I suppose I would describe them as all looking fit and trim and having a sort of hidden strength ready to be unleashed at any time. The angels don't become something the same way humans do, such as stronger, wiser, or socially higher. They simply are who they are. An unchanging permanence about them reflects their nature and calling established eons ago.

I also noticed that the angels had slight coloration differences. They were all bright, but some seemed to emanate a golden color. Others were more silvery, some had a hint of royal blue, and others were varying shades of white. It wasn't that they were these various colors in the sense of skin color as on Earth, but something that emanated from them. It wasn't on the surface but emanated from inside.

They wore no discernable clothing, but at times some seemed to have a covering over their bodies or parts of their bodies that were not actually part of them. I wondered if this represented an angel of greater authority or perhaps a particular assignment or mission they were currently on. And, although they were spirit beings, there was a solidness to them that was more impenetrable than flesh and blood. They were light years from the sort of floating incorporeal translucent apparitions that men imagine on Earth. The makeup of their bodies seemed to be the stuff of permanence, being formed from the tributaries of eternity. I could not imagine being able to inflict the slightest injury or pain on an angel, nor could any earthly weapon accomplish as much. The immortality of their being flowed from life and permitted no damage from the mortal man.

I vaguely recalled a description of spiritual battles between the forces and good and evil. I wondered how they attacked each other, and if injury was possible. Eventually, I would find this out on a personal level.

As to their individual identities, they all had faces as unique and singular as ours. In fact, in this regard they were most like humans. The bodies of the angels were, for the most part, similar to humans with hands, feet, arms, legs, and torsos. I would find out later that not all angels had the same appearance in this regard, but the vast majority seemed to look generally alike.

Odegeo allowed me the time to enjoy the breathtaking view and observe the beautiful panorama of the outskirts of the Heavenly City. There was electricity in the air, yet at the same time, peace and calm were part of the essence of all life in heaven. I could have stayed there at the entrance to the City forever.

Eventually, of course, it was time to proceed. Although, because of the awe of the landscape and stunning appearance of the many angels, I had been able to press down the worry within me regarding what must be awaiting me in the City. As we crested the top stairs and the City lay before and somewhat below me, my anxiety increased.

I saw the lightning in all its fantastic glory! It was a gleaming gold and a fiery red, a burning blue and a searing yellow, a blinding orange and a majestic purple. However, even the colors were ever-changing; some I could not even name. The colors of the lightning interlocked and shot miles upward and outward and danced between each other.

The lightning sometimes skewed in wild patterns and arcs in every direction, like a bolt of unpredictable earthly lightning. Sometimes it formed great spinning circles. Then, like a cosmic gyroscope, circles of lightning leaped in and out of each other, spinning like tornadoes at ninety-degree angles and in opposite directions. Sometimes the appearance was that of millions of diamonds sparkling in the most dazzling release of the radiance of light locked within them. It was chilling and awesome at the same time! Sometimes it seemed that there was some complicated but inconceivable pattern.

I could not grasp the design, pattern, or purpose, yet they were on the edge of my comprehension. My mind grappled with it but was overcome. I knew it meant something, but what it meant was beyond me. It was something of eternity and truth. I imagined that one day the meaning would be real, and perhaps I would perceive the depth of it.

I could see what I thought was the area of the Throne enveloped by a great cloud of extravagant light from this point at the outer rim of the City of God, but there was still a reasonable distance from this point to the Throne itself. As we walked forward toward the center of the City and some sort of the focal point of the presence of God Himself, many more stunning pieces of evidence of the Heavenly City's grandeur were in the endless displays of stone, gardens, trees, fountains, streams, and waterfalls. All of these were worthy in magnificence and stateliness of their presence in heaven.

But the visual opulence of heaven was not the primary source of its magnificence, as spectacular as it was. Life seemed to permeate even the gleam of the stones themselves. The life radiated from the Throne of the invisible One. So bright was the invasive intensity of the light that, as I looked at my hand, I realized I could almost see through my skin! I felt opaque in this searing luminosity, and I wondered if I was glowing as if blasted and saturated with radiation!

As we approached the Throne, His presence in one moment threatened to crush me or burn me. At other moments, a wave and a shiver of the thrill of life shot through me, life in a way I never knew—full, rich, abundant, dynamic, and an explosive feeling of life! My body undulated with waves of power flowing over and through me, and I feared that I might be disintegrating or bursting apart like exploding fireworks.

For the most part, my body seemed to be intact and functioning. However, I could never see God or perceive the Throne on which He sat. I could see a brightness, at times blinding, like looking at the sun and the blue, gold, silver, and green electric, dazzling arcs of power above the Throne. But I could not see a Person, Spirit, or a real Being.

"No man may see Him and live," Odegeo said. "Not with unwashed mortal eyes."

I could not approach Him; I could not comprehend Him. He was hidden from my sight. Yet from that place, that Person, all the radiance of sheer magnetic life poured out in a wild rush and frenzy, like trying to fill a cup with the waters of Niagara. Or like sticking your head out of the car window when the car was going a thousand miles an hour! I could see it in them; the citizens of heaven lived in it; they were all around me. In the deepest place of their souls, it electrified their being and streamed through them like the dazzling light of the sun in the vibrant royal blue of the sky.

At one moment, I found myself cowering in fear and dread and weeping. In another moment, I was lifted up to the thrill of an endless and almost promiscuous life. In my darkened state and the futility of my mind, I could only dimly sense the delight of His life, yet even I could perceive it and taste it. I wondered at the endless pleasures and everlasting joy to be found not only in heaven but even more remarkably, in Him. The glory would be not only in His creation but in His very being.

Suddenly, a deep and commanding sound, like the blast of the horn on a mighty battleship, emanated from the Throne. It crescendoed quickly, steadily, and ominously in volume. Everything else in heaven became eerily quiet. All of the Redeemed and the angelic beings stood in rapt attention. I sensed joyful anticipation in their faces as the sound grew steadily louder.

At one point, the noise was so loud and ponderous that I felt my body vibrating. The ground itself began to tremble under the weight of it! I looked around, which was not easy as the sheer magnitude of the now deafening noise seemed to penetrate my being with an almost paralyzing strength. Those in view were not afraid but relished this display of monumental power released through the nexus of sound. All the angels in front of me and the great and mighty angels at the Throne were standing.

And the volume increased!

Now it was actually forcing me backward like a hurricane-force wind. By its own acoustic intensity, the sound itself was driving me rearward! I stared at the Throne area from which the sound emanated, utterly mesmerized, unable to turn away, in a state of shock and fear, but totally consumed with this wonder. I felt the pulsation in the center of my chest and brain, and all my muscles began to twitch. Again, I wondered if I might explode or implode. My skin was rippling like the effect of a howling wind blowing across grass fields. Yet, there was no wind. It was the sheer voluminous sound! My vision blurred, and I closed my eyes in fear of damage to my sight. I bent over and vainly covered my ears as tightly as possible with my hands. I was sure my hearing was permanently injured, but far beyond that, I began to fear for my life. This had to end, or my body would quickly disintegrate!

Abruptly and without warning, it stopped. All was silent for an instant.

Then, a deafening pulsing cosmic thunderclap blasted for only a second but with such strength that I was thrown back ten feet. My hair streamed out momentarily behind me as if I were driving in a convertible going five-hundred miles per hour! At the same time, a series of phenomenal crisscrossing lightning bolts exploded straight up into the air from the Throne. The sound blast ripped instantaneously through my being with such an overwhelming and crushing blow that I felt divots in my skin and pressure on my eyes, pushing them briefly into my skull. Like the wind of a hundred tornadoes all at once, I was slammed by sound waves that knocked the wind out of my lungs, and momentarily I could not breathe.

I lay on the ground in a near catatonic state, distantly hearing the echo of the blast roll on and on throughout heaven, through hills, woods, and waters, for what seemed like hours. For some time, there was a roaring sound in my ears. As my wits slowly returned to me, I wondered what had happened and why. I felt my body, reassured that every part was still intact. Incredibly I had no apparent damage. Even my hearing seemed to be quite in order. To my amazement, I realized that the roaring I was hearing was the cheering of the Redeemed!

Like the response to an epic victory, the ovation and shouting seemed to herald the blast itself! It was a heavenly standing ovation that continued until it evolved entirely of its own accord into a spectacular song of worship!

Many among the Redeemed appeared to be writing something on pedestals standing in numerous places throughout the vast area surrounding the Throne. The cheering, singing, and writing all showed that it was not the first time this event occurred. Was it possible that this happened regularly in the City of God?

Although it seemed that the worship went on for a long time, the song ended, and a general return to normal activities took place before the Throne. However, a prolonged excitement and buzz was in the crowd after the Noise.

No single encounter in all my time in heaven was as stunning and extreme as this in its enormity and effect. I never heard it again during my travels in the heavenly realm. It was thoroughly unforgettable. I asked Odegeo what it was and what it meant.

"It was the word of the Lord," he answered.

"The word of the Lord? Do you mean an actual word as in a language? I didn't understand anything. It was just like a long building thunder and then a massively loud boom."

"That is like the word that He spoke while the Son walked the Earth. The Father spoke from heaven. Those who did not believe in the word of the Lord heard only thunder, as they thought."

"Then, sir, it really was language, not just noise?"

"It was words that His people understood perfectly, and they rejoiced greatly, for it was a great truth and revelation of Himself that many did not yet know. You are not of His people. To you it was hidden."

"Sir, may I then ask what He said?"

"You would not grasp the truth that was spoken. It is beyond your comprehension. Do not be dismayed or angered by this. Even the children of God who walk the Earth would not discern the meaning of this revelation. It is beyond all of them except for a few. Even Paul was not allowed to reveal all the mysteries of the third heaven that he saw. As with Moses who could only see the back of God in His glory, otherwise he would have died, so it is with the pronouncements of the Father at the Throne. The revelations in His very presence are sharp and piercing, eternal and unshakable, weighty and irresistible. To those who are unprepared, it is like looking into the face of God. The words may have destroyed you. It was by grace that you were protected although the immensity of the proclamation still overwhelmed you."

I had never before considered that truth and revelation were solid like this. In fact, my idea was that truth was vague and in a constant state of flux. My university professors had taught me so, and thus I had taught others. But here was some incomprehensible reality that so superseded even the more reliable constants of my universe that it threatened to undo me! How could a truth evolve into something beyond mere conception and abstraction, beyond thought and idea, and become so material that it physically moved me, against my will, by the sheer forceful gravity of its existence? This was mindboggling and an utterly foreign consideration.

"Sir, what you are saying is outside of my wildest reckoning. I never dreamed . . . I just never dreamed of the palpable existence of truth, an existence of truth as a thing. I can barely think of words to describe what I am trying to say."

"Yes," Odegeo answered. "And there is the existence of countless forms of truth, art, communion, and expression that are utterly beyond your imagination. Endless things that have not yet been revealed even to angels, though we have received the Oracles of the Morning that humankind has not yet received.

"Beyond hearing, seeing, tasting, beyond all the senses and the knowledge of our current estates, these are exponential in nature and infinite in measure and sublime beyond understanding. They are both simple and complex in their transcendent essence.

"The things He has prepared for us are hidden in the depths of His Being, and it is His delight to uncover them in His time, for His glory, and equally for our pleasure in Him. Music and color and all the meanings of the geometrical and all the depth of the most profound relationship and all the intimacy of the purest passion are only the beginning steps of eternity, joy, meaning, and wholeness. He has heights beyond heights of truth and experience and discovery that no one, not even Michael, has begun to scale."

My head was spinning. I had no idea what Odegeo was talking about. Still, I grasped that in God there existed things that no human (or angel, for that matter) in the most advanced state of thought, imagination, or dream had ever thought about, nor was capable of considering. These were totally outside our frame of reference, as much as pondering the beauty of a Rembrandt might be to a worm. But, according to Odegeo, God would reveal these things to His creation in eternity.

My head was still spinning.

Long after this inexplicable event, I took note of the worshipers before the Throne. These were the Redeemed, as Odegeo told me. They seemed completely unaware of my presence here in the City of God. There was an uncountable number at the invisible Throne. They were singing and laughing.

I didn't remember any laughter during worship at the old church of my childhood. In fact, I usually got in trouble for that sort of behavior in church!

A palpable radiance of joy was ascending from the worshipers. Many were bowing down, and many were weeping but without grief. These were the tears of utter gratitude, peace, contentment, wholeness, and the defining quality of heaven—delirious joy. The music and the singing were sheer joy. Sometimes the notes were ponderous and deep, and at other times they were sprightly, melodic lines that had the power and magnificence to have shaken the Earth had they been set free in our world! (Clearly, this music was too dangerous for Earth.) These voices reduced me to tears, and I found myself on the ground, weeping.

From somewhere not visible to me, the most robust and electrifying instrumental music sounded forth with such incredible strength and energy that the foundations of heaven seemed to shake at their intensity and volume. Many of the sounds were of recognizable sources: high and powerful trumpets and deep brass, drums (sometimes wild and what my mother had called "primitive"), and reed instruments of every kind, but many were completely new and unknown to me, like strings with an electrified sound and other sounds that can only be described as something that might emanate from the stars of heaven themselves!

The music of the instruments wound its way through the singing voices, and the sound rose up and down in varying crescendos and decrescendos. At one point, the music was swelling, rising, and exploding to such a climax that I thought perhaps my heart and ears would burst!

I was deeply torn by fear of the Throne. My lostness, failure, inadequacy, and downright repulsiveness were never more clear to me. I had a nearly irresistible desire to join the throng before the Throne, like Odysseus before the Sirens, knowing that joining their island would be the end of him, yet longing with an insatiable desire to race to hear their song. I was both a quivering, self-loathing sinner and a weeping, hopeful, nearly penitent soul!

I tried to approach the Throne. The nearer I came to it, the more I felt a pressure, a Presence, an Otherness. It was overt, like a forceful wind against my body but without any air movement. Or, like magnets held at their polar repelling ends, no visible force pushed me away, but the sense of His being was irrefutable and irresistible. And, somehow, inexplicably, personality and plurality were in it.

Finally, I could move no closer. I could not penetrate the Presence of the Throne, or rather *on the Throne*. I remembered science fiction descriptions of impenetrable force fields. Here was the real thing. I am confident that nothing could, unbidden, approach the Presence; no living thing, no celestial power, nor even the most powerful destructive invention of man could come to the Throne without an invitation. The omnipotence of Him who sat there, though in His fullness hidden to my eyes, was utterly without rival or equal and existed forever without any lessening. I could not approach. I would later learn that every attribute of the divine Being is infinite in its expression, eternal, and perfect.

Yet the Redeemed rushed by me, pulled forward in raptured magnetism to the source of their redemption. The same invisible force I could not overcome called them in joyful abandon to race freely ahead, undisturbed, to the place of wholeness, this mysterious Throne of God. I did not feel rejected by the Presence. There was no willful denial. I simply was not able since I was not redeemed,

I remained where I was, expending considerable energy in doing so. I was close enough to see something, certainly not what the Redeemed were seeing, but some Thing. What exactly I was seeing, however, was not at all clear. The brilliance of the light of the Throne never ceased in the least, nor did the phenomenal, ubiquitous lightning-like glory above the Throne. But there was some shifting effect going on in the light itself as it poured out from the Throne region, with hints of the depth of the Uncreated Immortal amid the dazzling brightness of the golden and silver hues, a royal blue, a fiery red, and other colors for which I had no name.

In the shifting of these colors was some bewildering multiplicity. Known colors formed impossibly complicated geometric shapes that instantly appeared to expand upon themselves, out of themselves, twisting and multiplying instantaneously into an infinite distance infinitely faster than the speed of light. It was somewhat like mirrors held together to reflect themselves into one another, but with a form and substance more real than the mirrors themselves.

It was as if, for a moment, I could see to the end of the universe or beyond, and I gazed in rapt, astonished awe, my mind seizing in explosions of stunned marvel both thrilling and terrifying. At one point, I thought I had fallen down an infinitely deep tunnel of arcing light whose end suddenly curved back upon itself in a multi-dimensional Mobius. While I gazed, my thoughts went on forever in wonder, as though eternity were caught up in this moment, and it was the only moment that had ever existed and ever would exist.

I was in an everlasting now; time was insufficient to calculate itself, and my mind expanded beyond the boundaries of sentience. I had stood in this place forever. There was no beginning. There was no end. There was only this ceaseless moment in which all things happened, existed, and ended. The linear sequential events of time were turned on a ninety-degree angle in a simultaneity of realization.

Then when the scene of the Throne changed and I returned to myself, it seemed the entire event had passed in only an instant, a moment too short to be measured.

I also saw something in the light at the Throne with a revolving sense to it. In the light itself, not that the light and color formed this, but within the substance of the light, there was a circular quality, yet undefined in origin or definition. It seemed to revolve in great wide round arcs, and then, somewhat like an optical illusion, the light revolved inside and around itself. But another similar shape was there as well, and then a third. The third began to orbit around the first two, but it was not so. In reality, the first circled the second and third. Then, much like the mind's ability to reverse the pattern in an optical illusion, or maybe nothing like that, the second orbited the first and third. And yet, they were not at all simply revolving light. It was light that was alive.

Then, unlike anything I had ever seen or would ever see, this light took on a living Being. Each living circle lived both within and without the other. Then the revolutions merged into one, then back into three. And as they returned to three, they began to grow, expanding in height, width, and length and then sharing geometric dimensions I could not comprehend. They were like parallels and shadows of those that existed in some chiasmatic relationship, but somehow in time, spreading forward and backward.

Visions came into my mind not through my own thought but simply and inescapably by being there. It was inevitable even for me, merely by being in His presence. And I saw a peeling back of history by images racing through my mind faster than I had ever thought or could possibly think: visions of oceans and ships, wars, great earthly kingdoms rising and falling, Rome, Greece, Persia, Babylon, Assyria, a horrific flood, a great tower, back still further to humankind in its virginity, to a great garden, to infant worlds, to another war of cosmic proportions, and still back to pubescent stars singing together in the heavens in the womb of the universe.

And behind that was only dim darkness. Then, in the shadowy darkness, at a distant point of nothingness beyond me, came again the three circles of dizzying living revolving light, now inestimable in size, filling the whole universe. But, no, the universe was overwhelmed by their presence, and they superseded it as the sun surpasses the flame of a match so that there was no escape. They were still orbiting each other, still coalescing, and separating over and over. The circles were still expanding, now exponentially, stretched out toward me and engulfed me before and behind, in time, in space, in motion, and into the very core of my soul.

Again overwhelmed, I collapsed. I knew no more.

And then I was back in heaven, far away from the Throne, lying on the ground. Odegeo was by my side, and he was speaking. "I have carried you out from the region of the Throne. Your meager soul cannot remain there. I do not think you can die here, but it is not safe for you so near the Throne. You are not yet of the Redeemed."

I was coming back to my senses. The memory of the

Throne was burning in my mind, swirling in my brain with a swarm of confusion, fear, and amazement. I was overwhelmed and could not speak for some time.

Two things I recalled from this moment with Odegeo. First, I asked him, "How long was I at the Throne?" I was baffled by the loss of linear reality. He answered, saying, "There is no known answer. You were near the Infinite, in the presence of the eternal. You were at the Throne in His eternal now. It is beyond the greatest of all created beings to understand that, for it requires both infinitude and omniscience. You experience time in a linear procession. For Him, that line of procession is turned on its end."

I didn't know what Odegeo meant; however, I did remember the second thing he had said, and I hung on to it: "You are not *yet* of the Redeemed."

My recovery from the Throne exposure took some time. I was not exactly weak, but I hesitated to stay in the City of God. I did not belong here, ultimately, and I sensed that. Whatever awaited me, it was about time to move on. Yet, I hated to leave. Odegeo concurred, telling me that I would soon receive direction. I had no idea how that would happen, but I trusted my guide implicitly.

I asked him about the Redeemed at the Throne. "Do they have the same type of experience that I had? I mean, I couldn't see anything that I could define much. Is that what happens to everyone?"

"No, not at all," he answered. "They see Him just as He is, and they become like Him."

"Humans become like God?" I asked, incredulous.

"Yes, in His transferable attributes. Their nature is transformed, confirmed in goodness. Faith is replaced by sight. Unchangeable peace comes in the deepest part of their soul. Their character is fully shaped in the likeness of the nature of their Savior and the knowledge of the holy. They are filled, at last, entirely with joy in His presence. They are conformed to the image of His Son, and they become fully what they were created to be."

I was silent for a while, pondering this. Joy, especially the joy, is what was apparent to me. The other things were matters of importance to the Redeemed, I understood, but joy was abjectly missing from my existence. I was barren in my own soul. But I could see the joy in everything, everywhere in heaven. It was conspicuous, living, exuding from the very ground of heaven, yet escaping me as though I did not exist.

Then I noticed (at a safe distance from the Throne) one of the largest colonnades near the Throne, a stunning marbled stone of gold with a pearl color. It appeared to extend out from a long silvery-blue tunnel-shaped structure. The tunnel may have issued from the base of the Throne itself; it was impossible to tell for sure because of the brilliance of the light of the Throne. At the open end, the site of the golden-pearl colonnade, angels were continuously coming out from the tunnel. Each angel seemed to be carrying something.

Occasionally I would see members of the Redeemed rushing toward that area and singing and shouting something like, "It's time! It's time! At last, he (or she) is come!" I could only catch a glimpse of this area, but it seemed to be a site of great rejoicing. Many of the Redeemed gathered around the colonnade, and a special song and even the sound of cheering would arise time after time as angels would appear bearing some endowment.

I asked Odegeo what that place was. He only answered, "To live is Christ and to die is gain. To be absent from the body is to be present with the Lord." I understood what the place was. Given my current spiritual condition, I knew it was a moment I would never experience.

Now while I was standing there in the golden joy and the brightness, I suddenly heard a noise from afar. It was a cacophonous sound, thunderous and sometimes very shrill and bombastic. It had none of the subtle, simple beauty and indescribable, thrilling complexity of the music or worship of heaven. The sound grew inexorably louder as it grew nearer. I began to realize that the noise was coming from the direction of the now far-distant Column from which Odegeo and I had ascended out of the dark place.

In the distance, as the noise grew nearer, I could begin to see a shadowy place in the air. It was an inexplicable darkness amid the impossible brightness of heaven. I became aware of a silence that had fallen among the angels here by the Throne. The citizens of this holy place (the angels, not the Redeemed, who seemed entirely unaware of any change in the atmosphere) were in a state of wariness and uneasiness.

Odegeo spoke suddenly and tersely to me, yet almost as if he were not speaking to me but voicing long-held anticipation. He said, "It shall not always be this way. One day there will be a complete and final end to this arrogance."

"What, sir? What do you mean?" I asked.

As I looked, I saw a new countenance on the face of my guide. Here now, instead of the beauty and peace of worship, was the embodiment of indignation. This was not a rage of fury or wildness but a sense of righteous anger. This was different. I had not seen him like this before. I would not have thought this possible.

"What is it, sir? What is going on?" I asked, growing anxious.

The next moment sent abject fear crashing through me, freezing my soul, as Odegeo turned, with a face of deep consternation and, perhaps, even a hint of fear (if that were possible). Looking directly in my face, he said, "The enemy of heaven has come. He is here, the one you know as Lucifer."

"What? No! Lucifer? That can't be possible! You mean the . . . the devil? How can he be here? I thought this was heaven! People are worshiping! The Throne of God is here! I thought there was no evil here! (Of course, it struck me that *I was there*.) Why is he here? What could he possibly be doing in this place?" With more than a hint of anger, I shouted all this, barely able to contain my dismay and alarm.

Odegeo's answer left me devastated and dumbstruck. "I believe he has come for you."

6

Encounter with Evil

Through all the insane and self-deceived years of indulgence, foolishness, and degradation, I had, more or less, convinced myself that this "serpent," this devil, this Satan, was a figment of the collective minds of religious zealots—a term I applied loosely to those inclined to such unenlightened thinking. Enlightened thinking was my high and noble search for meaning and truth, as I had sometimes dared to call it, no doubt in an attempt to assuage what I may have left of a conscience.

However, those distant memories lingered from long ago, ages it now seemed, thoughts from my adolescence that I was never entirely able to shake. Still, in my rational moments, I knew those tales of spirits, demons, and devils were more akin to fairies, dragons, and wizards than to real flesh and blood, real experience, and wasn't that the source of my truth? Reason and experience, my lord and my god. But those ancient memories pounded away. That song, that old song, something about the devil, a sly old fox, locked him in a box, throw away the key? How in the world could I still have remembered that? Why did that childish song throw my mind into such turmoil and anger even in my enlightened years?

Of course, near the end, as my life had careened toward that darkened Red Hue Room and that strange door lying on the floor with the bizarre chanting in that room and the hideous screaming face behind me at the last instant, maybe a devil didn't seem quite so impossible.

Could he have come for me, even in heaven, because he owned me? Perhaps in some moment of insanity, arrogance, darkness, or inebriation, I been idiot enough to swear some allegiance to this thing of hate, destruction, and malice?

In a panic, my mind raced through the many cultic encounters I had engaged in. The thought of them immediately induced violent shaking and profuse sweating. Had I vowed or promised something? I could feel the perspiration of fear beginning to form on my body. My memory leaped from scene to scene, desperately searching for some moment. I grew sick, my stomach wrenched, and I vomited. My terror overcame me, and I fainted.

"Awake, friend, awake," the voice said to me. I had collapsed onto the ground of heaven, and Odegeo was arousing me from my darkness. I woke to his firm voice and found strength in his presence, yet I was sobbing and quaking. My teeth were chattering from fear, and my muscles twitched in horrified anticipation of something beyond my wildest fears.

With a flash of insight, I realized that Odegeo was right. I was certain that this enemy of heaven was coming for me to claim his own. I stood there awaiting my coming doom. I saw no reason for my presence in heaven to be allowed to continue. I didn't belong here. Others could claim this blessed realm as their home, the place of delight, rest, peace, joy, and perfection they had anticipated all their lives. This was their inheritance, and they belonged. I knew I did not.

There was no hope for me now. I must have died when I passed through the Door in the Red Hue Room. My soul was simply waiting, enjoying a journey through what might have been, just to make my hell all the more miserable, now knowing what I would forever miss.

I attempted to gather myself as I realized angels were watching me. They had gathered around me, although they held back some distance, yet Odegeo stood close by. Somehow I reached inside myself, determined to "take it like a man," although the thought suddenly smote me that perhaps I was no longer a man … No matter. I must make a final good showing, not embarrass myself. The future would simply be what I have earned, my "wages," as I dimly recalled.

Then he came into view. He had no horns, no snarling twisted face, no sulfurous fumes or flames shooting forth, no ghastly (or ghostly) floating apparitions, and no barbed tail or pitchfork.

He passed under the enormous stately trees of heaven, through the magnificent arches, and over the outer stone courts. Despite the palatial opulence, purity of light, and divine complexity of symmetry, order, and flawlessness of their creation, as he passed through, a momentary dulling of the splendor transpired. As he approached the Crystal Sea, I noticed light dimming around him. The Heavenly Beings all still retained their brightness, that inner glow. Odegeo had grown more radiant as we had come nearer the center of heaven. That radiance was almost tangible.

But this devil, *the* devil, if he had once had that radiance somewhere long ago, it was completely gone, like the fading of a child's toy, luminous when held up to the light and slowly weakening in the dark, as the light fades farther and farther from memory. I intuitively understood that as heaven and He who reigns here is the very definition of light, this devil is the very definition of darkness. A distant recollection brushed across my memory of a story in The Book. Someone's face was shining from being in the Presence. Even on Earth, God's presence worked its miraculous brilliance on the otherwise dullness and dimness of human flesh.

This devil went beyond simply faded glory. Darkness was about him, as if the light of heaven refused to shine its glory on this dark thing, or perhaps this greatest demon absorbed the brightness but could not reflect its beauty. Still, it was evident that this was a being of power. His size alone was extraordinary, even in comparison to the angels. I estimated his height at five times that of an average man. And, although the spirit beings did not display an earthly sort of physical muscle, there was some sense of strength emanating from him, more than the angels I had encountered.

I said before that he was not at all as the earthly images had pictured him throughout the ages, but now I could see that was not entirely true. In one respect, it seems that the human artists did depict him accurately: he was deeply darkly, vividly red—a dark, somber red-like molten steel fired in a blast furnace, perhaps in the foul pits of hell itself. His whole body, or whatever flesh-like substance afforded his appearance, was red.

And the noise. I don't know where it came from. He was alone. There was no entourage of celebration. I recalled, and now I knew it to be abject stupidity, the declarations of reprobates, like me, who loudly proclaimed the fun, the debauchery, the wildly unleashed "freedom" we would all one day enjoy together in hell. What idiotic foolishness! Certainly, one essence of hell would be eternal loneliness from every being, especially The Being. Even if one might see others of the lost, no doubt that aloneness would saturate the soul of perdition for eternity. Hell would abound with the opposite of every good that fell from His hand in common and special grace.

There was no entourage of musicians with the devil, not even a foul dancing demon parade. Perhaps heaven would allow no such display. Or maybe one so deeply consumed with darkness and self could ultimately only be alone.

Like a rocket, a memory raced through my mind from far back. I must have been only seven or eight years old. How or why did I remember this? A visiting preacher on a Sunday night. What did they call him . . . an evangelist . . . said hell would be utter aloneness forever. It had frightened me badly, but perhaps not badly enough.

Still, there was this noise, although no musicians followed Satan. Earlier, I thought it to be painfully disordered loud music, but now it just seemed a series of noises, sort of a white noise with some indecipherable rhythm. I believe the noise must have emanated from his body, or perhaps even his mouth, for it only stopped when he spoke, as I was about to find out.

As the devil approached, his head turned this way and that, searching the angelic gathering. I knew he was looking for me, and I knew I had no place to hide. No one attempted to shield me, though Odegeo stood close.

A strange look of pleasure and malice passed over his bloodless red face when he found me. As I ventured eye-to-eye contact with him, perhaps the bravest thing I had ever done to that moment, he looked back at me in sneering triumph, but the malice never left his countenance. Then, what I dreaded the most happened—the devil called my name.

"Adam Sane."

There it was. My name. Adam Sane. Spoken by the incarnation of evil. It was the first time I had heard my name fully spoken since I had begun my cosmic travels, and Lucifer himself said it.

Hearing my name spoken by him, I was undone. My bravery left me. I collapsed in fear and quaked in my terror. The smooth, cool stone of the heavenly plaza, which I seemed to be melting on, was suddenly distant and hazy.

I groped around on the ground as a blind man in unknown territory. Darkness was descending. Heaven and its brilliant light seemed to be fading away. My vision was limited, and the scene changed to that of the dark planet from which I had first entered the cosmos. I intuitively knew I was seeing that world and returning to that place in great fear.

Now, however, I was on the planet, and something was happening. A vague, dim, blurry vision of a red room gathered in my consciousness. Then the image began to take on reality. I turned to search out the only hope I clung to, Odegeo. I could not see him except as a silhouette against a shadowy and grim fiery landscape as the red room gave way to something much larger. I saw movement behind him, beings lurching about in stilted and tortured pain, crying out for relief! There was a dim, red darkness to this place, like the skin of Lucifer himself. And there was the crackling, popping sound of burning. I heard the sound of fire reducing everything to ashes, yet the flames consumed nothing. It was merely burned in the red darkness on the strange planet, pierced by anguished, lonely, and desperate cries.

Back in the distance, black mountains were carved out against a deep reddish horizon, not a peaceful horizon of a setting summer sun, but a horizon reflecting the blazing and excruciating flames of perdition. Red spots dotted the black mountains, flaming areas in the blackness. The contorted beings were stumbling, wrenching, and screaming. It was a living death, and I was in it.

I also saw fissures in the ground, frighteningly deep sheer cuts in the terrain that seemed to descend for miles and from which the haunting red glow issued. But this was darker, almost like a black fire. And I saw strange inhuman shapes in the black fire, unspeakable forms, writhing in agony, yet with palpable hate and malice, a vengeful desire that stretched out toward me. A stench was in the air, and my lungs were burning as they once did in high school chemistry lab. What was that odor? Breathing it pained me, but I couldn't escape it. And then another worse scent, the smell of death and rotting got the better of me. I began to vomit.

I searched in the black sky for the Column of Light. It had been there on the planet of death when I first met Odegeo, but I could not find it. It was the one hope for me in hell. It had descended to this forsaken world, but now the Column was gone. I had no escape. This knowledge washed over me with a despair that gave way to profound loneliness. Even God Himself had deserted this place.

And all the damned were forever alone, filled with our guilt, malice, fear, greed, and hatred for heaven and hell—and even hatred for one another. We could not even acknowledge another soul in this place of abject misery and unfathomable pain. The victory we had won in our earthly lives, utter consumption of self, had now fully been realized. We had asked for it, begged for it, dreamed of it, and now it was ours for eternity. We had abandoned all hope forever and ever.

Still, the burning, pain, loneliness, stench, and endless death continued. My mind and senses were racked with the horror of hell, and the prospect of this existence forever was impossible to comprehend.

A burning, moaning soul stumbled passed me. I could not discern any gender, but the look on its face reminded me of a painting, *The Scream,* I think it was called. It was a picture of despair, desolation, and hopelessness. I reached for this tortured soul in the flames, thinking to give some comfort, but it recoiled from me and cursed me from its twisted face with the foulest language, swearing its anger at heaven. The smoldering soul ran from me in fear, loathing, and agony.

As it raced away, it turned and looked back at me. The look on its face is etched forever in my mind: the culmination of all the hideous, violent, despairing, horrifying, and demented nightmares of every human that ever lived.

I could not find Odegeo. I was lost.

Then the angel spoke my name and called to me from the Throne Room of heaven. Instantly I was back, among the citizens of heaven, to the place of purity, the golden-blue sky, and the very Presence of eternity.

"Odegeo!" I cried in relief and an agony of fear. "Odegeo! I was gone! I was lost! I was in . . . I was in . . ." I could not force the words from my mouth.

"No," Odegeo said calmly but firmly. "You never left my presence. You have been here all along. But you do not have the strength to look him in the eye. He has always had the power to confuse, despair, and deceive the mind. Do not look directly at him. You do not have the capacity for that, not yet. Even Michael, our Prince, did not revile this devil.

"Here, in heaven, Lucifer's power is greater than in your world, not less, because he is revealed to you as he is, no longer a shadow or passing spirit. You have given him much access to your mind for many years on Earth. He has great power over you, and peering into your eyes provides him an open avenue. He hopes to overwhelm you with fear and despair so that you will give up on heaven.

"Already you have considered that you do not belong here or are unworthy, and that is true. Yet, countless millions from Earth are unfit, yet they are here, are home, and rejoice. Remember that he has great power in twisting truth just enough to bring damnation. You were in a place of truth for many years of your early life, yet your enemy could distort the truth just enough to bring doubt and resentment upon you. And on this, you finally fed, bringing you to destruction. You must renew your mind in truth."

Then Lucifer spoke to Odegeo. "I triumphed over you centuries ago, gardener. Your flaming sword is gone, and your ancient garden was flooded. You cannot protect what is mine. I own it."

"Adam Sane is not an it."

"Nevertheless, it *is* mine. I have come to claim this soul for my kingdom. You shall not stand before me. It should not be here. This is a breaking of the law."

"It is not your place here in heaven to make claims for a human soul."

"I did not make the law, fool. It does not belong here and should not be here. It is mine and I shall take it now!"

Then Lucifer, in a rage of angry passion with death in his eyes, flew at me! Odegeo covered me, but the devil knocked him aside. I covered myself, closed my eyes, and screamed, "Please protect me! God of heaven have mercy!"

There was a sudden momentary silence and stillness. I hid my face and held my eyes tightly shut, wondering when the blow would come. I waited, clenched in terror, but nothing happened.

Then I heard another sound. This was not the noise of Lucifer, who had stopped (or been stopped) in his tracks, hovering over me, seeming unable to move. I heard a deep sound of power, a sort of rumbling in the ground. On Earth, this would have been an ominous sound, but here it gave a thrill of triumph and hope. I stood up and looked around, but not at the devil. There was electricity in the air that made my spine tingle and my hair stand up. Yet none of this frightened me. It gave me hope.

"Odegeo, what is happening?

"You cried out for mercy and protection. Now from the Throne, the Archangel comes."

7

Who Is Like God?

I looked up, and an angel came forth, with thunderous strength, from the Throne itself, which shone so brightly that I could not see it. I had not previously perceived the presence of this mighty angel because of the aura of the Shining Throne. The angel was indeed great in power and authority. An intense golden glow emanated from his being. He seemed to be the equal of Lucifer but also his opposite in goodness, wholeness, and purity. Then Odegeo whispered to me (I had not heard him whisper before, but he was paying deference to this mighty emissary from the Shining Throne), and he said, "It is the Prince of Israel." I did not know what this meant, but his confidential manner implied that I *should* know.

"Please, sir," I asked Odegeo, "what is his name?"

"To you, his name is Michael."

Even I knew this angelic name. I recalled old stories from my lost childhood. Michael was the Archangel, a representation of power and greatness. And awesome he was! All that Lucifer was not, Michael was—radiant with joy, vibrant with life, immeasurably old yet somehow youthful, peaceful yet with intensity, with a hidden strength beyond measure. I had a deep-seated desire in my heart to fall down and worship him! I understood the ancients and their unmitigated homage to the spirits of old. I restrained myself from such idolatry by the knowledge that such an act here in heaven would be received with instant and probably dire consequences. Yet the desire was there.

Then Lucifer spoke, but not to Michael. He stared dreadfully at me and never looked at Michael throughout the exchange. He addressed me again. "You have no right to be here. You must return with me."

I trembled in terror again, feeling nausea pressing against me. I dared not look at him as Odegeo had advised me. I did not know what to say, but then the mighty angel from the Shining Throne spoke.

"If there were no purpose in this, he would not be here. All present in heaven are here with a purpose." Although he was not shouting, Michael's voice thundered like the sound of many waters. It gave me fresh hope merely to hear him.

"Purpose has never brought any Adam to this place. Only by the cheap trick of redemption can he come here, and this Adam does not have that standing."

"The Lord rebuke you, Lucifer!" Michael's voice had raised in indignation, and the grounds and walls of the heavenly city trembled at his ire. "Redemption was far from cheap, as you well know. It was the greatest and most costly gift ever given."

"I know it well, *Archangel*." Lucifer sneered the word as he spoke Michael's title. "And I remember well that such an offer was never made to me or to the citizens of my kingdom!"

"It would not be made to humans except for grace. They have no standing before Him outside of grace. And, lest you forget, your estate was far different from theirs, you who were once the Anointed Cherub. You stood amidst the Stones of Fire and on the Mountain of God, yet your desire was corrupted. You were not born into rebellion; you chose it amid perfection, in the very Throne Room itself. Your choice made you. Their choice was made for them."

"I do not need your instruction on history, Archangel, told as usual with your pathetic devotion to humility. Your lecture does not change the violation of this Adam's presence here."

"Grace has bought this moment for him, and the moment is temporary."

"But this is a violation of the law!" Lucifer shouted.

"It is a violation of the law only if he remains here, apart from grace, which he will not, just as you will not."

"You turn the law about at your pleasure. He should not be here!"

"The Lord rebuke you!" Michael said with measured indignation. "He is here because of prayer and fasting."

"Not his! *I know him!*

"Certainly not his! But others have humbled themselves, prayed, wept, and fasted on his behalf. And the Son Himself lives to make intercession. You are here, Lucifer, without redemption and only for a season. Even you are here by grace. Do not think to deny his mitigation when you are here on the same terms and with no hope for reconciliation."

"I do not desire reconciliation with heaven! I am the captain of my fate. I would not serve in this kingdom of servants! I will rule or I will have nothing! I only desire what I deserve! You, Adam Sane, have no hope here! You are guilty and without hope. You have gone too far to expect redemption!"

But Michael again answered him. "You will indeed have nothing; in fact, less than nothing. And most assuredly will receive what you deserve, although you will not want it. You are ever a liar and the Father of Lies. Redemption is not under your purveyance. You have not foreknown the elect from eternity. How is it that you think to ordain the lost?"

The devil seemed to be taking on a deeper shade of red now, surely resulting from his growing anger at being denied his will concerning my presence in heaven. It occurred to me that denying his will was the essence of his trouble.

He responded to Michael but still had not given him a single glance. "Despite the drivel of your speech, I do not think to ordain anyone to anything, but Adam Sane is not saved and is not of the elect."

"Whether or not he is of the elect is not yet known to either of us. You presume much when you are not perfect in knowledge or justice."

"Justice? You proclaim justice? Can heaven claim justice while there is death, suffering, and pain for the innocent?"

"Your concern is not for justice," Michael said, "not in any way. This tactic is very old and has no merit in heaven or on Earth or under the Earth. Let us admit that your sudden interest in justice is only for the avoidance of your own culpability."

"Yet you do not respond to my prosecution!"

"It has ever been your deception to accuse heaven of injustice while you hide your own rebellion and convince men of their own innocence. Must we weary ourselves again with these words when you know full well both your guilt and theirs?"

Lucifer seemed to wince at these words, but he recovered and answered, "The guilt at hand is the guilt of heaven at having broken its own immutable law. Adam Sane has died, yet he stands here near the Throne from which the unredeemed are banished. Is the law not the law? You still do not respond to my prosecution!"

"What is your interest in the law? You yourself broke the law. Indeed, you were the first lawbreaker. You have tirelessly endeavored among humans to promote lawlessness and reject, nullify, vilify, and disgrace the law. Yet now you seem intent on enforcing the very law that you hate. But it is for your own vile purposes."

"I have no interest in the law. The law is His tool for subjugation, limitation, repression, and humiliation. The law is His tool for slavery! I will not be a subject! (Here the devil was shouting.) I will not accept any limitation to my desires! I will not be repressed, but I will express myself wholly! I will not be humiliated, but I will glory in my own greatness, not His! I will not be a slave, but I will be utterly free to indulge my own wishes! The law is your truth from which you are required to act. It is not, however, my truth. I create my own truth as any sentient and free being ought to do. I merely point out that you who are bound by His law have illegitimately violated the law at your own pleasure and convenience. You, who insist on unchanging, irrefutable, non-violable law, seem satisfied to break that very law to your own advantage!"

Michael said, "You are truly the Prince of Darkness. No one who violates the law is free. Freedom is only in keeping the law. Perfect obedience is perfect freedom. Whatever overcomes you, to that you are a slave. And you, Lucifer, are a slave to many things!"

At this, the devil began what sounded like a low, deep-throated howl.

But Michael continued. "The law is not something capricious or random and doesn't exist to lessen or enclose. Somebody did not create the law. It is. It *is* because it is who *He is*. It flows from the I AM. The law cannot be otherwise than it is. To be like Him is not enslavement; it is the only freedom, the only reality, the only life.

The devil's strange howl grew louder, shriller, and more intense as Michael continued to speak.

"You are not free; you are indeed in slavery. You know this though you deny it. From the morning of creation to the Day of Fire you are enslaved to what has overcome you. And there is no truth apart from His truth. All else is void. To create your truth, as you say, is to create nothing out of something. The ripples in the pond do not create the pebble that is dropped into it simply because they exist."

Now the howl turned into a sudden piercing scream. It did not seem to be an act of defiance or pending violence but a sound of intense, searing pain. For a moment, the sound took on the quality of horrific singing. This clangor went on for some time. I covered my ears, but no one in heaven moved. I wondered if they had seen this before. They simply waited.

Eventually, the scream sank down into a sort of quivering, angry-sounding gibberish. The devil's face, however, was now hideously contorted, and for a while, he seemed unable to speak. For several more minutes, his red-hued face slowly returned to normal, as if his facial muscles (if he had them), temporarily deformed, had relaxed.

Still, no one moved. I looked around, feeling the tension of the moment and a rising and ebbing fear as my stomach knotted and unknotted back and forth.

Finally, the devil spoke again. "You have not answered my prosecution!"

"The Lord rebuke you, Lucifer."

"You have not answered my prosecution!"

"Lucifer—" Michael began.

"You have not answered my prosecution! You have not answered my prosecution! You have not answered my prosecution." On and on the devil went, now mindlessly repeating the words.

Michael now stood quietly. I began to wonder at the devil's sanity. He seemed to have gone over the edge of rationality. The scene reminded me of a psychiatric ward I had witnessed during graduate school: the senseless repeating of words, as if the sound had meaning, but the people hollowly chanted the words like an incantation. He repeatedly chanted those words as if they were the only words in the universe, and he was alone in it.

Despite now thousands of angels gathered around, Lucifer was indeed utterly alone. Such, it seemed to me, is the very essence of hell. And such is the essence of utter preoccupation with self, like a downward spiral staircase collapsing on itself, with each circle getting narrower until it finally traps the descendant in an impossible grid of self-consumption and insanity.

Still, no one moved. Odegeo stood by me, and I saw on his face what appeared to be a look of compassionate pain (but without hope) and sorrow at the loss of something irrevocable, a loss beyond the reach of time. Even in this place, the very womb of redemption, here was one forever beyond redemption's reach, one confirmed in evil. It dawned on me that although my experience with the devil had been destructive on Earth and terrifying in heaven, there had been a day, eons ago, when the Earth was young, and the sun's rays were first warming that garden they called Eden, that Lucifer may have been a joyous brother, a family member, to those silently witnessing his crushing breakdown into his own empty, consuming darkness from which there was no permanent return.

Then, suddenly and unexpectedly, the devil spoke clearly and rationally again.

"I came to claim my slave and take it to my realm!" The devil still spoke loudly, but now his voice seemed distant and tired.

A wave of movement stirred the angels. I could hear them whispering, but I could not discern their words. As for me, my sickness returned as he spoke about me again. My stomach was knotted with tension, and my head began to throb with fear and consternation.

"He may only descend to your realm after the death of his body. This you well know. You spoke earlier that he died, but he has not died. Not yet."

"Then why is he here? It is not absent from the body, nor is it of your kingdom. Its presence here is doubly illegal."

Suddenly, Odegeo interrupted and spoke, "You, of all creatures, dare to address the law?"

Lucifer turned his malice from me at this point and looked spitefully at Odegeo, but still not at Michael, and said with a sneer, "If the law is to apply to all, I will address it at my pleasure, thou of the flaming sword! And I note that you are not at your post."

"I am not at my post, as you call it, because of your malice upon the world. The Lord rebuke you, Lucifer."

"Such you certainly hope for, child."

At this, I felt a surge of anger and came near to protesting the calling of Odegeo a child.

But, before I could speak, Odegeo responded.

"Lucifer, I understand your intent in calling me a child. So thorough is your corruption that you think to anger even the citizens of heaven with your barbs and darts. Do you still not know that those confirmed in righteousness by the power of Almighty God are immune to such acts of hate and cunning?"

At this, the scorn on the devil's lips twisted into something like a frown, and a deeper hue of red briefly swept over his body. Perhaps this was anger at the miserable failure of this baiting attempt toward Odegeo or perhaps malice toward all of heaven, for his arrogance and imagined superiority had no impact here. Or maybe, in the immenseness of his ego and self-worship, he knew an angel he held in contempt had bested him.

Yet, it was clear that Odegeo had not attempted to enter into a debate but had merely stated the truth. The devil, filled with malice, envy, insatiable conceit, self-consuming power, and the ego-desperate need to win every battle, could not imagine and had long since forgotten that not all are driven by the hunger for self. With shame, I understood all too well those motivations.

But now Michael was speaking again, and he seemed to be dismissing Lucifer from heaven. The devil was not going to claim me for his own, not yet, at any rate! However, I heard something ominous about the words of Michael toward me.

"Adam Sane has a destiny to fulfill within his choice of grace. I do not yet know the full extent of it, nor do I know the outcome, but the King has instructed me, by His grace, to announce the burden of Adam Sane."

I noted that Michael's authoritative words toward Lucifer required the devil to take his leave of heaven. He headed back in the direction from which he had come, to my enormous relief. The angels made a willing path for him, happy at his departure.

The entire appearance of the devil was completely hidden

from the Redeemed. They had been unaware of his presence. I do not know how this was accomplished, how it was even possible; I know only that the sovereign One who sits on the Throne of heaven could guard His children from the presence of evil, even the very memory of wickedness.

Michael, however, now turned his attention to me.

8

The Burden

I stood before Michael, although I was still more inclined to bow and worship, yet I knew by now that somebody would rebuke me for such an act. I was ready to hear my burden proclaimed. Whatever I was about to hear, I knew that I could make no reasonable protest, no sensible argument, and no rational defense.

Though I should be banished to the deepest pit of hell (I suspected I may have already passed through that place), I could not raise my voice in disagreement. I knew where I belonged, and I had already seen heavenly things that the lost are never privileged to see and the devout deeply long for. I was far from faithful! Yet, someone had handed me an extended season of grace that I could not explain.

With haunting wonder and curiosity, I recalled Odegeo's remark some time ago that I was being prayed for. And hadn't Michael said the same thing about me to Lucifer? I vaguely remembered a vignette about more things happening as a result of prayer than anyone can ever imagine or something to that effect. I now saw a definite possibility in my mind that the statement was true, however it was phrased.

Then Michael spoke. "You must travel back to your own world, but you may not return by the way you came. You must go along other paths, for you must learn of grace and faith. You do not yet grasp this. Your discernment is shallow, but it must be deep. And it will be, for you may yet be greatly used.

"Still, your destiny must be born out of your choice of grace, and to that end, even I do not know the outcome. In the moment of decision, you still have the will to choose otherwise."

"I don't understand what you are saying, sir," I answered meekly. "I don't understand at all. I have no business being here. I have no right to stand before you or be anywhere near the Throne."

"No one does but for grace."

"I don't understand grace."

"No one fully does. It was not offered to my race in the same way it has been offered to your race. It is a matter that will be discovered for eternity. Nonetheless, you may come to grace and learn of faith."

As I stood before the Archangel, the brightness of his being and the radiance of his power almost palpably buffeted my body. Although, incredibly, this seemed dim compared to the One on the Throne, whose form was utterly hidden from my sight, drowned in the impenetrable sharpness of the bursting dazzling light.

Michael's face was that unearthly combination of old age, years without number, and yet a youthfulness that was undimmed, untainted, and alive with a freshness and a newness as though he had been created yesterday. In Michael, as with all the angels, but more so in him, was a being who was a living contradiction: old but young, wise but innocent, glorious but humble, stern but kind, and powerful but gracious. These combinations did not exist in humans, at least not to this degree, and not at all in the ones I knew.

But I was perplexed. Michael intended for me to return to Earth, yet not by the way I had come. Of course, I was not sure how I had gotten from Earth, specifically from the Red Room to the dead planet and then to heaven. How was I to get back to Earth? Would Odegeo be allowed to go with me? He was my companion. I had strong feelings of love, friendship, attachment, and security with him and only him.

Even now, as I glanced about, I could not see Odegeo. Panic began to rise in my mind. I simply could not go forward without my friend. *How could I possibly find my way? How could I understand what Michael seemed to be saying I was supposed to do?* The journey was entirely overwhelming for me. *Where do I go? What do I do? How could I—*

"Do not fear," Michael interrupted. "Be anxious for nothing. The way will be provided for you, and you will find help in time of need and in ways you do not expect. The journey is as important at the goal."

"Please, sir. I'm frightened, I have no faith, and I don't comprehend grace. If I may ask, will Odegeo be going with me? I don't think I can bear whatever this is alone."

"You will have help along the way. Odegeo may travel with you at some time, but for now he has other ministry. You must remember what I said, the journey is as important as the goal, and it succeeds in the end by faith alone. If not by faith, you will eventually fail."

This quest was too much for me. I began to protest. "Who am I to take a journey of faith? I don't know how I even got here, much less why! Surely someone else could do this far better than me. I didn't ask to come here. This is impossible! I can't be expected to . . ."

Suddenly my voice stopped. I felt a lump in my throat, and

I literally couldn't make a sound. It didn't hurt, and I could still breathe normally, but speaking was physically impossible!

I looked up at Michael and realized I had been ranting at the ground. I was unable to look him in the eye *in my unbelief*. I understood that in heaven, unbelief cannot exist indefinitely. Speaking words of doubt is to deny the reality of the place where I was standing. Michael, who had been full of grace, mercy, and kindness until that moment, now looked upon me with a sternness that threatened to undo me.

"Blessings have been extended to you because of the faithfulness of others who love you," Michael said. "You have been chosen, yet you must choose. Will you proceed with the journey of faith?"

I had no qualms about continuing. The devil wanted to take me to hell and only moments before, he had been dismissed from heaven, giving me a reprieve. I did not understand all that Michael had said, but a faith journey was far superior to the other option. Perhaps my reasons were not all that pure, but it was a starting point. Beyond that, I suspected He knew my motives perfectly (whether or not Michael had that insight was unclear to me) and was still extending me a chance.

I also recognized that the whole deal had not been based on my character from the beginning. Apparently, this was all about the prayers of others on my behalf. I knew full well who it was that was praying, and the understanding caused me immeasurable shame.

But there was no doubt about my answer despite my ignorance, uncertainty, or skepticism. My misgivings about my beliefs ran deep even here in the place where faith becomes substance. It was not substance for me yet. I was still struggling with faith. Eventually, I would understand that faith is perfectly rational. The world treats it as an abandoned orphan because of our prevenient hostility and inborn sin. There is a *prima facie* from the womb, but it loses its grip quickly when life becomes earnest in its pain. I still doubted but couldn't deny the hope of the journey.

"I will proceed with the journey. I admit that I am uncertain about grace and faith, but the alternative is awful, and I'm afraid of that outcome."

"That in itself is the beginning of something," Michael answered. "Many in your world came to Him with less understanding and from a similar place of holy fear. The *object* of faith is what ultimately matters, not the *amount* of faith."

"Then, sir, what must I do to be saved from the devil?"

"Follow the River by which you stand, but you must go out from the Throne. You must leave this holy place and this holy realm and proceed to the place from where you will return to Earth."

"I don't know where that place is. I don't know how to get there," I said, fearful of the unknown journey and Michael's reaction to my doubt.

"That is the point of faith. You must trust God's goodness and leading. Yet there must be a beginning of faith, an instant in which faith becomes reality, a moment of faith that acts, borne out of grace. Even if you have faith that is only the size of a mustard seed, He will lead you. If you falter, He will correct you. The only true danger is in refusing the journey, that is, giving in to unbelief, *either here or along the way.* This is how greatly He values faith and trust. It is above all virtues."

"I will go," I answered with obvious reluctance.

"There is much that must be undone in your heart and mind. This requires a difficult road for you. Although there is a spark of belief in your mind yet there is much darkness and unbelief even though you have journeyed in the true Eden. You still are in a place of doubt. This can only be healed by merciful affliction and gracious chastisement."

I sighed deeply. "Then I guess I better get started."

I turned away from Michael and the place of the Throne of God and haltingly walked forward. I determined it best not to look back. Odegeo was nowhere to be seen. Much time would be passed and many miles trekked till I would see Odegeo again and under far different circumstances.

The worshipers still at the Throne were oblivious to me, so with a heavy heart, I began my journey alone. I passed through the City of God with all its regal splendor, enough to dwarf any mighty kingdom on Earth, and I headed into the unknown. It struck me again, forcefully, that I did not belong here. I was a foreigner in this land, heading into some thing or someplace that would require me to endure much difficulty. My prospects seemed quite dim. I knew I was still not a man of faith, not even a mustard seed's worth or whatever Michael had said. I wondered what "merciful affliction and gracious chastisement" meant. Whatever those words implied, there was no getting out of it now. I was between the proverbial rock and a hard place.

Maybe that is the way He wanted it.

9

The Glorious Redeemed

As I walked beside the river, as Michael had instructed me, still within the boundaries of the City, the fragrance and invigorating energy of the river filled my mind and heart. The effect of the river on me was like the ionic freshness after a spring rain or the thrill of young love. I wanted to lie down beside it, or even in it, and just rest and feel the joy and life of being by this stream of living water. I felt so alive.

The river flowed gently, sometimes with barely a ripple, but sometimes with the brush of a breeze, waves sprung, higher than the wind seemingly would create. The water's movement was almost in answer to some unknown desire to simply rise energetically in the joy of heaven as a worshiper suddenly moved to dance. Then the waves would rise and crash against each other, almost with the sound of clapping. At all times, the water was painted with the brilliant blues of the sky, the verdant green of the river banks, and the multifaceted colors of the mansions and gardens that marched alongside it.

Eventually, I walked out from the City of God, passing an endless parade of fabulous columns, fountains, gardens, colonnades, and porticoes. It contained every possibility of the most magnificent palatial city for the greatest and most exalted King in all creation—all of it in the rich and spectacular epicenter of heaven, with stunning light gleaming ubiquitously as though trying to light up the far corners of the universe with its radiant excessiveness. It was enough to make the famed earthly "city of lights" look like a ghetto of faint candlelight on a dark winter night.

The mansions that continued along both sides of the river (and could be seen spread out in broad and generous spaces and proportions in the distance) were alive with redeemed humanity. All the mansions were spectacularly beautiful, with indescribably lovely gardens and a heavenly permanence about them that was not subject to the effects of time and entropy. Some were strikingly similar to the palatial physical structures on Earth. Others looked more like a mammoth carving out of living rock.

Some seemed to be homes made out of the garden itself. Discerning where the garden life ended and the home began was not easy, or perhaps it was all one. Nonetheless, these homes were as tall and massive as any other. Some appeared as a sort of forest home, with trees and all manner of woodsy plant life making up the exterior walls. Many had animals playing in and around the garden areas. All sorts of animals were there, even some exotic looking creatures. One garden-type home seemed to have several bison foraging. I saw another one with a jungle theme where a lion and a lamb were lying together in peace.

Every mansion was thoroughly unique, and I began to wonder if each home was shaped and formed to express the love and passion of its owner. Between the mansions were more Edenic grasses, trees, and the startlingly beautiful inlaid granite plazas I had seen in and around the City.

Unlike Earth, there were no abandoned homes, fences, broken-down rusting items, sad tenements, signs of neglect, half-finished projects, and not a single example of the temporality or failure of men.

The river that flowed from the City of God bisected the land of the mansions on either side. The reflected colors in the river's waves were a palette of crystal blues, greens, yellows, golds, pale reds, and a silvery brightness, all flashing together as the occasional waves tumbled over one another. I would learn more later about the wind that moved the water. The beauty was breathtaking. I stood there drinking it all in. It helped dull the reality that I was alone.

But the redeemed were the real marvel of heaven to me! They were energetic, full of life and vigor, and present everywhere. They moved in and out and among their mansions, walked happily along the river, spoke greetings, even to me, and conversed with one another as they traveled in and out of the City of God.

I heard honest and often uproarious laughter everywhere, and many times I heard singing. Whether sung by one of the Redeemed or by many together, the songs often seemed spontaneous. Sometimes there were lyrics, and sometimes the singing seemed to have more of an instrumental quality made up simply of sounds of joy interspersed with what I can only describe as melodic laughter! I had never heard anything like it.

In the Redeemed I saw a depth of joy that was indefinable yet so profound and pervasive that it was impossible to ignore. It leaped from every cell of their spiritual bodies with radiance and energy illuminating their being, but it was not the same glowing or radiating of color effect the angels had. It was simply absolute fullness of life, perfect life, in which every moment is a joy, without drudgery, tiredness, boredom, or emptiness. Instead, it was full of meaning, purpose, and wholeness. Like those fleeting moments on Earth when the sky is royal blue, the sun is in its brilliance, and Earth is full of exploding green in the springtime. Or in the cool morning when dew is still on the grass, and life is wholly worth living because everything seems right and good, at least for the moment.

But, here, the wholeness was never-ending. In looking at redeemed humanity, it just seemed as though these people belonged here, like they were truly home in the place for which they were created.

The men of the Redeemed pulsed with strength and masculinity unseen in our world. Their power was not simply physical. (It was clear that no mortal on Earth could stand against any man of the Redeemed. I remembered a couple of older neighborhood bullies I would like to have introduced to these men.) They had a nobility, a royalty, about them that transcended humanity. They had confidence in their step and wisdom in their face that did not come from arrogance or conceit but from the intrinsic life of their spirit.

Every one of them was what any woman on Earth would have considered ravishingly handsome, exuding and throbbing manhood in the most powerful and, in earthly terms, alluring way. It was the very definition of manhood without the haughtiness and swagger, vulgarity, strained sexuality, bullying hierarchy, and all those earthly false notions of what makes a man masculine. There was nothing supercilious about this manliness. It was just the perfect balance of all the qualities of strength, goodness, intelligence, wisdom, faithfulness, and courage that define a protector, provider, and leader with authentic masculinity.

And the women of the Redeemed! Here was pulsing, physical beauty unmatched by any movie goddess or media icon. And this was true of every woman of the Redeemed! The perfection of both body and mind pervaded the entire being of each woman. Femininity was defined in these women. Every movement contained gentleness and modesty, loveliness and enticing desirability, sweetness and delicateness. Enthralling fragileness was wrapped in an assuring confidence of female essence, with demurring charm permeating the fullness of feminine sexuality in the most wholesomely desirable way. Every movement screamed out womanhood in its most joyful complementary delight.

In another place, the desire of lust would have overwhelmed almost any man surrounded continually by the sight of such flawless beauty. Here, this desire was utterly foreign and even repulsive to my mind. In my earthly life, the pursuit of lust had occupied much time and had flexed its powerful instincts in many places. Here, however, such desire was so unnatural and demeaning to the intrinsic goodness of these redeemed women that my mind had no place for such thoughts.

These women were pleased with their femininity. There was not the slightest hint of mannishness or the rejection of the blessed state of being female by God's design, unlike so many confused and deceived women of my modern and enlightened era on Earth. No, it is not all environment; the women of heaven were born for this. They gave perfect balance, in its sheer oppositeness, to the men's masculinity. And these women, like the men, carried a look of deferring wisdom in their eyes, joining themselves with the True Groom for whose delight they were ultimately created, even beyond the state of helpmate.

How sad now the poor pathetic estate of fallen humanity seemed. What a shadow of man and woman the earthly inhabitants had devolved to. We appeared pale, weak, dense, and stumbling compared to these people. Humanity was like the terminal patient lying on the hospital bed: breathing with difficulty, unable to control its wastes, eyes sunken in to the skull seeing only indistinct shapes, a pallor of gray on the skin, and a heartbeat slowing nearly to a stop. In our womb, in that ancient Eden, we had traded all the life of heaven for the lie of hell.

And again, an old lost church memory rushed back to me—a song about this world not being our home; a sermon about being strangers and visitors in this world; a Bible passage about citizenship in heaven. I had missed it all, ignored it all, or even more accurately, rejected it all as I was so caught up in my worldly pursuits, especially in my teen years and off to college. Again, I saw the lights of the old sanctuary where I sat Sunday after Sunday with those diffusing fixtures hanging from the ceiling giving off their soft, warm yellowish light. The old organ would be playing hymns, and my mother and father would be singing those old songs humbly with joy, contentment, and peace that I arrogantly had finally come to hate, thinking them to be the domain of fools.

But redeemed humanity silently shouted to me that I was the fool. In heaven, every human was the picture of perfect health, beauty, strength, and intelligence. Their spirits were alive with the eternal dynamic life of God Himself. It was like the freshness of a burgeoning green spring day, the very smell of life, health, and joy. It was the thrill of being filled and knowing one's good purpose. The realization of those same marvels that had always been elusive was now entirely, permanently realized. Then there was a sudden noise behind me, then a voice.

"So, you finally made it!" the voice loudly proclaimed. I heard a delight in his voice, and although I could not see him, I could sense the twinkle in his eye. I turned around, knowing already who was standing behind me, too close; he always stood too close, but somehow with this man, you didn't care. He was full of life, love, and joy. To be in his presence was to realize a higher level of energy and spirit.

I turned and saw a familiar face, recognizable but profoundly different from his face in his earthly life. Now he was radiant, strong, and boundlessly energetic. He had always been full of energy, but now he had no trace of the inevitable weariness that comes upon all humans from time to time. He was full of deep joy, like an underground stream that feeds the land above it with richness and greenness.

It was Pastor Gordon Lachen. He was the man who had been the preacher in the church of my youth. What I saw most deeply in this face here in heaven were the things I had remembered most clearly about him from life on Earth. He had had a fullness of life and energy. He had been a man of great joy who laughed easily and honestly. It was so unlike what passed for comedy among those I knew, which demeaned those not like us, implied perversion and crudity in every context, and flaunted haughty pretensions. Much of it was forced and hollow, the pseudo-intellectual drudgery of the Gnostic elite.

But here was a man as real and solid as the Earth. He had been without pretension, arrogance, or guile.

We greeted one another with great pleasure.

"You're here, but something doesn't seem quite right, eh?"

"Uh, no sir, it isn't quite right. I'm afraid I don't quite belong here."

"Ahh," he said, laughing. "I think you will someday! I think you *will* belong here. You know (he winked at me), you could've come the standard way. I believe you sat through many a sermon when I told you that." He seemed almost gleeful in reminding me of this.

"Yes, Pastor, you did. I see my foolishness now. But how did you know I was here, and how did you know that I didn't come by the . . . well, the standard way?"

"The angels told me what was going on, and they knew that I would want to see you very badly. I'm quite glad, of course, that you see the foolishness of your ways! That's a step in the right direction. You see your foolishness, eh? That's good, that's good! But you don't have to call me Pastor anymore. I appreciate the sentiment, but there's really only one Pastor, one Shepherd here. And that isn't me!" He laughed heartily, and I was so struck by his mirth and the twinkle in his eyes that I joined in. It was such a joy to see him laugh. Just like on Earth, his whole body shook when he laughed, and he leaned forward almost like a diver ready to splash into a pool.

I realized that as a child, I had loved Pastor Lachen. Why hadn't I believed his preaching? He was as genuine a man as you could ever meet.

Then, as though he were reading my mind, he asked me with sudden seriousness, "Adam, what kept you from the faith?" He had always been capable of going in an instant from uproarious laughter to the deadliest gravity.

"I'm not entirely sure, Pastor—"

"You can call me Gordon," he said, interrupting. "Although that won't be my name forever!" He had a delightful grin and a look in his eyes that I had seen in Odegeo as well; that look hinted that I should know what he meant, but I didn't.

"OK, I'll try to remember to call you Gordon. And the answer to your question is that I am not entirely sure what kept me from the faith. I wish I knew. I don't understand what happened to me. I really regret it all now."

"Regret, eh? Well, that's a start. It's not really quite good enough in the end, you should know that of course, but it's a start."

"What do you mean Pastor, uh, Gordon?"

"Why don't we walk along the river? I may be with you for quite some time." He hesitated, a chuckle rising in his voice. "Regret may mean you're just sorry you got caught!" Then he winked at me again, which made me laugh. Then, just before breaking out into loud laughter, he managed to blurt out, "And you got caught for sure this time!"

The full measure of this understatement, perhaps the greatest of all time, sent Pastor Lachen into a fit of laughter that also irresistibly drew me into it. Even as I was enjoying this undeniable charge of pure humor, I thought it both strange and ludicrous that I was laughing heartily at the result of my own moral failure. I had always laughed at my shortcomings but in a completely different way. I used to laugh at my missteps to convince myself and others that they didn't matter; I was above that adherence to ancient mores! It was cynical laughter that at once both absolved me from guilt, I hoped, and contemptuously ridiculed the commoners caught up in the morality ruse that was being pulled over on the less erudite.

But Gordon saw me laughing, which only evoked more from him. The mere sight of him in the grip of pure, joyous, free, untainted, holy laughter was the cause of such deepening mirth in my heart that eventually, we were both laughing so hard that tears streamed down our faces. It wasn't merely about the joke. It hadn't been all that funny; it was just some spontaneous joy welling up and producing uproarious laughter.

At some point, we must have fallen to our knees because we found ourselves helping each other up when the laughter finally subsided. It was indeed a comical moment worthy of healthy laughing, but somehow it didn't seem that our exchange should have resulted in such abandonment of senses in the fit of laughter that had overwhelmed us. Something about being in heaven created a fundamental change in perception, even in me. Joy was everywhere, unavoidable, and delicious, bursting out constantly in every atom of creation and every cell of living beings.

"Yeah, I got caught," I finally answered, setting off another round of wild laughter that eventually found drool coming from my mouth in a complete loss of dignity as I gave myself over to the joy I felt. Eventually, we regained a measure of composure.

"You know, Gordon, I spent a lot of time with the angel Odegeo. It was amazing and enjoyable, and he had such a peace and strength about him. But we didn't laugh together like you and I just did."

"Yeah, angels don't get it," he said, chuckling.

"They don't get what?"

"Humor, jokes, comedy. It's not that they don't laugh, they certainly do, but it's not at funny stuff, exactly. I've used some of my best material on them. They just give me that blank stare. It's a holy stare, of course (Gordon winked at me and chuckled), but blank!"

"But it's not a matter of any lack of joy?"

"No, no, not at all. I'm not suggesting anything like that. Angels have profoundly deep joy in the Lord. And peace is a pervasive quality of their being. But they are spirit, you know, ministering spirits sent out to render service and all that. Well, maybe you don't know, but you should! I preached on that more than once!"

Gordon crinkled up his face just like he used to do on Earth when he was making a big point in a sermon. "Anyway, their nature is just fundamentally different than ours. Maybe they don't need to laugh, at jokes I mean. When you've lived in the darkness that we came out of, laughter is all the more necessary. It's a gift from God. But, to them I think it seems a strange gift, something unique to flesh and blood.

"But, to get back to the original point, regret is a starting point, but it won't get you all the way to repentance. Regret can be the result of too many other things. Repentance comes from godly sorrow."

I decided to change the subject. "Where does this river go?"

Gordon laughed. "Changing the subject, eh?" I hadn't fooled him.

"The river flows into the Crystal Sea a few miles ahead. The Crystal Sea goes on for hundreds of miles, to use the earthly measure. It's not wide, like you would think of an ocean on the Earth. It's more like a river that's, I don't know, forty miles wide and hundreds of miles long. This whole land is a part of heaven, but it's not the whole thing. Eden, which you walked through, is part of heaven. It is one hundred twenty square miles but separated from this heavenly realm by the Throne. There are other levels of heaven to be sure!"

I responded to this statement with a look of amazement,

but Gordon said, "You should've known that, Adam!"

"I get that feeling all the time," I remarked.

"I've not seen the other levels yet, but I think we all will see the fullness of heaven eventually, all *believers* I mean." A pained expression came over his face. "I've not even seen all of *this* level of heaven, not by a long shot, but some of the Redeemed told me that this whole land is fifteen hundred miles long from the City to the far end, what we would sort of think of as east and west, and fifteen hundred miles wide, or sort of north and south, although directions don't exactly work the same way here. I'm still trying to figure that one out. I always loved maps in my earthly life, although I was no cartographer. But the size or rather the dimensions have significance. I don't suppose those numbers mean anything to you?"

"Uh, no, not really."

"Hmm, I probably never preached on that subject! All right, you're off the hook!" he said with a characteristic wink. "But, Adam, where are you headed? I've not been given all the information about your presence here. I know that Michael addressed you, which must have been quite a moment, but I don't know all of what he said."

"I believe I'm supposed to follow the river to the Crystal Sea and walk alongside it till I come to some realm beyond that. I have to get back to Earth, somehow on my own, and apparently that means going to the far end of, uh . . . heaven, I guess."

"I don't think you'll really be on your own, at least not all the time. In fact, I've been sent to accompany you for a while. The far end of heaven, at least on this level, which isn't the eternal heaven, is actually where the Crystal Sea ends. Two rivers flow out of the Sea in opposite directions and wrap all the way around the outer borders of this land. I think the rivers go all the way back to Eden, one on the north and one on the south, for lack of better terms. You probably haven't noticed it yet, but there is no curvature on the horizon."

"Now that you mention it, Gordon, I remember standing quite high up in Eden, with Odegeo, and looking out over a vast distance. We were probably several thousand feet high and you're right, there was no curvature."

"Interesting, eh? I don't quite get it, but we are on a flat plain, so to speak. I don't think we are on a planet. I don't think heaven is necessarily subject to all the natural physical laws that we were used to. In any case, at the far end of this land, where the Crystal Sea ends, there is another realm. The citizens of heaven don't go there, at least not the human citizens. It's the only way to and from Earth since the Column was broken."

The comment about the Column piqued my interest. "You mean there used to be a Column, a Column of Light that went to the Earth?"

"Yes, exactly. A Column of Light. Near the City of God. You came here in a similar one I understand. The one to Earth was destroyed a long time ago."

"Why would Lucifer want to destroy that?"

"He didn't. The Lord destroyed it in a judgment on humanity. You probably don't remember the story about the Tower of Babel in Genesis chapter eleven, although you should. I preached on that! Great sermon, too, by the way."

Now I was truly fascinated. I had heard of the Tower of Babel story, although, sadly enough, not so much from the Bible. There had been strange and somewhat oblique references to it in the occult reading I had done. I was not about to admit that to Pastor Lachen. I remembered the name of Nimrod related to the Tower of Babel. Nimrod seemed to have a significant place in occult history, and many legends had grown up around that name. It struck me that, of course, I remembered names and details about occult matters, but the knowledge and memories about the Bible had almost completely left me, despite the many years of church and my own parents' efforts to teach the Bible stories. Darkness stays in the heart of man while light is elusive to the lost.

But the Column had a special appeal to me. It had taken me to heaven. Of course, that Column had not taken me to heaven from Earth. In fact, as I now understood, it could not have. There was no longer any Column on the Earth to take any human to heaven. I wasn't even sure how I got from the Red-Hue Room to . . . wherever I was when I regained consciousness, but this was something to pursue another time.

"What did the Tower of Babel have to do with the Column?"

"Well, the people of that time weren't stupid. Our era on Earth doesn't give previous generations much credit. That's because of the arrogance of humanity in believing that the human race is getting better and smarter, when in truth the opposite is happening. And many humans also believe that morality doesn't matter, as though it has no impact on human intellectual growth. Ridiculous, Adam! Humanity is at the shallow end of the gene pool now and will continue to devolve.

"But you asked me what the Tower of Babel had to do with the Column, right? Well, the people of that era could actually see the Column in the sky, probably especially at night. It was still there. I don't know how high it was off the ground, but they knew that they could build a tower to reach it. They knew it was possible, and when they reached the Column, all they had to do was figure out how to get inside. And they would have, as you can tell by the Lord's remark about the situation. Then they could have had access to heaven. I'm pretty sure this was all inspired by the enemy. It seems consistent with his character in Isaiah fourteen and Ezekiel twenty-eight. You know, I—"

"I know, Gordon, I know. You preached on that, and I should know all about what you just referred to, but I don't. I don't have a clue!"

"Well, you should. Anyway, the Lord not only confused their tongues, but He also broke the Column, and it has been unused to this day."

Then something hit me suddenly, like a thunderbolt. "Wait a minute, Gordon! Did you say a minute ago that there is another way back to Earth, somewhere in the land beyond the realm of heaven?"

"Yes, I did say that. When angels are sent to Earth for ministry, they go that way. And when Satan enters heaven, he usually comes by that route. In fact, there is great conflict in that realm, angelic conflict."

"You mean the angels fight with each other?"

"Well, angels and demons, which are fallen angels. Yes, they are at war. I preached several times on Ephesians chapter six, you know, spiritual forces at war in the heavenly places? No, you probably don't know. (He winked again.) But it was some of my best preaching. I quoted Tozer and Lewis all over the place!"

"Actually, I don't know about Ephesians whatever it was, but I do know something about that war. I saw some of the other side in my years of darkness."

"That's why the Redeemed don't go there, because of the war and the darkness. In this heavenly land we are untouched and untouchable by that war. Although Satan may come to the City of God, he may not enter the realm of the Redeemed. There is a boundary he may not cross. The Redeemed are unaffected by his presence."

So, I have to go through that land to get back to Earth?"

"If that is what you were commanded, then yes."

"How do I get through? Where is the route back to Earth?"

"That I don't know. I'm sorry, Adam, but I have a feeling no human in this realm knows for sure the answer to those questions. I will tell you what I know, but let's save that discussion for another time. The moment will apparently come when that conversation must be had, but let it be later rather than sooner. That land is a land of angels in both of their natures, and little is known about it. Even the Scripture doesn't say much. No one in the heavenly lands has any interest or desire to go there. We don't seek the edge of evil as we used to often do. There is no more craving to dabble in even the slightest evil or open the door to even the smallest degree to play around with the darkness. It is utterly over for the Redeemed."

"I'm not of the Redeemed."

"I'm sorry, Adam. But I do believe I will be going with you all the way to the far end, where the Crystal Sea ends. Beyond that, I don't know what is to happen, but you can be sure that you will not be left alone permanently. Some battles you have to face alone, or so it would seem. Remember, the key to all things on your side of eternity is faith. He risked it all, in a sense, to see faith. He doesn't play cosmic dice with the universe, but He does value faith, trust, and belief that is uncoerced and freely chosen. He values this above all things, even to the risk of the soul. What He values is what *is* valuable. Faith, Adam, faith is *everything*. All else is merely results."

10

The Knowledge of the Holy

We walked on in silence for some time. I was pondering all that Gordon had said. The scenery was ever-changing and impressive. The river was on our left side, and across the river, perhaps a mile wide, were many mansions with more in the distance.

For the first time, I realized the river was at the bottom of a valley. On both sides, the land rose in a gentle slope so that the mansions of the Redeemed could be seen on each side of the river for many miles up the hill. Many in the distance glinted the reflected light of gold, silver, bronze, blue, green, orange, red, and yellow; some had an almost prism-like effect. I didn't know how this could be since no light source existed. No sun here lit the sky with the brightness of its fire. In heaven, light was everywhere. It just seemed to exist somehow, almost of its own accord. The landscape was dominated by the lushest of green exploding with life. This was life without death, abundant life, perfect health, vitality, and vibrant richness without limit, including in my companion. My Redeemed companion.

Suddenly, just as I was about to ask my friend about a marine-looking mansion, a strong wind came and began to stir the waters of the river, which until now had been mostly quite serene and peaceful. I hadn't felt much breeze in my heavenly travels, but this wind steadily and quickly grew stronger, as if a storm on the horizon was rapidly approaching (although there was no storm) and increasing in intensity as it came closer.

As the wind blew more and more briskly, the waves rippled, grew choppy, and gathered up like giant columns of teeth on a ripsaw the entire length of the visible river! The wind was now a gale, and our hair and clothes flapped violently. What was happening? The words of Odegeo raced back to me now! Was this it? Was the Son arising from the Throne? Panic struck me! He was coming, walking through the land, and I was not ready! My legs crumpled, my stomach tightened into a suffocating knot, and I could barely breathe. I began to wretch and moan and howl in fear. It was too late! It was too late!

Seeing my consternation, Gordon shouted into the force of the wind, "Peace, Adam, peace! All is well! Just watch this marvel!" He was laughing!

Then a most extraordinary thing happened. The waves rose out of the water of the river! Momentarily they retained their saw-blade form, but then the wind swirled the air-bound waves into a confusion of thousands of massive, blended streaks of water, great planes of water spinning like a top until they broke into millions of droplets! The droplets soared even higher in the wind and, a moment later, started falling like a heavy mist across the landscape. It swept over us, tingled, and seemed to sparkle as it fell on my face. And every drop of this divine rain glistened as though the light of glorious diamonds was contained in the billions of falling, whirling beads of moisture.

Nothing on Earth had prepared me for such a sight. It was like a shower of light itself, a new kind of light, a water light. In heaven, everything, including the rain, is packed with an essence, an abundance, of light. Gordon laughed joyously and held up his arms as if to receive as much of the misty rain as possible. The water sent exquisite chills all over my skin, and goosebumps formed in a delightfully thrilling and refreshing soaking. This rain was not normal! There was something of divine life in the water falling on my skin.

For the first time since I entered heaven, the ever-present light dimmed as moisture saturated the air. An almost Earth-like essence was in the scene around me, which included a heavy soaking moisture, dampness, and humidity in the air. There was filtered light a little bit like a cloudy overcast day. Because the "storm" didn't last long, it reminded me, ever so briefly, of rainy days on Earth.

This rain mist was how the land was watered, and the plant life stayed fresh and rich. Although this was my first experience with seeing the source of it rolling over the land, it was not my last. On many occasions, as Gordon and I moved inexorably, and regrettably for me, toward the end of the Crystal Sea and whatever awaited me there, the river or sea would rise with the wind (the "saw-waves" as I began to call them) and send the rain mist dancing across the ground, drenching thoroughly everything in its path, including us.

Unlike on Earth, when everyone ran indoors to avoid the threat of a severe storm and getting wet, here in heaven, the Redeemed would come out to welcome the rain and stand or even seem to dance in it, obviously with deep joy and refreshment. I would often hear singing when the rain mist came, and great laughter would rise from the mansions during these showers of heaven.

The rain mist was almost electric as it tingled on my skin and brought a sweet but chill effect on my body. I might have even tried singing once myself, but I knew no songs of praise like the citizens of heaven did who made such a joyful noise.

"That rain was a life-giving pleasure," I said to Gordon after the mist and my anguish had passed. The storm was moving up the gathering slopes in a radiant glistening rhythm of blues and greens, saturating the mansions and all the life of heaven on the hills and into the distance. In a remote way, it was like watching the passing of a storm. I remembered the days of my childhood when summer storms flew through; we went outside to watch them streak the sky with darkness and see the vertical haze of sky rays of drenching rain that could be seen miles away.

"Yes, it is wonderfully pleasurable. And I understand what you are saying, but be careful there, Adam," Gordon said with sudden seriousness.

"What do you mean? Be careful about what?"

"The rain is merely a tool. Nothing more. It does not give life. Do you understand me?"

"I'm not sure."

"Well, Adam, you must realize that only God gives life. I know back on Earth, people tossed around remarks like you just made and especially about the life-giving sun and the life-giving oceans and all that nonsense, but that is a great error and a great offense, so be careful that you don't tolerate that kind of thinking. God created all those things, but He is not the same as all those things. The creation reflects Him, but He didn't create the world for you or anyone else to deify it. In fact, He is utterly different from His creation."

Gordon was so insistent and direct about this matter that I began to feel bad. "I'm sorry, Gordon. I meant nothing offensive when I said it."

"I know you didn't. But living on Earth, humans become so ingrained with wrong thinking, poor judgment, and indifference and apathy about truth and the reality of a Christocentric universe, that they constantly say things that are misinformed, downright foolish, and even offensive to God. When those professing themselves to be wise say that the sun brought about life on Earth, what they are ultimately doing is crediting the sun, an inanimate ball of gas, with being the creator on some level!

"Adam, that is simply sun-worship and idolatry, ascribing to the sun or the ocean or gravity, of all things, what belongs solely to God. It's bad thinking and horribly misguided. People, even Christians, are so lazy in their thinking it's revolting. I have a dear friend here who once wrote that the most important thing about any person is what they think about God. He was absolutely correct!"

"Okay. I suppose you're right."

"Just imagine if you and your wife had a child. Are you married, Adam?"

I hesitated to answer. "No." I knew my view on the topic would be scorned in heaven. "I've actually held marriage in disdain. I'm sorry. I know that isn't an acceptable position to hold here. And I imagine you have preached on that topic," I said, hoping my nod toward comic relief would alleviate a sudden sense of inadequacy and failure. I knew Gordon would not approve of the type of relationships I had had with women. I didn't even really approve. I knew my pleasures were mostly that of a user with little interest in real love, the type of love that I had seen in my parents: genuine caring, commitment, and selflessness. I had a feeling that Gordon knew I had engaged in such acts, and I was hoping to head him off with my attempt at humor regarding his preaching.

"Marriage is an honorable God-ordained estate, but we all mess things up to one degree or another, eh?" Gordon looked at me with raised eyebrows that betrayed an intuitive understanding of my moral failure. "But," he went on, "my point is really about who gives life. So, imagine you and your wife having a baby. Now you have to understand that every parent is secretly, or maybe not so secretly, convinced that their child is the brightest, most beautiful, and most wonderful child ever born."

Gordon began to chuckle and then said, "This example might be even better if I used grandparents, but anyway, you're a brand-new father, and you are as proud and happy as you can possibly be with your new baby. You and your wife are absolutely in love with that kid, as you should be! You consider the possibility that this is the greatest, most significant thing you have ever done in your life. You look at your child, and you say to yourself, 'This is good. This is very good.'

"Now, imagine someone comes along and tells you that the child isn't really yours. They claim that your wife, although she still has the scars to prove it, didn't give birth to the baby. A terrible mistake happened, but the child isn't really yours. You had nothing to do with its birth. This person is very persistent, and no matter how much you try to show him the truth, he just continues to defy you and insists it's not your baby. Then, to add insult to injury, he starts telling everyone else that the baby is not yours. He even cooks up some phony pictures or makes up a timeline to show that you couldn't possibly have had this child, and he calls this proof.

"Imagine that everyone else starts believing that this man is right, and you, the father of the baby, are wrong. You're not the father after all. Eventually, you and your wife are the only ones that believe the child is yours; no one else believes you." Gordon paused. "How would that make you feel?"

It was an apt analogy. "I get it, Gordon. I understand. Only God gives life."

As we continued walking along the river that flowed directly from before the Throne to the Crystal Sea, perhaps twenty miles, I saw several bridges spanning the entire width of the river. These bridges were two or three miles apart.

As with everything else in heaven, they were spectacular in appearance (although tame in comparison to what I would see later). One bridge was completely golden in color, and another was all silver. The brightness of the bridges blazed in the beauty of the radiant light of heaven. Each bridge was different. Some had high arches and cables supporting their respective streets and were very earthlike in their structure. One was very low, barely a foot or two above the water, and seemed to be made of rich reddish wood beams and planks through the whole length of it. I could not tell how it was supported or if it even was supported! (I suppose in heaven even bridges can walk on water.) I wondered what happened to this bridge when the powerful winds came and lifted up the waves and drove the rain-mist onto the land.

Other bridges seemed to have far too little support by way of beams, trusses, and cables, yet they were quite solid. I observed many residents, both angels and the Redeemed, passing over the bridges. Some of the bridges defied the laws of earthly physics.

As I had learned by now, He was not bound by the natural or physical laws. And He was inclined to violate the laws men so desperately lean on and trust in for security and stability whenever He wished. I would never have thought such a thing in my former life. I was quite sure that if there was a God, He was bound by the same rules as everyone else.

In my irrationality, I believed that even if a deity somehow created the laws of the universe, the deity was still subject to them. I was not alone in my delusion. Countless blind guides lead the blind, like me, in all the halls of learning that I had haunted. Brilliant men with minds of stunning intelligence, yet trapped, unknowingly, inside the black box of their own narrow and rigid humanism, straining with all their might to find the answers to the "whys" of existence, but utterly determined to keep the light from shining the humbling truth into the midst of the dark places of their thoughts.

I was quite curious about one thing in particular regarding these amazing bridges, and I asked my guide about this. "Gordon, who built these bridges? They are astounding!"

"Marvelous, eh? These were built ages ago, although they never age in the least. They were part of the celebration of the newness of the Earth and heavens when the foundations were laid, the morning stars sang together, and all the sons of God shouted for joy. But there is better than this to come."

I didn't know what Gordon was talking about. I was pretty sure it was something from The Book (maybe from a sermon!), but I was hesitant to show my ignorance yet again.

We were passing what Gordon had said was the last river bridge, a tremendous silvery-gray cantilever bridge with seven supporting piers across the river. Many of the Redeemed were coming off and going on the bridge. As we momentarily stopped so that I could admire the structure, I noticed someone coming off the bridge onto land, happily greeting everyone he saw, someone that looked oddly familiar, yet distinctly different from the memory I had of the person who came to mind. As I watched him, even his gait was reminiscent of my earthly memory.

Then he turned his face toward me, and even from a hundred feet away, I realized with shock that this was indeed him! It was the old man from the street I had grown up on, my neighbor, the last person I ever expected to see in heaven! I was stunned by his presence here. He was my nemesis even as a child, a man whom I and everyone else had hated. Perhaps every neighborhood has that one person who lives to frighten the children with his spiteful darkness, enforces the minutiae of nonsensical civil law to his advantage, and cares nothing for social graces or neighborly politeness. This was Frank Henderson, the man from my old neighborhood. He was redeemed, and he was in heaven.

11

Frank Henderson

I feel shame in admitting that I was not pleased to see Frank Henderson here in heaven. I especially noted that he was a redeemed resident, and I was not. He belonged here, and I did not. And I felt some graceless irritation that this man had made it, and I had been left out as if I had been a victim of a conspiracy to keep me out of paradise! My immediate thought was that this arrangement was impossible. I knew I was a better man than he! It was fine to talk about forgiveness and this thing called grace, but this dark, bitter, and intolerant man in heaven? Ridiculous, so I thought.

I immediately turned away as if I had not seen him, pretending to be looking at some other heavenly scene with great interest. This practice I had nearly perfected on Earth: culpable avoidance. I did not want to see him, this Frank Henderson. What was he doing here? What right did he have to enjoy this perfection, freedom, and guiltless joy?

This man had been a thorn in the flesh for everyone on our street—a busybody, a nosey mean, hateful old man bent on making everyone around him as bitter and miserable as he. We had even developed a nickname for him, given his penchant for policing the citizenry and constantly attempting to create situations in which he could use the law to harass neighbors. We called him Inspector Henderson, behind his back, of course. And it had seemed in my youth that he had it in for me, especially me.

But he saw me.

"Adam? Adam, is that you?"

Unlike the Throne in the City of God, where the Redeemed had been oblivious to my presence, here I was noticed by all the passersby, which were many. Frank saw me and recognized me. I tried to quickly start a conversation with Gordon, pointing at some distant sight in the opposite direction. Gordon looked at me strangely.

"Adam Sane?" The old man persisted. *Old* was an anachronistic hangover from a world where entropy mercilessly ruled with an iron fist. Frank was no longer old. In fact, he had grown young, mocking all the formerly vast and impenetrable wages of sin. Where grace reigned, those wages were utterly abolished (Another had paid them), and I remembered something about sins being as far as the east is from the west.

It struck me that nowhere else does anyone *grow young*. It was inevitable: we grow old. Period. This was merely another case of the magnitude of the diametrical opposites of the DNA of Earth and that of heaven. Down to the very molecular level, the polar opposites of the two realms exist as the very definition of irresistible glorious eternal life and inevitable crushing, unending death. Like a slap in the face, the revelation struck me anew: Frank Henderson had wholly emerged in the irresistible, glorious life.

I, Adam Sane, was submerged in the inevitable crushing death. Yet, I still rebelled at realizing his presence in heaven and my exclusion from the state of the Redeemed as though there were flaws in the system itself, not in me. After all that I had seen, understood, and experienced with Odegeo and

Gordon and at the Throne of God Himself since that night in the Red-Hue Room, I still held rebellion in my heart! How is such darkness, blindness, and greedy, self-possessed, shriveling shrinking of the soul possible?

"Adam?"

There was no escaping now. Frank was coming near. I turned to look and feigned surprise. I was about to lie and say I hadn't seen him, but the words died on my lips.

No! You cannot tell a lie in this place. It had been my way of life, falling far too easily from my lips, but not here! I knew I was a liar and hadn't even cared about it in my earthly life. I had even joked with my friends about my pervasive dishonesty, telling them on one occasion I had considered answering yes on a job application about speaking a second language.

"I speak English and Prevarication." I laughed derisively, arrogantly confiding in my friends that the proprietor of the auto parts store was so dense that he probably wouldn't even know what *prevarication* means. We laughed heartily at the hard-working man, behind his back. I was a haughty, lying, conceited coward. "Yes, sir, I learned Prevarication while studying in France."

But not here. You cannot lie in heaven.

So, I weakly responded. "Hello. Is that you, Frank?"

Gordon looked at me with some surprise, not because I knew someone in heaven, but because of my hesitation and lack of enthusiasm.

"Adam!" Frank said, "It is so wonderful to see you here!" I am heading to the City, but what a good appointment it is to see you on the way."

Then his countenance subtly changed as he gazed at me, realizing with some uncertainty that I was not of the

Redeemed. It was evident by my appearance. Although I was physically healthier and fitter than I had ever been, by far, I was not of the Redeemed.

"It's great to see you, Frank," I said, meaning that it was not great and I didn't want to see him. The composite of the statement helped me avoid the boldness of a lie.

Frank immediately recognized the truth. "I understand, Adam. And please believe me, I don't blame you a bit."

"It's okay," I said, trying to sound magnanimous and hoping to disengage the conversation.

"No," said Frank. "It was not okay. I mistreated and hated everyone in my life, near and far. I caused children like you to stumble. I know what I deserve, a millstone, a drowning in the deepest hole of the sea. I know the verse well now. My greatest regret in not getting saved till I was on my deathbed was the inability to beg for mercy from everyone I hurt.

"He saved me, Adam. He forgave me—even me, the least-deserving man who ever lived, and yet grace was abundant and free. I can't explain it. I could only receive it. One exchange on the last day of my life! A moment of humility and real sorrow, not simply regret or remorse, but sorrow over my pathetic self, an instant of faith, was all it took to secure me forever. Seventy-five years—mostly of anger, bitter hatred, and resentment—all washed clean in an instant. How can there be anything but thanks and praise forever?

"A man came to my room on that last day, another man I had mistreated out of bitterness, and he told me about forgiveness and grace. He also told me about sin and hell. And he had the courage to speak the truth: 'If you think your life on Earth has been misery and pain, your future, your forever, will make this life look like your honeymoon with Rachel.' He knew right where to hit me, Adam.

"Rachel, my lamb, the love of my life! We had met when I was only twelve and she was ten. I loved her instantly, even at that age. Fourteen years later we were married. I was in heaven and thought my life would be bliss and happiness, but within a year Rachel was dead.

"I watched her die. Her disease-ridden body shrunken and weak, her skin was a sickening splotchy, flaky red, almost like she was covered in blood. Her joints were swollen and intensely painful. Her breathing was labored, and at times she could barely draw a breath. She was so frail and could hardly speak at the end. Her last words were of love and devotion to me. And then she died. My life ended right then and there. I was undone. I swore hate, anger, and defiance against the God of heaven forever. How could He take my Rachel? She belonged to me; no one else could have her!

"Foolishness, Adam, foolishness. She was His all along, not mine. I didn't weave her body together in the womb. I hadn't known the number of her days and the hairs on her head from all eternity. I hadn't been the One who created her to share my joy forever. And, seriously, would she have traded fifty years on Earth, no matter how good they *might* have been, with the utter joy, happiness, and perfection of heaven? Would she, would anyone, want to go back to that fallen, painful world after having tasted the richness, purity, and fullness of divine eternity? Was it true love that demanded in my darkness that she come back to me? What would love want for her, Adam? Fifty more years on Earth?

"But I was ignorant, a fool. I thought I was God. I'm not

saying grief, pain, and loneliness don't exist for the believer. They do, and they should for a loss like that. And I understand a season of anger. God is big enough for that. But this anger and hate consumed me for nearly fifty years. I grew more and more inwardly obsessed with my own bitterness, coddling it, justifying it, obeying it. And anger brings a twisted pleasure— not a pleasure that grows a person and brings positive feelings and satisfaction to life but a dark pleasure that justifies meanness and strokes its own sense of deserving.

"I truly believed that no one had ever suffered like me. And as I turned in on myself with my anger, the result was that I was sick most of my life with one malady or another: ulcers, headaches, depression, constant body aches. I blamed all of these on God. When I heard, accidentally as I called it at the time, about others who had suffered similar loss in their life yet recovered with great faith and love for God, I called them idiots, misguided fools, tools of a cruel tyrant, a God delusion. And my hate spilled out ever more.

"So, as you well know, Adam, I caused everyone in my path, and then some, misery and anguish. I wanted to spread my disease. No one should be happy since I was not! No one should be at peace because I was not! No one should have love because I did not!

"I screamed and raged at children. I plotted foul, ridiculous, petty schemes against my neighbors who were good people, just to enjoy watching their misery. I caused trouble and dissension at work. I spewed lies and gossip about coworkers. Everywhere I turned, I brought pain. But I always blamed Him. It wasn't really my fault. I was a victim of a cruel god.

"But then, do you understand this, Adam, that last day of my life! Oh, thank heaven, thank God! He spared me for one final day, one final chance! He foreknew me from eternity, and He brought me to that final point of utter weakness and utter frailty. He kicked every prop out from under me: my health was completely gone, my money, and there was plenty of it, could not deliver me from this long, dark night, my business had been taken over by others, and even my anger, which horribly had sustained me over the years, could no longer cause me to lash out at anyone!

"No one cared about my death, and no one grieved at my passing. Not a single person, Adam. Hear me. Not one human being visited me in the final month I was in the hospital, dying. Even the medical personnel had nothing to do with me! They flew in and out of my room and tried to ignore the venom in my soul. Every single thing I had stupidly held on to, no matter how evil, foolish, or empty it was, was stripped away. I was dying of the one and only disease that could have pierced my tiny soul. I was dying of the same disease that had taken Rachel, my lamb.

"The agony in my heart was indescribable. But here was a strange and startling thing. At that moment when I learned of my terminal disease, when the incredible reality of it hit me that I was dying like Rachel had, I had a moment of clarity, an insight that this was beyond coincidence. It was arranged by an intelligent Designer that I should die like my beloved Rachel fifty years earlier had died.

"This was no mere accident. Even in the midst of a disease that was killing me, and it didn't need to kill me had I not ignored it for months until it was beyond human medical treatment, the tiniest glimmer of realization came into my mind: *there was design in this!* It could not have been an accident! It could not have been mere coincidence given the monumental odds against it!

"I actually considered this a mercy, a mercy of the severest form, but a mercy, nonetheless. To die like Rachel was, in my mind, a suffering on my part that in some way gave a vicarious sense of her death. I deserved this! I deserved to suffer! She did not deserve it, but in the mirror reflection of my suffering I had a sense that there was something greater at work.

"There was a quiet, gracious, willing suffering in her body, my Rachel, my lamb, that anticipated the future, a fifty-year down-payment, that she died for me. She died the way she did so that I could die with the dawning realization of mercy. Did she know? It didn't matter. *He knew!* The light was faint, but there it was.

"And over the final month of my life I held on to that thought secretly. I told no one, but for the first time in fifty years I saw something outside of myself. And then this man, the only one that came to me, came into my hospital room and told me the truth. As he explained about grace, mercy, forgiveness, heaven, death, judgment, punishment, and hell, I still resisted. Though death stood at the threshold, and the grim reaper held his scythe for a final blow, I resisted!

"I didn't resist so much because of hatred for God because I now saw the design at work even in my death, but I resisted now because surrender meant *admitting my whole life had been utterly wrong, wasted, and without purpose!* Even in my condition, that admission was grueling and detestable.

"And, even more, it meant that the most important thing in my existence, my misguided loyalty to the memory of Rachel, had accomplished nothing, had proven nothing. Everything was collapsing around me, Adam. Was there nothing I could hang on to? Nothing to commend myself for? Not a single good, no matter how twisted I had made it. And the answer is no, there was nothing for me. I had not a single thing to offer of myself.

"But, Adam, when I heard about the cross, when I heard about His suffering and how he suffered, what crucifixion does, I could resist no more. I was overcome. I was undone even as I had been when Rachel died."

"I know," I said at last. "The cross involved suffering."

"No, you don't understand, Adam. The suffering alone would not have won me. I'm ashamed even now to tell you that. It should have been enough, but for a soul as shriveled up and blackened with sin and unbelief as mine, the suffering of Christ on the cross in and of itself was not enough.

"But listen, Adam, do you know what happened to the body of Christ leading up to and during the crucifixion?"

"What do you mean?" I asked. Frank's fire and adamancy in his story was pulling me along now with its own energy.

"His entire body was scourged by Roman whips that were laced with glass and stone till he was covered with red bloody welts. He received so many violent blows to his face and body that he was covered with purple and blue bruises, to the point where He was unrecognizable. Large wooden nails were driven into and completely through His wrists to hang Him on the cross. His joints were pulled apart while He hung on the cross, till they were swollen and discolored. Can you imagine the pain, Adam? His muscles cramped so badly that they would no longer function. His legs and arms were swollen. He asphyxiated like a deadly asthma attack. Finally, a spear was driven into His heart to assure His death."

"I didn't realize how bad it was," I answered, wondering at the point Frank was driving toward and so deeply intrigued by the excruciation and, at the same time, the joy of the story.

"It was far worse than you and I can possibly imagine! His suffering was unimaginable physical agony, and I haven't even mentioned the abandonment by His Father, which was even worse than the physical pain! But no time for that right now. I'm only telling you the basics of His suffering, but here is the point. Adam, listen to me. Do you know what Rachel and I both died of?"

"Well, no, Frank. I'm sorry, but I don't know."

"It's fine. Of course, you don't know. We both died of Lupus, Adam. Rachel died because medical care was unable to cope with Lupus at that time. I died because of my stupidity and stubbornness. Lupus is treatable, but I ignored it till it was far too late. Do you know what the symptoms of Lupus are?"

"I have no idea," I said, again wondering where this was leading and fascinated by the excitement and agony on his face.

"Remember I said that the tipping point for my soul was the realization that there was design in my death? I died like Rachel, the exact same death! What are the odds, Adam? But listen to this! The symptoms of Lupus are joint and muscle pain. The joints become red, warm, and swollen. It causes inflammation and bleeding from the blood vessels that leads to blue and reddish spots on the skin. Lupus causes arthritis pain in the joint areas and especially the wrists! Lupus causes blood red sores and a purple rash on the skin. It causes inflammation of the heart sac that brings on terrible and sudden pain in the left side of the chest. It creates swelling in the hands and feet. It causes lung problems and decreases breathing capacity! Do you see, Adam?

"Not exactly."

"I not only died like Rachel, but Rachel and I died with the same symptoms that Jesus had on the cross! I saw in that design a God who was calling to me across the centuries. No, my suffering was nothing, absolutely nothing, compared to His, but the design, Adam, *the design* in it was astonishing to me! I looked back over the centuries that had passed since the cross, and I suddenly knew He had died for me. Not for me only, but somehow beyond all the impossible intricacies and improbabilities of time and chance this had been arranged for me to know Him! And, Adam, if that is not enough, He has arranged such intersections of grace, overwhelming the cosmic level of hopeless odds, for everyone who has ever come to Him. Want proof, Adam? Ask yourself, *What are you doing here?*"

I did not respond immediately. His story was so astounding and told with such deep passion and joy that I felt frozen into a silent respect of the moment.

Was he correct? Was I here beyond the wildest of odds that any bookmaker could imagine for an "intersection of grace" as Frank had called it? Odegeo and Michael had both hinted at this—no, more than hinted. There was a purpose here that still baffled me.

I had been intending to take part in an occult experience in the Red Hue Room. Had an intersection of grace transformed what was purely intended for evil into something possibly of eternal import? Prayer and fasting had been offered on my behalf. Gordon had said he had never seen parents intercede as relentlessly as mine.

But how can something so trite and commonplace occurring in human history, and something planned solely for the purpose of evil, be transformed into a work of God? A thought occurred to me. *Was not the cross the same type of event?* The bloody murder of an innocent man who was just one of thousands that the Romans violently destroyed, without a second thought of regret in their singular and unswerving pursuit of Roman justice.

It appeared so normal on the surface, just the daily turn of events in the culture of the era. Business as usual in the first century: a no-name soon-to-be-forgotten religious zealot with a Messiah complex cruelly put to death in a random series of events, cause and effect to be sure, but wholly random in the overall course of history.

Yet, it seemed transformed by a divine appointment into something of incredible significance. Even if it was not the only truth of divine provision (I was not sure yet. What about the many others claiming their path to God?), it was a moment of profound importance. Millions of people had died for this One, and millions more would give their life at a moment's notice, my parents included, because of that cross. He was loved like no other human who ever lived, and the institution of the church, no matter what I thought of it or whatever contempt and accusations the skeptics through the ages hurled at it, existed for the sole purpose of bringing people to the One who died on that cross.

The events leading up to my disappearance through that door appeared so arbitrary. My choices, decisions, purposeful seeking out of evil, and (I realized with sudden earnestness and surprise) my similarity to Frank Henderson in running away from God in defiance. Yet, they all converged on a singular point in time when divine sovereignty relentlessly broke through in hot pursuit of me across the wall of rebellion and the barriers of space and time to extradite me from my womb of wickedness and deliver me to this intersection of grace.

Yes, it had to be true. He was calling me from darkness into light. Whatever my intentions had been, whatever Frank

Henderson's intentions had been in the misery and emptiness of his life, the Hound of Heaven was inexorably pursuing me, bringing together unbelievable odds, intersections, to draw me in.

Then I awoke.

A thought struck me. Darkness broke upon the glimmer of light that flickered in my soul. Like the snuffer I had used as a child in my own church as an appointed acolyte dousing the candles during something called Advent, I suffocated the light that threatened to dawn upon my soul.

"That's an amazing story, Frank, but really, it's not fair for you to be here, you know. You don't deserve heaven. At least I recognize I don't have any right to be here. And if I don't deserve it, well, let's be honest, you certainly don't."

"Yes! Yes!" Frank nearly shouted. "That's the point!"

"I mean, after all, there are plenty of people who were better than you and yet may not have made it here, as I understand it."

"You're right, Adam! You're right about the fact that there are plenty of people better than me who are not here and never will be. But that's not the point!"

"Well, what *is* the point, then?"

Frank looked at me with compassion and empathy. He knew the life of unbelief struggling against the immutable and irresistible truth of the One who had laid the very foundations of the universe. The fearsome power of death and the true horror of death that lay beyond death had gripped him and had come dangerously and horribly close to claiming him as its permanent resident in the vise of eternal darkness, pain, and fire. He knew my fight, and he was filled with compassion.

But my question was posed in a tone that was close to

reliving the false nobility that had sometimes afflicted me in my earthly life, although I did not realize the affliction at the time. Striking a pontifical pose, I would defend some indefensible act or some "modern" (read as vapid and self-absorbed) group or some transient and shallow view or philosophy, all for the sake of being forward thinking, progressive, modern, intellectual, urbane, socially engaged and cutting-edge on any socially minded cause. The cause didn't really matter; it was the appearance of brilliance and the air of collegiums that mattered. Yet, as with the temptation to lie, I knew that such vanity and hypocrisy simply would not fly here in the long run. I held my foolish tongue from further murky words. Frank continued with great urgency.

"Adam, don't you see it yet? No one deserves heaven! No one! Believe me, friend, you don't want what you deserve!"

Then Gordon spoke. "Think of it this way, Adam. Just for the sake of argument, let's say you needed a million points to get to heaven."

Points. This was perhaps a perspective that even I could grasp.

"The best human who has ever lived, and remember this is all just an illustration, is at zero. The rest of us are all in the negative. The best humans on Earth are not only far from the required one million points, they are hopelessly forever in the negative. The difference between the best human ever and the requirement for heaven is impossibly far apart, an unbridgeable chasm. Adam, you and I need a million points, and we can't even get up to zero!"

I said nothing, but I vaguely recalled Bible verses from far away, from a different life that I had led. Memories came back to me, phrases like "fallen short" and "no one is good" and "all died because all sinned." How these verses came to mind now after many years without giving them a single thought was a mystery to me. I must have learned these notions eons ago, but they had been lost to my conscious mind till this very moment. But the darkness was still gaining ground here in the light of heaven.

I was torn. In the midst of this place of perfection, I found myself offended at two things. First, the inability of humanity to satisfy God. Were we that bad, that evil? Bad *things* happen. Societies can create bad or difficult circumstances, but aren't humans basically good, or at least at some level of moral equilibrium? Capable of both good and bad, yet influenced by a negative environment? How could a loving God hold us guilty for that? And second, Frank's presence in heaven was mystifying to me. An anomaly. How could he be here, but I hadn't made it? Where was the justice in that?

Wait a minute. How does a society of good or at least morally neutral people produce a negative environment capable of motivating the wickedness obviously pervading our whole culture? That was a problem I had avoided contemplating, probably because I had no good answer and had never heard a reasonable explanation from all my learned gurus.

Then it occurred to me that the very thought that I believed Frank to be too evil to be in heaven was perhaps an indication of at least the potential for great wickedness in humanity. Still, Frank had gone through terribly painful and unfair circumstances at the loss of his young wife! Of course, he had done bad things; he had been the recipient of a terrible roll of the dice. My mind rebelled at the thought that life was merely the arbitrary result of a cosmic game of chance. No, it simply cannot be! Was Frank culpable given the hideous misfortune he had suffered? Could anyone, including God, expect anything other than a life a misery and anger from Frank?

Then I was smote with another realization. This one hurt. Perhaps Frank did have an excuse for the darkness of his life. *What was my excuse?* I had been raised in a good home with loving parents, good-hearted brothers, endless opportunities, and a multitude of the material things the world had to offer. My environment should have produced exceptional ethical standards. Yet, there was no denying I had done evil acts in my life, rotten things to people who deserved better, manipulation and usury toward women, greed and dishonesty for my own gain at the expense of others, and the list went on and on. My environment could not be blamed for my wickedness. *It was me, my heart of darkness.* The argument against personal culpability was failing for me.

And there was Frank. The argument to justify his sin would not stand either. Many people had gone through pain and suffering as bad, or even worse, than Frank. They had not fallen into a life of hate and bitterness. I recalled people who had suffered horribly, finding peace, contentment, and even purpose in the midst of their darkness.

Frank, it seemed, had purposefully pursued the night. He was so dark that no one had even visited him in his dying days! Frank was capable of terrible evil, but it still seemed that someone could have taken a few minutes to meet with an old man dying of a horrible disease. No one had the time, the concern, the interest, the hope, or the compassion for this pitiful old man? Even if Frank was an unbearable and mean-spirited old fool, could no one find the kindness to visit him, to lift his burden for a moment?

Again, all the "basically good people" I was unwittingly

investing my judicial hope in were too self-consumed, unmercifully busy, and blindly disinterested in a hopeless and, I must admit, hell-bound elderly human being. It wasn't right. Even those Christians didn't seem to care much. Maybe Gordon was right. Even the best of us is still in the negative.

And then, of course, I realized that in holding up the word *Christian* and categorizing them, no matter how obliquely, as "the best of us," I was admitting that something was in them that was different. I had no delusions about myself regarding Frank. I knew that I would not have visited the poor old man. Acknowledging the charity of the Christian, even in the slightest measure as holding to a higher ethical standard, was admitting that there was a standard of goodness that was virtuous and greater than me, that was outside of me and my Machiavellian ideal.

One of my mantras had often been a declaration about my "rights." I saw now that even that assertion implied something greater than me—some thing or some One granting those rights. Otherwise, they could not exist apart from my menial and individual attempt to create a value system. And that was the whole point; this judicial "good" I was quantifying was greater than me. And these rights granted to me were clearly beyond the level of governmental authority, and besides that, every government disagreed on rights and privileges and freedoms.

This matter was far more foundational.

I can't say that the ilk that I had come to call "friends," a word that should have meant more in my little society, had much interest in anyone or anything but themselves. One from our group had checked into an addiction clinic at the peak (or should I say the low point) of his process of self-destruction.

He had finally owned up to his need and personal inability. Not a single one of his "friends," of which I was one, had visited him or followed up upon his recovery, ever! That was despicable of us but strangely and ironically wholly predictable.

On the other hand, my parents had made a regular habit, as did Gordon, of visiting church members in the hospital and sick neighbors and giving generously to organizations that helped the poor and infirm. In them was an undeniable interest in others who paid nothing back to themselves. It had that scent of unconditionality that carried the fragrance of a God of grace.

My parents weren't perfect, but they were growing toward something greater than themselves. They were becoming like that Something. There it was: kindness, grace, faith, compassion—a standard of goodness foreign to me but alive, well, and screaming out to me about my failure, inadequacy, selfishness, and, yes, sin.

A thought struck me. Only one person had visited Frank Henderson in his dying days. I had to know. "Frank, who was it that visited you on that last day before your death? Who was it that helped you find heaven?"

Frank smiled broadly, and tears formed in his eyes as he laughed from sheer joy. He looked at Gordon. Gordon laughed, that infectious easy irrepressible joy-filled laughter of his. He looked at me, his face crinkled up and his eyes squinting in his own unique way.

He chuckled and said, "Didn't see that coming, eh?"

12

Along the Crystal Sea

I had much to think about.

Frank left us, heading to the City of God. He could not be delayed any longer. No one hesitated, much less disobeyed, when that call came. But this was not a perfunctory duty. It was a glad and fulfilling day of joy for the Redeemed to go to the City. I was beginning to think that the Redeemed's visits to the City of God were as regular as attending church had been for my parents. Everyone here went often and habitually. Rather than the drudgery of church attendance for the growing skeptic I had been through my teen and college years, these worship attendees in heaven lived for these moments before the Throne of God.

When, during my college years, church as a lifestyle had abruptly and permanently ended, this gave rise to painful and profoundly divisive confrontations with my parents when I was at home, which was part of the reason I quit going home. At first, I had lied about my lack of church attendance, but eventually out of some misguided and vain independence, I proudly told my parents I was done with church. They were devastated.

From what Gordon had told me somewhere along the way, discussions about God dominated conversations even in heaven. Learning about Him, apparently, was a permanent condition. There were countless topics on which to converse, education was very big here, but it always came back, one way or another, to God. He was and is the prima facie.

"In Him we live and move and have our being, and He leads us into all truth" Gordon had said. I had a feeling he was quoting here, but I said nothing due to the risk of being reminded of a long-lost sermon! Gordon had added, "We can never exhaust the infinite; we can never fully discover the eternal. If it were not so, then He was not God to begin with." It sounded suspiciously like something Odegeo had said.

Gordon told me that there had been periods on Earth when education had reflected this heavenly practice. Except for remote pockets of religious educational fervor, which now received considerable academic abuse and elitist scholarly disrespect (so Gordon said with surprising earnestness and a complete lack of his usual mirth), this God-centered curriculum had passed into history.

"That Ivy League school you attended started as a seminary, Adam."

"I didn't know that." It was a surprising piece of information. "In fact, that is shocking. They hate God. There was no sense in soft peddling it. It was the underpinning of half the programs of the university shtick. God as a theoretical concept and a philosophic talking point isn't so bad. They don't mind that, but a real God with real *moral* demands? That is a different story, one with which I had wholeheartedly agreed. (I now dimwittedly hoped that He had not noticed.) I've been there and lived that life. You know, they believe they have moved on to greater enlightenment."

"So did Adam and Eve."

"I doubt if the people in that university believe in Adam and Eve."

"And they will no doubt find themselves in the same predicament as Adam and Eve did."

I was not entirely sure what that predicament was. Still, I knew it was not a good position in which to be, and that the intelligentsia of my alma mater was dead wrong about the existence of those two progenitors of the human race. I would have been laughed at—no, actually scorned out of the college for saying that out loud. Yet, even in my state of vast ignorance, the truth of the origin of the human race was beginning to grip me.

The hundreds of miles of walking, which on Earth would have been laughable to even think about attempting, was passing quickly. With no real need for nightly sleep, indeed, there was no night and little need for any type of rest, we moved with great speed.

Sometimes it appeared as though we were covering more ground than seemed possible. This was not at all to my liking since I feared what lay beyond the border of heaven. I tried to put this out of my mind and often succeeded due to the splendor around me. I wanted to stop and linger (and stay permanently), and each time I suggested such action to Gordon, he would respond with something like, "Nothing good can come from disobeying Michael," or, "He gave you a command, not a suggestion," or, my personal favorite, "Taken leave of your senses, eh?" Gordon always said that one with a wink and a crinkled smile.

We proceeded on our journey. I marveled continually at the wonders I was seeing, although in my darkness on Earth, I had ignorantly and stupidly joked about "the torturous and miasmatic concept of eternity and the wish-fulfillment philosophy of heaven." It was from a presentation I gave in a scholarship application jury lecture before my senior year at a particular Ivy League university. (Yes, one that used to be a seminary.)

I now recognized that heaven was the greater reality, and no torture here! We rarely needed to hurry, despite the regrettable speed at which we were moving, unless it was simply to see some amazing sight that caught our attention, and we could barely wait to get there to explore it. Gordon had by no means seen all of this realm, in fact, very little of it. Some of what I saw for the first time was also his first experience.

Soon enough, the river expanded as the banks gave way, widening rapidly to form the Crystal Sea. Gordon had said it was about forty miles wide for the whole length of it. We walked on what, in my mind, was the north side of the sea, for I considered myself heading west. This was merely a convenience to keep my simple wits about me. I took some comfort in having a sense of direction, even if a heavenly compass would have made a mockery of my bearings.

As with the river, there were many mansions along the sea. And in the same way, the estates stretched on into the distance as far as I could see, although they were never crowded together in the slightest. The Heavenly Realm was quite spacious and open. Being by the sea, we were at a low point geographically, so the view was limited in the distance.

It seemed that far off, mountains were rising high into the sky. I had no doubt that these must have been far away because my vision was so clear in heaven, and the air was so clean and pure. Although I could not depict individual mansions on the mountains (they must have been hundreds of miles away), I was sure of their existence.

The land along the sea was open and some of it was covered with tall, beautiful grasses of many shades of greens and browns. Some had soft feathery plumes of white, cream, or yellow on top. Others had a striped effect on the grass itself, either running horizontally across the leaves or up and down the full length of the blades, which could be as much as ten feet tall. And much of the grass was like that in and around the City of God, perfectly manicured and thriving in the most vibrant of green.

And trees were there, although not dense as in the forests of Eden that Odegeo and I had traveled before reaching the City of God, but beautiful and stunning trees, nonetheless. Every tree was perfect in its shape and spread. The leaves were colors of every shade of green, yellow, gold, silver, and purple. They were all fresh and spring-like in their radiance and hue. Sometimes it seemed that they moved and swayed of their own accord, without a necessary wind, as though they were breathing deeply in the wholeness and richness of the light and air.

The Crystal Sea itself had a translucent blue hue. It was often calm and as flat as a tabletop, but the water had a definite directional flow toward the west. From time to time, the strange wind would rise up and begin to lift the waves. This always meant the rain mist was about to cover the land and water the abundant and extravagant plant life. Even when the wind was not blowing, the Crystal Sea had a sparkle in it and a dazzling, almost piercingly deep effervescence to the water. This may have resulted from the ever-present lightning still visible above the Throne.

So powerful and pervasive was the brilliance of those pyrotechnics that their flashing and histrionic beauty could be seen throughout the entirety of heaven. It drew worshipers almost hypnotically to the center of heaven, although there was nothing in the least hypnotically induced about the worship by the worshipers. All were utterly alive and aware in the whole capacity of their being, and never more so than in worship. My insolent, ridiculous, and prejudiced earthly view on "the opium of worship" was now an embarrassment. It was the title of an idiotic paper I had written for a philosophy of religion class in grad school. The professor urged me to consider expanding this idea for my Masters' thesis! Yes, the university that used to be a seminary now proved to be not only wrong, but humiliatingly shallow and foolish. True worship, I now understood, was the most profound realization of life, truth, and reality. It was not the dulling trance-fed state of a brainless automaton that I had accused worshipers of being. My parents knew how to worship in the right way.

As we walked along the Crystal Sea, new wonders arose. The Sea stretched to the far end of this heavenly realm. It occurred to me that bridges had been along the river, but the sea was forty miles wide. How would the Redeemed transverse the Sea? I posed the question to Gordon, but he simply said, "Wait, just wait."

We continued to admire the mansions of heaven. In some places, many were grouped somewhat like a small city. In other areas, mansions stood alone. The arrangement was very much like Earth. I wondered if this somehow reflected the owner's personality—solitude versus extroversion. Each was unique and reflective in some way of the one for whom it had been prepared. I suddenly realized in all the time that I had spent with Gordon, I had never asked a question that now seemed an obvious one.

"Gordon, I'm sorry."

"Well, I accept your apology!" Gordon laughed and winked at me. "What in heaven are you sorry about?"

"I just feel like I've been rather inconsiderate. You've spent an enormous amount of time with me, and I have not had the decency to ask you about yourself! What about your life, what about Eileen, what about your heavenly home? Where do you live, Gordon?"

"No need for an apology, Adam. You've had a few other matters to try to assimilate, eh?" Gordon chucked along through his words.

"I suppose, but still . . ."

"And remember, you didn't come here for my sake. I came to meet you for your sake. You've been through difficulties, I know that. You've seen things in heaven that human eyes seldom get to witness. Although you aren't the only one who has been allowed this privilege, it *is* rare, very rare. Your life on Earth was hard in many ways, and things were not great with your parents."

"Yes," I said, "but that was by my own choosing, my own arrogance."

"I understand. But you know they never gave up on you. I never saw parents, or grandparents for that matter, who persevered so faithfully in prayer, fasting, and bringing their heavy hearts before the church without fail. In all my years in ministry, no one ever had the amount of intercession you've had, Adam. I don't say that to shame you, but to remind and assure you of the absolute unconditional love of your family."

I sighed deeply. I had avoided thinking about these matters. On Earth I had avoided it due to my conceit, pseudo-intellectualism, love of my darkness, rejection of values that represented something archaic and limiting, and ultimately because of the God who was chasing me but whom I could not escape. Since entering heaven, I had avoided these thoughts for entirely different reasons, which I knew would make enormous demands on me. Whatever the needs might be, I wished I could return to that home, that family, that unconditional love, and live all those early years again. I longed for that.

But wait, the fasting . . . Hadn't Odegeo or Michael said something about that regarding my presence here? Maybe it was time to change the subject again.

"But, Gordon, what about your mansion?"

"It's quite a long distance from here," Gordon said, pointing in the direction I interpreted as northwest. "Far out of our way. I'm afraid we cannot visit."

"It looks like there are mountainous areas far up to the north."

"The north?" Gordon said. "Well, if that seems north to you, okay. It is in that direction where I live, and yes, mountains are nearby. Farther out, at the very edge of this realm, is a band of mountains that runs just outside the river that encircles the whole land. The mountains form a great barrier all the way around the whole of heaven, just like the river does. I don't know what is beyond them. I have only been to the edge of the realm once."

I was about to respond to what Gordon had said when in the distance, a bright light was glinting off something above the sea. It looked like a structure of some type built high out and over the Crystal Sea. It must have been a momentary reflection from the pervasive lightning above the City, but a reflection off of what?

I wanted to hurry on to see this sight. It must have been

many miles ahead since it was not clearly visible, even given the air's purity and my improved eyesight. I had a sense of what it might be from a comment or two that Gordon had make earlier. If I were correct, this could be a sight to dwarf all others I had seen in heaven.

13

Dr. Kakos

I was about to urge Gordon to press on to whatever the spectacle ahead might be when I felt a firm prodding on my shoulder from behind and a commanding voice addressing me loudly as, "Sir!"

I turned quickly to see who it was, especially since being noticed and known was hardly a common occurrence for me in the Heavenly Realm! Gordon was beside me; who could be behind me, attempting to get my attention? To my astonishment, at least on the level of seeing Frank Henderson, before me stood a memorable and influential figure from my collegiate days, a renowned and scholarly professor from the university, who had fed my disdain and contempt for the religious training and "indoctrination," as he had called it, of my youthful years. It was Dr. Marlas Kakos.

I am certain that the look on my face betrayed my shock at seeing him of all people as a member of the Redeemed and a resident of heaven. (Had I not thought the same thing about Frank?) His immediate amusement indicated he read my surprise.

Before I could even comment, he said loudly with great joy, "I'm surprised as well, Mr. Sane!"

"Dr. Kakos! I . . . I . . ."

"Do not know what to say? That is fine, Mr. Sane! Very

fine indeed! Whom of my students would have ever expected this?"

As on Earth, Dr. Marlas Kakos had a booming voice, which he never minded using to his advantage and which had lent power and persuasion to his opinions, no matter how wrong it now seemed that they had been. His large and imposing physical presence had added a ubiquitous aspect to his authority. As unforeseen as Frank Henderson's citizenship in heaven was, I had a sense of Dr. Kakos' presence here being perhaps even more unexpected.

By the time I had taken his courses, he was nearing the end of a long and distinguished career. His white hair, which he had combed straight back in the style of the era in which he had grown up and had never given the slightest thought to changing, was receding and thinning. His goatee, also pure white, had somehow added more strength to his intellectual authority. He had been rather thick, though not fat, and walked with a cane, but not for any ambulatory need. The cane, as he well knew, seemed to add something to his aura of intelligentsia and was a throwback to the days when professors ruled the university in unquestioned brilliance. His always grayish suits, a feature for which he was known and seemed nearly obsessed with in terms of color, were somewhat oversized and had hung on him in a loosely undignified way. His jowls were prominent and sagging and had an odd way of quivering when animated, which he was often.

Although my friends and I had a great degree of respect for Dr. Kakos, we made much sport of his quivering jowls. Our insolent imitation of his vigorous tirades probably looked much more like an aged bulldog shaking water off its body than Dr. Kakos ardently defending his opinions. But his influence was unquestioned. He had written books and articles polemically advancing a Nietzschean worldview, a universe without God, without absolutes or a designed purpose. Dr. Kakos' most famous mantra was, "The only purpose in life is what you create it to be; the only values that matter are those that you create for yourself; the only truth is the one that works for you."

Hardly a Christian mentality!

Although he was somehow perfectly recognizable to me, he now looked very little like the dignified, aging, well-fed, and pompous professor under whom I had studied. Now, in heaven, he was trim, muscular, with a full head of rich flowing hair (still white, however). He was still large compared to most of the Redeemed I had seen, and like Frank Henderson and everyone else, he seemed to be in the bloom of health. He had a quiet peace in him now (a quality he had never mastered on Earth) and eyes filled with mirth. He always had a quick wit and a clever sense of humor, but it mainly had been turned toward sarcasm, sharp-tongued comebacks, and sardonic anecdotes.

Now, even though I had been in his presence only briefly, I could see deep joy welling up from his spirit. If I were to guess his age, I would have said perhaps thirty to thirty-three years old. (It suddenly struck me that all of the Redeemed looked to be about that age.)

Despite his presence in a high ivory tower, Dr. Marlas Kakos had been highly influential among his students in his university department and probably in many other quarters where his apprentices advanced his vital opinions. He was a materialist, hardly a friend to people of faith, the church, or any religious system.

Now, however, I understand that some religions and faiths

have nothing to do with God. In the strictest of definitions, Dr. Kakos was highly religious, but that is an entirely different matter. And yet here he was in heaven, with a place among the Redeemed? This I had to hear!

"Yes, sir. I am rather speechless," I said. "I don't think any of your students would have expected you to end up in heaven, and, of course, we didn't even believe in such a place. That is, nothing personal, Dr. Kakos, but you were, uh, not really the type to uh . . ." I stammered for words. I was intimidated by his presence, even here in heaven, although I don't believe he had any intention (anymore) of intimidating me or anyone else, for that matter.

"Not really the type to what, Mr. Sane?"

I felt uneasy for a moment and thought I had put my foot in my mouth. Then I noticed the mirth in his eyes, much like Gordon before he would break into laughter.

"No need to answer that, Mr. Sane. You are absolutely correct in your assessment! Hardly anyone could possibly be a more unlikely candidate for heaven than Doctor Marlas Kakos! Not the type? No indeed!"

Here Dr. Kakos laughed quite freely and with abandon. Gordon joined him as they shared the joy-drenched delight of heaven. I laughed as well. It was a humorous moment to be sure, but their gladness seemed of a different caliber than mine—something I could not yet touch, something fundamental, not simply circumstantial.

Gordon and Dr. Kakos did not know one another, so introductions were made. The first order of business in heaven among new friends (there are no *acquaintances* among the Redeemed in heaven) is in telling each other the story of how they came to God. I had heard most of Gordon's story over the time that we had been traveling together, so most of what he related I already knew. However, the tale that Dr. Kakos told, while nothing like Frank Henderson's saga in the details, was nonetheless every bit as extraordinary in substance. And it was clear that the tale of his discovery of God was directed to me far more than toward Gordon.

"As you know, Mr. Sane, I was of the unfortunate mindset of skeptic in regard to all things spiritual." I noticed that Dr. Kakos did not say he was *a skeptic*, but that he was skeptic. Almost as if it was an entire defining category of which he was the executive officer.

"My parents did not raise me in this manner of thinking. They were devout Christians; however, I became a devout philosophic materialist. When I reached the height of my intellectual maturity—do not confuse that with wisdom, Mr. Sane—all things in my thinking were reduced to materialism, and therefore, all things were measured by materialism. I can only imagine the dismay and dread in my parents' hearts as they recognized the older I became, the more I was turning from their belief system to one diametrically opposed to all that they held dear."

Still idiotically and needlessly concerned with impressing the great sophist, I started to interrupt him with a comment about the existence of loving parental care yet their implicit naiveté and the evolution of modern thinking about family structure and the place of the necessary village culmination doctrine and its important impact on child development. Of course, this would only have revealed my own disingenuousness and artificiality, but thankfully, he cut me short, recognizing my pathetic pseudo-intellectual attempt at relevance.

"Stop, Mr. Sane! I am presciently aware of your condition

and relationship with your parents. I will tolerate no remarks, no matter how contextually significant *you* may think they are, that in any way demean, defame, degrade, devalue, deport, or denigrate your parents! You think them provincial, simple, and a bit vacuous? Be careful, sir! You are no doubt unfamiliar with Saint Paul's magnum opus? Chapter one, I believe. Is that correct, Reverend Lachen?"

I was completely lost, but Gordon seemed to sense Dr. Kakos' direction.

"I think you are referring to verse thirty," said Gordon. "'Slanderers, haters of God, insolent, arrogant, boastful, inventors of evil, *disobedient to parents* . . .'"

That was a particularly painful list to hear. It seemed that I fit all those categories, but I recognized especially the last one was where Dr. Kakos was headed.

"Interesting, is it not, Mr. Sane? Do any of those maladies appear applicable?" He paused, unfortunately waiting for me to answer.

I hesitated and then stumbled on my words but admitted to the power of his. "Yes, they do, Dr. Kakos. I feel the sting of your words."

"*His* words!" Then suddenly Dr. Kakos softened. He spoke quietly and humbly. "Can you see, son, how these negatives that Saint Paul strings together in this chain of malcontent character all relate?

"You and I both fit with stark congruity into this sequence paradigm. Our matriculation through this series of dispositional contraction led us, almost with a degree of inevitability, to the final flaw which Reverend Lachen mentioned. And that one is not the least of those evils. Indeed, it is perhaps the most serious of these ills, though few recognize the catastrophe and tragedy of this transgression. In fact, many inveigle others to such betrayal by representing this behavior as having an elemental psychological relevance and the formative importance of rebellion!

"The others' sins, for the greater part, represent mere unholy contempt, but the last one strikes at the very nature of God's creation, the fundamental character of willing humility and joyful submission, of ordained authority and autonomous headship. It most profoundly reflects the very nature of the Trinity of God and the eternal proceeding of the Son and all the matters of redemption, which, we can be quite certain, He does not take lightly. That temperament of disobedience most deeply reveals a disposition toward not only parents, *but to God Himself.* There is a direct and undeniable relationship. No one who dishonors his own parents can honestly proclaim love for God. The two simply cannot abide together.

"You and I, Mr. Sane, have been of the dishonoring party. We pretended we were not. We called it something else. Few devices of the enemy are more effective than that of nomenclature revision and this example is of paramount implication.

"We were modern: the new cultural designers, evolutionary and revolutionary. Concomitant, however, with our modernity was the oldest of all prevarication, flowing again from the Squamata itself as it had in the womb of humanity. God is a liar, or perhaps He has not told *all* the truth. We can find something better, and we have! Yet, among our kind, and this includes you, the lie was celebrated! It was encouraged! I was a willing participant in such vacuity and inanity not only for my own part, but also in decades of promoting such vile and dissentious lies.

"This is, in fact, why I was sent to you. The similarity of our pasts is striking. My parents, much like yours, never ceased to pray for me. They involved many others in their intercessory ministry for their wayward, self-absorbed son. Until their dying days, they sought the Father for their own prodigal."

Dr. Kakos paused for a moment. I contemplated what he had said. "As far as I understand, Dr. Kakos, my parents are the only reason I have been allowed this visit to heaven. If I have dishonored them in my life on Earth—"

Dr. Kakos interrupted me with a wave of his hand and a dark glance. "There is no *if* in that equation, Mr. Sane. Such a statement causes me great concern in your acknowledgment of your own culpability and speaks of a certain pusillanimous avoidance."

"You're right, sir." The truth of his statement couldn't be denied. "There is no *if* in this matter. I still fall into traces of my arrogance and insolence at times, but I recognize greater than ever the debt I owe to them as well as the pain I have caused them. Whatever happens in the future, and I don't know what that may be, I do hope to thank them. Although I am sure I can never repay what I owe, I desire to see them and thank them."

"By the grace of God," Dr. Kakos said, "the first moment I arrived in heaven, I was permitted by His goodness to see my parents. I cannot begin to tell you the joy I had with them, and although I knew I was utterly forgiven by God, as far as the east is from the west, the unburdening of my soul to my father and mother was a blessing beyond comprehension. The great, renown, and brilliant Dr. Kakos! I wept deeply. I prostrated myself before them. I begged for their mercy, which of course was unnecessary in an absolute sense, but all that my soul needed.

"My soul, Mr. Sane! Do you hear me? My soul, which I had spent a lifetime denying, was in heaven! Forgiven, redeemed, *saved!* The very words I had held in rapturous contempt were now the joy of my existence! I had been a materialist, reducing everything in the universe to one reality. I was the definition of the modern materialist!"

"Dr. Kakos, how did you come to reject the philosophy you had promulgated and defended all those years?"

"I did more than teach and safeguard it, Mr. Sane, I lived it. It is a wonder that I retained my sanity for so long. Remember the Nietzsche class? I will commend Nietzsche on this level, he lived what he believed. Most philosophers do not. They refuse to carry out their purported beliefs to their logical end. Otherwise, they should live in anarchy and hedonism. But they cannot do that, and on some basic level, they understand that the most innocent minutia of daily life, not to mention the necessities of career, family, and institution, among others, cannot possibly exist with any order or sensibility in the very context they advance. That is because they know in their mind, in the deepest part of their souls where God is calling to their spirits, that their philosophy does not and cannot work in real life. He has set eternity there.

"Nietzsche, however, lived his beliefs with great vivacity and all the consequences. And this drove him to insanity. He took his masks, their impossible contingencies, and the necessity of utter uncertainty to their logical end. He lived the darkness, and it destroyed him.

"He was braver than I was. That is not a commendation of Nietzsche, but simply a recognition of his commitment to his belief system. I would not go all the way, but I went further than most. Yet even there I found questions in my reductive materialism to which there were no answers. Or rather, the only cogent answers of any didactic quality were not found within the discipline of what we called science. Our pursuits were not true science, of course, they were something else. The authentic scientific answers kept pointing in the wrong direction from our presumptive conclusions. Oxymoronic, Mr. Sane, do you see it? Presumptive conclusions!"

"Yes, Dr. Kakos. I understand. The idea of a presumptive conclusion is a self-contradiction."

"Correct, Mr. Sane. Those who claim the very exigency of objectivity are blind to the fallaciousness of their assumptions, reasoning, and conclusions. The derivation of the problem is not simply the inability of human reasoning. In many regards, my colleagues had the greatest minds and the most profound thinking facility in the world. The quandary, however, is a spiritual blindness. It was this spiritual blindness that kept me from admitting the truth of what was destroying my materialist constructs.

"The first deleterious crack in my materialist foundation was centered on the atheist maxim, 'The absence of evidence is the evidence of absence.' You might even remember me quoting this in class?" I shook my head and started to comment, but Dr. Kakos stopped me with a wave of his hand again. He was in full professorial pedagogy now, somewhat reminiscent of his earthly demeanor in his passion.

"No matter, it was an axiom I held dear. What if, however, we are using the wrong instruments to measure the evidence? Or what if the instruments do not yet exist? The history of science is replete with occasions in which statements of an absolute nature are made based on testing and observation by inadequate tools, inept scientists, or sheer conjecture in the hope that one day some appropriate apparatus might be invented.

"I had done this myself concerning my writings on the brain and the mind. I attempted to make firm conclusions on immeasurable qualities, thus invalidating my maxim! The absence of evidence means nothing whatsoever if science has insufficient means to measure and test.

"It is one thing to develop a hypothesis that manifestly recognizes the admission of uncertainty and assumption. It is another thing entirely to proclaim absolutes to the degree of eliminating even the potential for discussion! That is not science; it is a paltry, oblivious, and unsubstantiated form of philosophizing, but it is commonplace and an execrable practice among some in the scientific community.

"And Mr. Sane, what if the object of the test refuses to submit to the conditions of the test? What if the object of the test proves to be inscrutable? Must we therefore conclude that this is evidence of absence? Taken in this context, you can see the absurdity of the proposition! And it is beyond simple absurdity. It is arrogance to the extreme.

"I have spoken with Isaiah on this matter, and he finds it quite insidious, especially given his theological perspicuity. It was he who reminded me of the great apostle's lucidity when he wrote, 'Professing themselves to be wise, they become fools.' Fools indeed, Mr. Sane.

"But there were other vexing issues. For a materialist like me, who insists that the material is the only objective reality and the existential measure of all things, the development and acceptance of the idea of dark matter brought into focus other matters that, when subjected to the same evaluative criteria as my acceptance of and belief in dark matter, were rejected.

"My presuppositions were creating an irreducible conundrum. I began to perceive the inherent contradiction in what I had previously considered to be a unified field of thought. I should add that this process was the result of the Lord God opening my eyes, not genius on my part. It was perhaps not a solely unilateral work of God, as the process of enlightenment does not exist exclusively in a vacuum. There is an aspect of partnership or interplay. A response to light brings more light, and an honest and hopeful curiosity in seeking brings more direction; the calling ordains the electing.

"I have spoken often and at length with Jack about this, and he has far more intelligence and wisdom in the matter than I, a solecism incarnate by comparison, and Jack agrees. Yet without the initiatory pursuit by the Lord God of the human soul, there is no seeking or searching response. Let us be honest, Adam, there is no interest in the corrupted human heart in the things of God. We love Him because He first loved us. There are no other alternatives."

I wasn't clear on what effect the belief in dark matter had on Dr. Kakos, nor half of the other things he said. I thought I might know who Isaiah was, but the name of Jack was completely lost on me. I didn't see the connection. It had always been difficult to see the connections he made. Whether they were just intellectually too deep, a distinct possibility, or it was simply a matter of the maze of his dangling thoughts and excessive vocabulary, I often was at a loss. He was a great intellect, but his teaching was sometimes incomprehensible. "But, what about the issue of dark matter, Dr. Kakos?" I asked. "I'm not sure I see what you are saying."

"Only this, and I will keep my remarks brief." (I chuckled to myself at the prospect of Dr. Kakos keeping his remarks brief.) "Physicists now believe the vast majority of matter and energy in the universe is made of dark matter. Various conditions in our universe, such as the gravitational forces that galactic density requires, are found to be inadequate. The accelerating expansion of the cosmos, rather than the decreasing speed that traditional physics—and common sense—would predict, are paradoxical. The answer to this predicament? Science creates dark matter and dark energy *ex nihilo*. I am certain, Mr. Sane, that you recall the study of these matters?"

I started to answer, but again, Dr. Kakos waved me off and continued.

"No matter. To the point, first, dark matter and dark energy must be fundamentally different than all matter we have observed or measured in any way. Second, dark matter, which is understood to account for the preponderance of matter in the universe, has never been visually perceived and cannot be measured much less found by any known instrument. The idea of dark matter and energy is entirely based on its supposed effect. No one has ever seen, smelled, tasted, heard, touched, measured, tested, or directly observed it.

"Despite these two scientifically profound difficulties, most scientists blithely accept dark matter and dark energy as realities. I am not saying it does not exist, Mr. Sane. Perhaps it does, and perhaps the Lord God created it to perform the very functions that physicists postulate. However, do you see the dilemma I had as a materialist? The same rationale I used to reject and vehemently and abrasively assault the things of God, I openly disregarded when it came to the subject of dark matter.

"How did I live with the contradiction? How could I remain intellectually honest, holding one view of the existence of dark matter quite by faith and rejecting another view on the basis that faith was inadequate without material proof?

"It was only by the gracious work of the Spirit of the Lord God that my eyes were opened, and I began to grapple with the illogic of my belief system.

"Shall I mention the Anthropic Principle and the difficulty it created for my worldview? Every necessary parameter, regardless of how narrow the tolerance that is needed for human life, is met on Earth. The list of essential categories is extensive, yet without fail, all of them are perfectly suited for life on Earth, especially human life, which has exceedingly narrow ranges in all the fundamental components. The more assiduously I searched for reasons to disbelieve the evidence of design, the more coherent and inescapable the idea of design became."

I am not sure quite what motivated me to think that I needed to remind Dr. Kakos of anything. The man was brilliant and had probably forgotten more knowledge than I would ever gain in my lifetime; but one thing I needed clarification on, or so I thought.

"Dr. Kakos, all that you are saying about the narrow parameters for life on Earth is certainly true, but isn't that the very point? Is it possible you are getting the proverbial cart before the horse?

"The process of . . . Well, there was a process that succeeded in developing life exactly suited to the environment. In fact, that is the only type of life that could have evol—er, *developed* on Earth, life that was suited to the planet. When you imply that the parameters were met by some external creative power, it really means, doesn't it, that the parameters themselves chose the process and its conclusion? It was selected, it was—"

"Adam, please." This was the first time Gordon had spoken in quite some time. He was shaking his head. His eyes were closed, and the joy that had been a constant in this countenance was gone. "You don't understand what you are saying. You have forgotten where you are." Gordon opened his eyes and looked at me. I saw sadness and an almost fatherly look of deep concern.

The look on Gordon's face was painful to me. I knew I had disappointed him, which upset me. I loved this man. He had indeed become very much a father figure to me, and I didn't like letting him down.

I had seen that look on my father's face many times in my earthly life, and although I usually feigned disinterest, in my soul I felt pain at those moments. My father was a man of incredible integrity, goodness, and faith, and he deserved better than my inappropriate disdain. And I was unaware at the time of how my rejection of his values and my defiance against what he held dear (and, in fact, my defiance of all authority) caused deep anguish for him and created in his mind the sense of abject failure in his fathering.

His disappointment in me had nothing to do with any lack of love or caring on his part. I had given him every reason for disappointment, yet though it hurt him and pained me deeply, for reasons that are beyond even my own comprehension, I remained bent on rebellion and self-seeking. No son can long bear the guilt and sting of letting his father down as monumentally as I did. It will result in seeking balm usually in places and ways that only increase the separation, and, as in my case, tend toward self-destruction. As I would eventually learn, there is no circumventing the fifth commandment of honoring one's father and mother.

"Alright, Mr. Sane." I suddenly knew that I was in deep trouble. I should have kept my mouth shut. I had heard that remark from Dr. Kakos before and had seen that look on his face. Even in heaven as a member of the Redeemed, Dr. Kakos was ready to pounce. On Earth, the attack would have been mostly about his ego and the opportunity through debate, a generous description of his mostly unilateral arguments to humiliate his opponent, which I had been the victim of three or four times in his classes.

As I was about to find out, however, this was not about his agenda. I remembered the term "righteous indignation." That was something my father in particular often expressed, usually when hearing or reading about some new aspect of "this sick society!" Dr. Kakos was now more interested in defending the truth than in intimidating, embarrassing, or triumphing over an opponent.

"Shall we discuss probability?" Dr. Kakos began again. "The probability of life developing through time and chance is so infinitesimally small that the suggestion of it is nearly preposterous. If, however, you insist on embracing that position, very well; but let me remind you that probability informs us that time and chance as a creative mechanism is an exceedingly *unscientific* hypothesis. The odds, if you will, are monumentally and ludicrously against this eventuality.

"You must accept your position *completely on faith*, Mr. Sane. Probability chooses no sides! It simply reports. What it reports is that evolution is so remarkably close to impossible, impractical, and unfeasible, even given the billions of years that biologists and physicists insist upon for the age of the universe, that the idea would be banished in any reasonable and sagacious discussion of origins. Were it any other theory with the same deficiency of substantiation, no one would attempt to stellify it. It would be mocked and receive a just vituperation."

For some reason, I could not let go. Perhaps it was the awareness of the desperateness of my view and some faint hope that other options in the origin of humanity and the implications of relieving personal responsibility might present. I trudged on in my stupidity. "What about the matter of mutations, Dr. Kakos? This is the very core of the—"

"Stop," said Dr. Kakos, and he gestured with the familiar wave of his hand. "Are there any observable mutations that create *new* (Dr. Kakos strongly emphasized that word) genetic material? Not variations within a species, but new genetic material that brings substantive adaptive changes? All mutations introduce destructive non-violable changes. All.

"Given that the evolutionary process would require continuous positive mutations, without *any* negations for thousands of centuries, and yet we never observe a single mutation that introduces positive genetic change, you must admit if you insist on this position, it is very *unscientific!* You may hold to it if that is your inclination, but please recognize what the data articulates so unmistakably.

"And what shall say we of DNA? The information found in DNA, not just the molecular structure or the code, but from where did the information in the DNA originate? Beyond DNA itself, there is no instrument for the evolution of information! The existence of the information is without precedent, without explanation. It demands a Mind that purposefully placed the information. Evolution makes no rational accounting for this."

I had no response to the barrage of facts. It was time for me to shut up. I should have known better than to attempt to debate Dr. Kakos. *What was I thinking?* And I now fervently hoped that Gordon would forgive my audacity.

What I had seen and experienced in heaven, with Odegeo, in the heavenly Eden, at the Throne, the encounter with the enemy of my soul, the grace and protection of Michael over me, the love and compassion and friendship I had felt from Gordon, the stunning story of Frank Henderson, the utter nature of heaven itself—these should have overwhelmed me and quieted me.

I had noticed a pattern. I would be immersed in the joys of heaven and respond to something in my heart and mind, when the old darkness would suddenly invade my soul. My heart would harden, and I would be full of self-doubt and even defiance, though I did not show it as blatantly as in my past life, it was there in my being.

I knew Lucifer was not causing this. I understood that the enemy of heaven was the source of unbelief and many other things, but here in the heaven realm, I could not blame him. This was only my darkened heart. Shame began to creep upon me again as it had repeatedly done far earlier when I was on the other side of the Throne, heading toward the City of God with Odegeo. Then I had frequently fallen into periods of grief over my sin, shame, and the fear of what lay ahead. Perhaps I had wandered too far from that sense of need and inadequacy. In all that I had been through I knew the reality that something in my soul had changed. A certain veneer of goodness and joy had covered me, but there had been no ontological change.

Even amid glorious heaven, even in the presence of this utterly changed and thoroughly redeemed brilliant former rebel, even within shouting distance of angels around me, I held to my defiance, wavering somewhat, but still grasping the darkness. Such is the corruption of the human heart.

14

A Prisoner Set Free

Now it struck me that in all the discussions with Dr. Kakos, I had not heard the story of how he came to God. I wanted very much to hear that, and this would be a good distraction for my present state of mind.

"It seems," I said, "that a lot of things were piling up against you intellectually. Were you purposely studying these matters?"

"My purposes for investigating these matters in a systematic way initially were drawn from a thoroughly reprehensible motivation," he answered.

My own search for "truth," which ended up in occult activities, the very means that God had used to bring me here, had been of the same nature. It had been a less than admirable attempt to remove God, or at least what I sensed were His demands, from my life.

Kakos continued, "Like Voltaire, my intentions were for the elimination of religion, at least the Christian religion, because of the moral requirements I knew it made on my malevolent and decadent conduct. Ostensibly, I addressed all religions for their repressive and despotic governance. I also used the tenuous and misinformed argument depicting religion as the basis of so many wars, proving it to be a pointless blight on humanity.

"This created a justifiable, *a priori* reason for the abolition of religion. Its sentient eradication would consequently bring a new era of libertarian self-determination and the permissive realization of otherwise denied autonomy for mankind. Of course, Mr. Sane, that noble-sounding selflessness was all simply superficial putrefaction! What I really wanted was freedom to pursue every pleasure without culpability!"

I looked at Dr. Kakos with genuine surprise at hearing that such low and base purposes drove him. The realization that this man of great influence and brilliance was primarily driven by little more than his desire for unmitigated pleasure was stunning! How many more were likewise motivated by such unsavory impulses?

"Yes, Adam, the fundamental stimulus in my career pursuits was mostly selfish pleasure. I am sorry, regretful beyond description, to have used the gifts the Lord God gave me for such insalubrious reasons.

"Yet as I unremittingly continued my pursuits, for years on end, mind you, even acknowledging the pleasure-driven selfishness of my ego, there were certain relentless facts that persistently intruded. All of the matters I mentioned previously, and many others were leading me to an inexorable conclusion. The pervasiveness of the possibility of an actual designer of life was eventually inescapable.

"I perfectly understand the thrashing about of my colleagues on Earth. They are desperate to find a reasonable and rational way to discredit, discount, or disprove the Lord God. However, they cannot. Not from an objective, lucid, and coherent propositional basis. The longer they search, the more obvious this becomes. The more obvious it becomes, the more desperate, and in many cases the more irrational, their efforts become. Believing lies, skewing studies, and misrepresenting facts. I did it as well.

"Such is the desperation. And all the while, the Lord God was calling, patiently waiting, and extending unfathomable grace. I know now that the longsuffering prayers of my parents were breaking up long-hardened ground and my heart of stone was, miraculously, being softened.

"However, it took something else to bring me to my senses. You never knew of this, Adam. Few did, at least initially. Even my professorial contemporaries, for the most part, did not know until the progression of the problem reached an unmanageable point."

"Know what, Dr. Kakos?" I was curious and slightly anxious about what he was about to say.

"Adam, I went through a period of insanity. I finally lost my mind. Near the end of my career, at the height of my distinguished professional glory and the greatest breadth of influence, mental illness overwhelmed me. That is why I felt such kinship with Nietzsche, even despite his lostness. No, he is not of the Redeemed. But, like him, madness came over me. All the contradictions I was living in the realm of my learning and the darkness of my personal life, the dishonesty in my scientific proposals, and the duplicity in my philosophic pontifications—not to mention the pervasive guilt that I could not eradicate despite the years of fervent unbelief.

"It all collapsed on me. The doctors called it Acute Porphyria, but in the end, all that mattered was the teleological point. It was a circuitous, subterranean, ignoble, debasing, yet propitious path to travel!

"Ah, but the grace and glory at the finish! Of course, as you know, or perhaps not, I was not the first man in history to travel that auspicious route to its soteriological conclusion." (I didn't know if I knew that or not.) "Can you imagine, the great Dr. Marlas Kakos, institutionalized, medicated, legally medicated, Mr. Sane, restrained, intellectually impoverished, under the comprehensive dominion of others, without self-determination, without motivation, without the fecundity of my previous life? All of these were the utter contradiction of all that I had been."

Dr. Kakos suddenly paused, which was unusual for him to do during an address. He seemed now to be so moved by his story that a flood of emotion was coming over him. Gordon's eyes were brimming with tears, like the spilling of waters over the edge of an inundated reservoir. Dr. Kakos had begun to falter at the mention of grace, a moment that was not lost on me! The memory of grace for him was the tipping point, as it had been for Frank Henderson.

Then, out of the tears, both Gordon and Dr. Kakos unexpectedly broke directly into a joyful laughter that sounded something like singing. At first, it reminded me of many moments in Eden with Odegeo when I had seamlessly moved from tears to joy and laughter. The thinnest of lines had existed between those two radiant states of dynamic pleasure. But this was different.

I watched them with intrigue and hope, but I sensed that this was not something I could share with them on the deepest level of being. It is not possible to describe this laughing-singing expression. It was not like anything I had seen before. Hysteria or loss of control had no part in it, nor any trance-like quality. Indeed, I had both seen and personally experienced similar states, but only in altered conditions of consciousness, a result of various stimulants, legal and illegal, physical and spiritual. And there had always been a hollowness to it; it was temporary, external from my being, and craved more in a way that lessened who I was and increasingly fragmented my personhood.

But Dr. Kakos and Gordon were both fully in command of their faculties and seemingly transcended to a higher plane of life, not a lesser one. I was again observing, but not participating; this was an ongoing condition for me in heaven. It did not seem appropriate to interrupt this moment. I stood respectfully and waited.

Finally, Dr. Kakos collected himself, although not out of embarrassment or confusion, and spoke again. "During my occasion of mental illness, everything I had built my life on was stripped away.

"At first, I dealt with the illness surreptitiously. This, however, was only successful as long as I could deal with it on my own terms. Eventually, as hospitalization became necessary, I was unable to manipulate the circumstances clandestinely. There was an ever-widening circle of knowledge about my status.

"I had a few visitors in the hospital, very few, which undoubtedly said something about both me and my important and highly dignified colleagues, but I deeply resented that! I wanted no one to know, and it seemed, for the most part, that my friends, given their level of concern," he said, rolling his eyes slightly, "for my well-being did not want to know much either. I would have done no better had a colleague undergone the same adversity.

"Yet, as the illness progressed to its full-fledged state of mental incapacitation, I could not hide. I remained in that condition for several years. The day came when I no longer knew who was visiting me, or if anyone was visiting. Near the end, I lost control of my conscious mental processes and was unable to deal with my most basic needs. At times, I wandered the grounds of the institution in a near animal-like state."

I could barely believe what I was hearing. The story that Dr. Kakos was relating so violated my memory of him and the admiration I had for him as an influential intellectual who seemed to have resolved every issue of life's deepest questions, that I found myself in something of a state of disbelief. I even began to feel sick to my stomach. Not Dr. Kakos . . . Of all the people I had ever known, no one was as confident, aware, and settled as he.

"Dr. Kakos, I'm in a state of shock. You, of all people, were so . . . so . . ."

"So utterly wrong, Mr. Sane. The Lord God says I was a fool. A materialist such as I, who draws every breath by His grace and goodness, used those astounding gifts to deny Him! We profess our wisdom but promote our foolishness."

"But how did you . . . how did you get out of your condition? What happened to bring you to a place of religion?"

"A place of religion, eh?" Gordon said suddenly, with an air of disquiet. I did not understand why he seemed to be concerned by my remark.

Dr. Kakos glanced at Gordon with pursed lips. I remembered that disconcerting look from many years before. Some agreement passed between them that I did not then comprehend.

Dr. Kakos continued. "Here is the most marvelous thing of all. It was not some tremendous mind, gifted genius, or brilliant philosopher that finally helped me. No, because that is what *I* would have wanted: an exchange with a fellow genius, a cerebral and scholarly interplay with profoundly deep intellectual discovery leading me out of my darkness through luminous and mercurial logic. In the end, I could have claimed that with the help of so-and-so, who ultimately would have very little to do with my deliverance, I saved myself! Through my efforts and a daring look within my psyche, I diagnosed my lugubrious disease and triumphed over my despair through sheer willpower, courage, fortitude, and intelligence!

"But the Lord God would have none of that. It was a Bible, Adam, a Bible left in my room at the institution. Dusty, ignored, pushed to the back of a drawer. How long it had lain there, I do not know. Yet there it waited for me for years, perhaps decades. Placed there by some servant of God I do not yet know, although I hope that He will allow me to discover that person here among the Redeemed and the placement graciously designed by the Lord God in response to the fervent, longsuffering prayers of my parents. Knowing one day I would enter the world of dementia in that city, in that hospital, *in that very room*, the Lord God prepared for me.

"And one day I discovered that Bible. In all my contempt and excoriation of religion, especially the Bible, it was an extraordinary thing to consider; I had not opened a Bible since my childhood. I had little idea what it said.

"Not surprisingly, none of the treatments for Porphyria had been effective. I was not advancing in my recovery. Out of abject despair and fear, in hopelessness, I opened the Bible. In stunned disbelief, the first thing I began to read was about a man, a king, who in the midst of and because of his glory and arrogance, fell into insanity that had been predicted by a servant of the Lord.

"My mind suddenly cleared, and I felt a dawning in my consciousness. My senses began to return to me with great alacrity. The king of Babylon, Adam, that was me, and I knew it! The Lord God had given me a moment of clarity, a brief respite from the insanity that had reduced me to a state of complete dependency and humiliation, a chance at choice. And the breathtaking result for the king of Babylon: he was healed! This was hope beyond hope. It was stupendous and utterly unforeseen! The fact of his humiliation and change of heart was not lost on me.

"After reading that account, I turned to Genesis and read as one famished for words. I scarcely slept or ate. I read the entire text of the Holy Scriptures in three days. I know that the medical personnel had immense apprehension over this, at least briefly, thinking I was slipping into some catatonic or delusional state, but the truth is that I had finally begun to find myself.

"I began to read the Scriptures again as soon as I had finished, but this time with even greater clarity of mind, searching for answers to life. I did not read maniacally as I had those first three days, but I did read and study with great hunger. And my mind was restored, renewed, and transformed. It was only a matter of a few more weeks, and I was released from the institution.

"I went back to my home for rest and more study. I was completely astonished at the Scriptures. I had never imagined the wealth of wisdom and knowledge contained within its pages. With great lucidity, the Bible addressed all of the questions of my existence, Adam! And when I finally came upon the story of Naaman the Aramean, I was quite ready to surrender. For only surrender will do, do you understand?

"As the slave girl said to the mighty Captain, "Had the prophet told you to do some great thing, would you not have done it? How much more then, when he says to you, 'Wash and be clean.'

"And I did, Adam. I washed, and I was cleansed! I could add nothing to His work. I had nothing to give, offer, or merit. *It was all by grace.* The great Marlas Kakos was emptied of himself and surrendered at last! All the battles I had fought, the rebellion I had breathed, the dark that I had multiplied, were all released to grace! And it was all brought to fruition by insanity, the breakdown of my once-brilliant mental faculties. No other act of Almighty God would have sufficed. My ego, arrogance, self-perceived glory and greatness had ascended to the heavens. Only in total loss of myself could I finally see myself. I saw at last the light of grace.

"Without warning, In the midst of my surrender, ardent and clear visions of my parents and my sister, Anastasia, flooded my mind. I saw them in prayer at an altar, weeping with friends, grieving in great pain and sorrow over me. Adam, I had not wept in years, perhaps decades, but the flood overwhelmed me now and years of hardness, like the steel of a hammer, were swept out of existence.

"To have gone from being the man I was, a man of incalculable arrogance and baseness, to a broken man throwing himself at the foot of the cross and crying out like the publican for mercy is a transformation that is beyond human ability and comprehension.

"I, Marlas Kakos, now praise, honor, and exalt the King of Heaven. I thank Him for the mental illness, for it was a means of grace to me, a prison from which flowed the only path by which I could find Him. Bless you, prison of mental illness! And I say with another,

"It was granted to me to carry away from my prison years on my bent back, which nearly broke beneath its load, this essential experience: how a human being becomes evil and how good. In the intoxication of youthful successes I had felt myself to be infallible, and I was therefore cruel. In the surfeit of power, I was a murderer and an oppressor.

In my most evil moments, I was convinced that I was doing good, and I was well- supplied with systematic arguments. It was only when I lay there on rotting prison straw that I sensed within myself the first stirrings of good. Gradually it was disclosed to me that the line separating good and evil passes not through states, nor between classes, nor between political parties either, but right through the human heart and through all human hearts.

That is why I turn back to the years of my imprisonment and say, sometimes to the astonishment of others about me, 'Bless you, prison!' I have served enough time there. I nourished my soul there, and I say without hesitation: 'Bless you, prison, for having been in my life!'"

15

The Bridge of the Crystal Sea

I had no words for Dr. Kakos. To say that I was stunned would be an understatement of epic proportions. All that I knew of Marlas Kakos and all that he represented to me were wholly turned upside-down.

After some departing remarks, Dr. Kakos took his leave of us and appeared to head toward the City of God. I watched him as he went and wondered how this transformation could have taken place. If anyone else had told me the story of Dr. Kakos, I would not have believed them.

My mind reeled as I considered the stories of both Frank Henderson and Dr. Kakos. My conceptions of God, His workings, and His interest in humanity had been wrong. Two men from my past, whom I had met here in heaven, who were very different from one another but both came from a place of abject unbelief and rejection of God, both were now of the Redeemed. And in both of them, I saw the similarities of my apostasy.

At first, I had thought that meeting Frank Henderson coming off that bridge at precisely the right moment was sheer coincidence. But after the encounter with Dr. Kakos, not an accident, the idea that the reunion with Frank was purely by chance disappeared wholly. Both of these men and Gordon too had talked about grace. They had received a gift of inestimable and indescribable value that they did not deserve.

Still, the question plagued me. Was I on the same level as they had been? I could see *their* rejection of God, *their* unbelief, *their* evil. Had my life been lived in that degree of darkness? Gordon had mentioned the one million points illustration. I was hopelessly in the negative as is every human, according to Gordon. Frank had told me about the intersections of grace. He believed everyone experiences these, and he obviously believed my presence in heaven was such an intersection. And Dr. Kakos had vehemently and diligently worked *against* God, yet he had attributed the opening of his eyes as an act of grace, something he was incapable of doing on his own.

As I stood reflecting on Frank, Dr. Kakos, and then my life, I realized I had answered my question. Yes, I was every bit as dark, unbelieving, and sinful as they. I had no more business in heaven, of my merit, than they. At times during my trek through heaven, I had seen glimpses of my sin and felt the pain and shame with great depth. I had feared the Throne of Heaven because of this very problem. Yet, at other times, the knowledge of my inadequacy had slipped away and my rebellion crept in. During moments with both Frank Henderson and Dr. Marlas Kakos, my dark nature had rebelled against the truth they were proclaiming to me. I was not grasping something about this grace.

"We need to keep moving, Adam," Gordon said, interrupting my reverie.

Happily, the joy and mirth had returned to his eyes. His countenance gleamed again with the delight of heaven. I suddenly remembered getting a glimpse of some sight ahead that I had seen just before Dr. Kakos tapped on my shoulder. I was eager to move on and see whatever it was that had shimmered high in the distance.

We began to walk again. As we moved forward, ever so slowly a construction did indeed become more visible. The first clear view revealed a mammoth structure that slowly came into focus in its entirety. The pure clear air of heaven allowed for no hazy uncertainty. And, the flatness of heaven, apart from hills and trees and mansions, generally meant that the whole thing was visible at the same time, not just the highest peak. Upon recognition of its form and clarity of the sight, my breath was taken way.

It was a bridge, the bridge, the mother of all bridges! There was an immense presence about this bridge. The towers were enormous in height! These were at least three times the height of any other I had seen in heaven, or on Earth for that matter. The suspension cables were the thickness of large trees. And the color of both the towers and the cables was a brilliant, orange-coppery color that shimmered. At moments there seemed to be a brilliant reddish hue or a silver and golden cast that played upon the surface, but the orange-copper color was constant, and it was bright!

As we approached the bridge, which took some time because it was visible from many miles away, I realized that the "road" of the bridge was not like that of an earthly bridge. It was not cement or asphalt, but it was a living surface of grass! Green and vibrant, like all other life in heaven, this was lush rich grass. I had never dreamed of a bridge with such a covering, but why not? This was not a bridge for semi-trucks, tourist buses, cars, or pickups. This was for the pleasure and contentment of human feet and perhaps angels as well. And the width of the road of grass appeared to be several hundred feet across. Many of the Redeemed were traversing the bridge. The whole site was utterly spectacular!

As we finally came near the bridge, I stopped and stared in awe. I realized as I gazed at this wonder that more than grass was on the road of the bridge. Farther up the span of the bridge, a variety of trees were growing in the road. Some were quite large and stately, others were smaller but covered with blossoms of many colors. Never had I imagined such a thing.

On the other hand, why not? Heaven pulsed with life and vibrancy! Why should a bridge, especially one of this magnitude, not serve as an arboretum?

Gordon waited patiently for me. I think he was laughing quietly at the sheer enjoyment of my stunned amazement. I shook my head in wonder and could only utter, "Wow" over and over again.

Finally, I managed to form a question. "How long is it?"

"Well," Gordon answered, "it spans the whole width of the Crystal Sea, so it's at least forty miles. In the middle there is a passage down to the island."

"Island? There's an island?"

"Yes. You can actually see it quite well from here, Adam, but you have been so taken with the bridge you haven't even noticed the island."

I looked out at the sea and sure enough, plain as day, there was an island, a sizeable island that the bridge still soared above, but was accessible from the bridge. "Do I see buildings on the island, Gordon?"

"Yes, oh yes!" he answered. "They are mansions, homes like you have seen all through our travels. Many of the Redeemed live there, and some are very unusual people."

"Now that is saying something!"

"The island is halfway across the Crystal Sea, right in the middle. It's many miles long, and I would guess perhaps ten miles wide."

"Do you think we could walk on the bridge? Could we walk out to the island?"

'Yes, certainly," Gordon said.

We strolled over to the wide entrance. The overwhelming magnitude made me feel like an ant crawling onto the Golden Gate Bridge. I looked straight up at the full height of the orange-copper towers rising above my head and felt a moment of dizziness. I steadied myself against Gordon's shoulder and regained my balance.

The slope of the bridge rose quickly. On Earth, it would have been an exhausting climb, but now in the bloom of health here in heaven, I was able to practically sprint up the incline. By the time we reached the full height of the bridge road, we were far above the surface of the waters of the Crystal Sea.

I went to the side of the bridge and peered over the rail. I may have been in heaven, but the distance of the potential fall still gave me a sense of uneasiness, a hint of vertigo. I drew back from the edge. I suddenly wondered, could I die in heaven? It was a question I had never considered till that moment. I decided to ask my guide, but he brought up the topic before I had a chance.

"Adam, the way you backed up from the rail gave me the feeling that you're afraid, like you might plunge to your death if you stand too close!"

"It's a long way down to the water! Plus, I'm not real comfortable with heights. What if I did fall, Gordon? Would I die? Could I die in heaven?"

Gordon paused, obviously thinking through that question. It was the first time that I had seen him appear uncertain in response to a question since we had met in heaven. "I'm not sure how to answer that," he said. He put his hand to his chin, a leftover trait from his earthly life and a sign of deep thought. It was a vaguely familiar gesture to me even though I had not seen it in this realm.

"There is no death in heaven. Death exists solely in the realm of sin. It's a consequence of sin, whether physical death, spiritual death, or eternal death. By definition, there can be no death in heaven; yet, technically, you're not supposed to be here either." Gordon paused again. "Of course, the Lord is not bound by technicalities!" He chuckled deeply with crinkled eyes at his comment.

"I suppose anything that might happen to you, any dangerous thing, is foreknown by God, so He would have prepared circumstances to keep you from harm, I think. Unless, of course, an accident, which is a necessarily inaccurate word especially in heaven, is some event that the Lord would use to help you recognize your need, which frankly, I don't think you do yet. We also must factor in the persistent intercession of your parents, among others, on behalf of your soul. Death outside of Christ would seem to be a virtual impossibility given all that they have done for your soul and the fact that you are here, an indescribably unusual event.

"On the other hand, the Lord simply will not violate His allowance for free will in matters of salvation, His electing purposes notwithstanding. I suppose in the moment of greatest insight you could still choose against His will, as you have in fact being doing all along." Gordon paused again then finally spoke. "I don't know what the answer to your question is. I do know that the outcome is not hidden from God, and He would have foreknown it, so His allowing of it would be, must be, good. All that He does, Adam, *all* is motivated from His love, goodness, and holiness."

For the most part, I followed what Gordon had said, but the remark that really hit me was that I had been choosing against His will all along. I had not seen it that way at all while I was doing it, but now it struck me with such force that I could not deny what he said. I had been choosing against Him all along, whether I was with Frank Henderson, with Dr. Kakos, with Gordon, and even at times with Odegeo.

The possibility that I could die was a difficult proposition to accept, yet there seemed to be an aspect of it that must be true. I could not unravel the logic, but practically speaking, if I fell off this bridge . . . And what about the future in the realm that Gordon had referred to as the battle lands? Death there might have an entirely different availability.

I felt a strong desire to keep moving up the bridge. I promised myself to stay away from the edge. No sense in testing any theories at this point! And as was the case so often both in my life on Earth and here among the Redeemed, my decision was to delay, to change the subject, to put off the choice. Deep in my soul I knew this could not go on indefinitely.

I made no response to Gordon other than nodding and feigning agreement, but I began walking further up the bridge.

"All right," he answered.

I pushed the conversation out of my mind. It was actually quite easy to do given the spectacular views around us.

It was strange to walk on a bridge, high above the blue ocean, yet feel the coolness of grass. It was also odd to look out at a vast horizon and see no curvature. At the zenith of the bridge, I could see the mountains Gordon had mentioned that circled the realm of heaven. They must have been high indeed since, according to my guide, the mountains must have been hundreds of miles away to the "north" and "south."

Still, with no planetary curvature to figure into the equation, calculating what the size might be was difficult. In any case, they were clearly visible from this distance.

The colors of the mountains were somber reds, probably sheer rock sides, vivid greens, definitely vast areas covered with trees and perhaps other foliage, a mix of purple and gray, many shades of brown, and some very dark, nearly black. But this is too simple. Many shades were between all these colors plus peaks of every size and shape—some jagged, some smooth, some ascending to unknown heights, and some lower. These were predominately green, and some areas of brilliant blue, which I took to be great areas of water in the mountains.

The enormity of the view and magnificence of the grandeur suddenly struck me with a haunting sense of my own insignificance. Instead of inspiring the worship and wholeness that the Redeemed enjoyed at the marvel of His creation, I suddenly felt almost hollow. The overwhelming beauty hit me with an austere sense of isolation, a strange aloneness in my soul. I did recognize some victory in acknowledging the reality of my soul, as I was no longer a convicted soulless materialist. Still, there was an odd emptiness at this moment. A pang of vacancy twisted my stomach.

My mind remembered beautiful but poignant music I heard long ago that had the same effect on me. How was it that something of such extraordinary splendor could now bring such an awareness of unfulfilled purpose, of remoteness from real meaning, of lostness from a life of promise? I was just existing. I longed in my heart for something I could not grasp. I had no solidity, no chest. The glory of this place revealed the bankruptcy of my existence. With tears in my eyes, I turned to Gordon and said, "Why does this hurt so badly?"

"He has set eternity in your heart. That longing for eternity, for life, is what is hunting you, Adam. You will never be truly at rest until your soul rests in Him."

The weight of it was too great for me. I wept. Many of the Redeemed were passing by and looked at me, not with condescension or judgment, but with compassion and mercy. To what degree they understood what was going on (a human, not of the Redeemed, traveling through heaven), I don't know. But at no time did any one of the citizens of heaven treat me with anything but kindness and respect.

After some time of just sitting and wondering, again, at the marvel of my presence here, and at the same time having a sense of lostness, uncertainty, and a hurtful regret over my past life, I stood. Gordon, as always, had waited patiently for me.

"I think if you persevere to the end of your journey, you will understand," he said. "I think one day you will join the Redeemed, Adam. I believe great hope is in this and great purpose in your presence here. It is not for nothing that you have come to this place."

I took some comfort in Gordon's words and thanked him again for staying with me for so long and being my guide, not just geographically but in every way possible.

Eventually we moved on. Ahead, however, the bridge was bending downward somewhat, and I saw that we were approaching the island. From the bridge was a long grass-covered walkway down to the island. The intricately patterned railing along both sides of the walkway were of the same marvelous material that shone with the orange-copper brilliance and color on the towers and cables. Beyond the island, the bridge soared up again and marched forward to the far shore across the Crystal Sea.

Just before we descended the path down to the island in the middle of the Crystal Sea, I turned my eyes once again to the mountains. I noticed now that there were also many thread-like, effervescent vertical lines with a dazzling, sparkling sense of movement to them. I stared at these for some time and finally asked Gordon what I was seeing.

"Waterfalls, of course," he said.

What the height and width of a waterfall must be to be seen from hundreds of miles can only be guessed. Yet, like this mammoth bridge that we were walking on, the sites of heaven were spectacular and often on a grand scale.

"Some of the Redeemed live right in the presence of the waterfalls. Their houses are continually misted by the falling water. Some, I have heard, live behind the waterfalls, between the falls and the mountains, and some make the water the very walls of their mansion. These loved the sea in all its glory and power.

> *For the Lord is a great God and a great king above all gods, in whose hand are the depths of the earth. The peaks of the mountains are His also, the sea is His, for it was He who made it, and His hands formed the dry land. Let the heavens be glad and let the Earth rejoice. Let the sea roar and all it contains, the world and those who dwell in it. Let the rivers clap their hands. Let the mountains sing together for joy.*

I had no doubt that Gordon was quoting from the Bible. I lamely responded saying, "Yes, indeed." It seemed inadequate, but I felt some response was necessary. I wondered if perhaps we might eventually make our way over to the mountains and waterfalls. What was it he had said? "Some make the water the very walls of their mansions." I wasn't entirely sure what that meant, but it would no doubt be amazing to see!

Yet, the island was ahead, and now we were climbing down the path toward it. "Does this island have a name, Gordon?"

"Yes, it certainly does!" he said with surprising earnestness and emphasis. "It's called the Island of the Temple."

Something struck me about that name that was not altogether comfortable. Memories of occult-centered novels, spectacular action movies, and uneasy thoughts of the activities of secret societies flooded my mind momentarily. I remembered (vaguely as usual) old strange and disconcerting stories from church about a temple. But that was on Earth. This was heaven. A heavenly temple. Was this, like Eden, what we had passed through, the heaven-born original?

Before I could even ask about the temple or a visit to it, Gordon announced, "But before we see the temple, we must see someone who lives on the island. He must grant access to you to visit the temple."

I was almost afraid to ask, but I summoned the courage. "Who is it we must see?"

"We must see the Lawgiver."

"The Lawgiver? Who is that?"

"Moses! Adam, you are going to see Moses!"

16

The Man of Vision

Moses! Even I knew that name. I admitted to my ignorance of the Bible, but Moses' name was legendary. Had anyone asked, I would have acknowledged that a real Moses had lived once upon a time, but the supernatural wonders he experienced had naturalistic explanations.

But Moses was real now. I didn't fully understand Gordon's remark about the Lawgiver, but a few moments of thought brought back memories from movies and Hollywood special effects, memories about Moses on a mountain and the stone tablets with commandments written on them. That was all I could specifically recall. I didn't even know all the commandments, but I intuitively knew (especially here in heaven) that I had broken those commandments, all of them.

I was having a moment of lucidity. These flashes of clarity came and went during our travels. Even an occasional moment of penetrating insight was infinitely better than my darkness on Earth, where I had reached a point of no recognition, understanding, or perspicuity. At times it became all too clear who I was, how little I belonged here, how deep my inadequacy, how utterly I lacked any merit. Eventually I realized that this was tied up with grace, but I did not perceive it wholly yet. At other times, even here in this place of perfection, and even with Gordon at my side, I fell back into unbelief and doubt.

Doubt is far too kind of a word to describe the human condition. Doubt implies some potential for rational rejection, some reasonable cynicism, some credit to the doubter for careful consideration of the question. This has *nothing* to do with unbelief.

This moment of clarity reminded me of my obvious moral failure; yes, that is what the Lawgiver was all about! Those commandments revealed my sinfulness, whether I remembered them individually or not. That much I knew. I allowed the reality of that word, *sin*, into my mind. It was a word that I had carefully avoided, even in heaven.

The mere mention of the Lawgiver had shifted my whole mentality to my failure. I hated the Law. I understood little of the Law, despite the brave efforts of my parents and my pastor, who was at my side, to teach me. The law seemed to create in me more rebellion! It seemed impossible to obey this law. It was a standard by which I could not live.

The answer, in my mind, was to reject it, pretend it did not exist, treat it as irrelevant, and deny the One behind the Law. I now recognized that I was not alone in my efforts. Indeed, I believe this desire to flee from the Law is the motivating force behind all the libertine philosophies, humanist worldviews, and all the false religions on Earth.

We had descended the path to the island and stood at what seemed like to me the "east" end. The island stretched on for many miles toward the "west." The greater length of the island had been on my right hand as we had approached it on the bridge. I didn't see any temples. Like many earthly islands, this one seemed from our vantage point to be mostly forest. The heavenly trees were much more densely packed than almost anywhere on the mainland, and no visible break was in the woods except for a path, a wide path lined with majestic trees and wide, colorful gardens.

The trees were enormous! These were the largest trees I had ever seen anywhere in my life. Even in the heavenly Eden, the trees had not been like this. Their wide, thick trunks and extraordinary height gave the impression of great strength and, in a sense, age. The sheer enormity of the trees combined with the denseness of the undergrowth, including other trees, shrubs, many large fern-like plants, and countless other vines and bushes and all manner of foliage (a horticulturist's dream), and the darkish greenness of the atmosphere in many areas (even the radiant light of heaven was quite dimmed) created in my mind a sense of oldness like an ancient forest on Earth.

I could smell the woods with a hint of moisture, a mossy scent, a touch of the freshness of a spring morning, and the unique effervescence of living green things. It was an aroma to rejoice in! I knew this was not like a forest on Earth because here there was no death, and all this plant life, from the tiniest blade of grass to the greatest Redwood-sized tree, was in perfect vibrant health. Yet, here more than anywhere else in heaven, there was a hint of Earth-like nature.

As we walked, we came to the mansions of the Redeemed. All of them in this region of the island were tucked away among massive and stately trees. The mansions themselves formed an organic unity with the trees. At times, much like with the waterfalls Gordon had mentioned, the trees became a part of the structure of the home, sometimes serving as a wall or even a roof.

As we walked the path, the gardens and forest continued, and occasionally Gordon would inform me who lived in certain homes. I began to realize that the names he was saying sounded like names of Bible characters. "That is the home of Nicodemus . . . Over here is where Malachi lives . . . This mansion belongs to Josiah." It seemed that many of the saints of Scripture lived on this island.

"Is everyone who lives on this island from the Bible?" I asked.

"No, no, not at all, but there are many from the days before the Lord walked the Earth who still desire to be near the temple, or at least the memory of the temple, for the temple now lies mostly empty and dormant. Those living here are those who loved His temple but seldom, if ever, saw it celebrated and used in Jerusalem in the way the Lord had intended. And now it has been made obsolete, yet there is a purpose it still serves as you may very well find out, Adam."

"Does the temple still serve the same function? I mean, weren't priests wearing robes and animals sacrificed there?"

"On Earth, in Jerusalem, yes there was animal sacrifice for sins and so forth. But, no, Adam, no temple can serve that original purpose anymore. I have had many discussions with great saints on that very topic. The temple has been forever replaced by the fullness of grace in the fullness of time."

Grace again, I thought.

"This temple, which is really the original, serves as a permanent reminder of what it pointed to, what it foreshadowed, and the degree of grace necessary to atone for sin, really atone you understand, not merely cover sin."

"No, Gordon, I don't really understand."

"Perhaps you will when we get there, if you are able to hear from Moses."

The path we walked, like all the realm of heaven, was beautiful, overflowing with life, striking in its array of colors from the trees and the flowers that varied in size from minute to gigantic. We occasionally walked over small streams, or through them, which reflected in varying measures the vibrant blue of the sky and the striking hues of the flowers.

At times the depth of island foliage seemed almost jungle-like. Its thick, dense growth, while never barring the path, at some points created a roof over the path, completely enclosing the path in a green luminescence of pervasive life. Even as we were passing under a long length of the path with large bushes lining either side and willow-like trees joining together above the path to form a living green tunnel, a sudden drenching rain came up from the river, or rather, the Crystal Sea, driven by the powerful and curious winds that delivered the water throughout heaven.

The mist came over the land, but this was an unusually strong and lengthy downpour. The fact that the waters of the Crystal Sea surrounded the island no doubt explained the heavier rains and the tropical nature of the island. We walked out of the tunnel and into the mist. The warmth of the rain combined with the gentleness of this wind that moved the rain reminded me of summer storms from my own childhood. I closed my eyes and smelled the sweet and rich life smell of the rain (it was the smell of green) falling with such freshness on my face. I could see the light of heaven, even with the moisture-saturated air, shining through my eyelids.

I was transported through sweet memory back once again to a delightful place, running with happy abandon through warm July rains, of laughing with my brothers as we stomped through the puddles in a contest to see who could splash the muddy water the farthest, of perfect days, rain or shine, filled with perfect peace, playing together with such serenity and freedom in the complete security of our family. Oh, to go back to those days and the fullness of that life! And even as a child in the midst of this ideal life, a voice had been calling to me from somewhere else, hinting that this was merely a fleeting taste of the joy to come. Heaven was hailing my soul, calling a child to come to His embrace.

Gordon had said that He had set eternity in my heart. I knew this was true. I had grasped the tiniest corner of eternity as a child, as all children do in fleeting moments of release to heavenly wonder, in all its beauty and fullness. I comprehended it to the degree I could understand this thing of perfection and completeness. Then later, as a young adult, I threw it all away.

The rain had stopped. I was pulled out of the depth of my reverie, but somehow the rain and the longing for the simplicity of childhood, when life made some sort of effortless sense, and the flood of memories of peace, warmth, and contentment had all conspired together to reach far back in my memory to a song from my childhood. It was dancing about in my mind, unconsidered for years on end and probably taught to me in a smallish dimly lit room in the church basement by a loving, gray-haired lady. She later would become the generic object of my derision. I don't remember her name, though she deserves better treatment. I have no doubt there were thousands of such ladies who loved, cared, taught, and prayed for tens of thousands of children like me. Perhaps some prayers, even by faithful gray-haired old ladies who live to serve and leave their mark of joy and faith, are not answered.

But the song I distantly remembered. It was about a man named Ezekiel and dry bones mysteriously connecting together, and somehow this was all "the word of the Lord." The song, though from far away, was surprisingly clear in my mind.

It was a sweet, comforting memory. I mentioned it to Gordon, who, of course, immediately knew the whole song and text. I think he was preparing to sing it to me, but suddenly his eyes lit up with excitement and he said, "Adam! Would you like to meet Ezekiel the prophet? I believe he lives very near!"

I wasn't exactly sure I wanted to meet Ezekiel. I knew next to nothing about him except this song that I was sure did not originate with Ezekiel himself. It seemed that he was an Old Testament name, which for some reason made me even less inclined to make his acquaintance. Still, Gordon was visibly enthusiastic about this opportunity, and I knew that I owed such a debt to Gordon, that if he thought we should visit Ezekiel, then I should at least make an effort. I agreed to meet Ezekiel, and although it would eventually prove to be one of the most powerful experiences of my life, upon entering his presence, I almost immediately regretted it.

We inquired as to the whereabouts of Ezekiel's home. It was very close, just a few miles away. I noted how impossibly far this would have been in any consideration of walking distance in my earthly life. Isn't that what cars are for? But here it was a joy to walk.

The people we asked about the location looked strangely at me when I told them that we wished to visit Ezekiel's home. It was clear to all that I was not of the Redeemed, but this was the first and only time in the Heavenly Realm when it seemed that my status as an unredeemed human resulted in doubtful stares in regard to visiting Ezekiel. I almost had a sense that we, or I at least, should not proceed. This was disconcerting to say the least and gave me cause to reconsider the visit, especially since I was not entirely in favor of this direction.

Gordon, however, did not seem the least disturbed, and I

certainly had no reason to doubt his wisdom nor had any previous interactions with Redeemed humanity to give me any cause for alarm.

We continued on, taking paths through the marvelous woods and gardens of the island, and I was thankful for no automobiles or public transportation in heaven.

Very shortly we were standing and gazing from some considerable distance at Ezekiel's home in heaven. It was set in the middle of a very large (hundreds of acres it seemed to me), round treeless glade, unlike any other place I had seen on the island.

As we came out of the dense woods that made the vast circle around Ezekiel's land, we saw Ezekiel's mansion, and we stood in rapt wonder—and for me, a substantial amount of fear. Before me was a home, a dwelling place. Perhaps *habitat* was the best description. This was utterly different, startlingly so, than anything I had seen in heaven, or on Earth for that matter.

Ezekiel lived in a storm. In the middle of the otherwise peaceful glade, surrounded by the immense beauty of God's nature, was a storm—the home of Ezekiel. Wind was swirling wildly, in a ponderous cloud filled with areas of both deep darkness and lightning-like brightness darting fire or some type of piercing red lightning flashing constantly within. At times, it seemed as though small tornadoes were flung out from the edges of the storm then sucked back in to resume the ferocity. A brilliant, glowing but indefinable metal-like substance seemed to be inside the storm. This was not the house itself, but it was somehow part of the storm. In fact, there was no house; the storm was the house.

The entire time we were in the glade and in the presence

of Ezekiel, the storm never ceased its fury in the least. Sometimes it spread out to take up more of the glade, and sometimes the wind of the storm pulled it back into a more concentrated area, but the storm raged on. And the storm was not thundering ten thousand feet in the sky. It was on the ground. It did extend many hundreds of feet into the sky, but unlike an earthly tempest, the main strength of this storm was at ground level—Ezekiel's home.

I looked at Gordon, and I could tell this was new to him. Even he did not know of Ezekiel's storm, at least not the full extent of it. Gordon appeared to be enjoying the thrill of this moment, however. The electrifying minutes before the onset of a huge storm were always full of excitement for me. The charging tension of the radical change in the air pressure, the oncoming surge of wind bending the trees into precarious shapes, the ominous blackening of the sky, the fierce squall line of clouds forming like a cosmic saw blade across the horizon, and the hammering downpour of the wall of rain approaching menacingly across the fields.

But this was different. This storm, as far as I could tell, never ended. The exhilarating thunderstorms I grew up with normally lasted a few minutes, blowing quickly over us to the next county. Here it seemed permanent. That was astonishing, unnerving, strange, and radical. Gordon was animated and excited while I was uneasy and edgy. I wondered what to do next and if it was possible to convince Gordon that we should move on.

"How can this be, Gordon? How can he live in . . . that?" The storm was loud. The wind howled, and I had to shout.

Gordon laughed! He laughed excitedly but was unable to provide an answer.

"What do we do now?" I yelled.

"Just wait and enjoy this marvel, Adam! I have never been here before. I have heard rumors of Ezekiel's home, but it is far greater than I imagined!"

The storm, as with any storm, I suppose, was ever-changing. We watched with endless fascination. Eventually, as rationality returned, I felt more at ease and was able to appreciate the wonder of this site. When I remembered that there was no hurt or harm done in heaven (at least not to the *inhabitants*), some measure of calmness came over me. The storm was real, to be sure, and it seemed to me, a mere mortal, some danger might be present, but I had come this far safely, and it was not likely that whatever protection was over me would be removed now. I had made it over the bridge, after all!

Then we saw a man standing just outside the circle at the base of the storm. I don't think he had been standing there for long, or maybe the storm had moved slightly and revealed him. He waved at us. I felt some dread when I saw him wave. It was not just a greeting, it was a welcoming wave, beckoning us to approach! Despite having achieved some level of calm, I had to summon all of my valor for this moment. Gordon went boldly forward. Not wanting to be ashamed of any lack of courage and not wanting to be left alone, I followed closely behind.

The storm was louder the closer we got. The howling wind was very real; our hair and clothing whipped around and slapped our flesh. The brightness of the piercing red lightning and that dazzling, glowing metal was blinding. Directly above my head, the clouds whirled around in furious and threatening shades of gray, black, fuming blue, and angry brown. We were near to Ezekiel now. I wondered how we could possibly communicate given the shrieking of the wind.

Now we were standing with Ezekiel, and he was inviting us *into the storm*!

"You should grab hold of my arm!" Gordon shouted. "I don't think you need to hang on tightly. It's not that kind of threat but hold on to my arm anyway!"

I had no qualms about his directive. I grabbed his arm tightly for I was terrified again. Stepping into darkness blowing with fiery darts of light, we walked ten, twenty, thirty feet, deeper and deeper, into the maelstrom. I thought I might be picked up by the gale and blown around like an autumn leaf on a windy day. We moved farther into the storm, fifty feet, a hundred feet, and it became darker, but with flashes of lightning so close I thought I should be burned alive (although I felt no heat). Then, stepping over a dim threshold inside the storm . . . Perfect calm!

Incredibly (we were not in a room or building), I could see the storm still flailing all around me. There were no windows or walls, but as though in the eye of a hurricane, all was calm and even quiet. If I were to step but a few feet back, I would be engulfed in the storm again. Nothing visible protected us, yet the storm for all its effects, might as well be a hundred miles away.

The calm area where we stood was about a hundred yards in diameter and seemed to have a round quality. Against all odds, there were furnishings and something that seemed very much like a small pond. The ground where we stood consisted of granite, like the stunning, brilliantly colored granite that I recalled from the City of God.

Gordon was ecstatic! He immediately began to speak with Ezekiel about the wonder of his home. I was numb, due to the strangeness of the bizarre place where we were standing, and

I was frozen into silence and curiosity as I beheld this man who stood before me.

He was tall and bearded. I couldn't remember seeing many beards in heaven. He was, of course, in the most robust health imaginable, and his appearance was like all of the Redeemed: of an indefinable age, combining youthful exuberance and deep maturity in some sort of peak of perfection, an astonishing masculinity (as with the women who were the very definition of femininity) and a glow that exuded the fullness of life and joy coursing through him.

But the most memorable and riveting aspect of Ezekiel was his eyes. I looked at his eyes and somehow knew instantly that this man had seen God. He had seen God in ways that perhaps no one else ever had. I wished then that I knew the book of Ezekiel, for clearly this was one of the most extraordinary men who had ever lived. I could not even tell the color of his eyes, but they were bottomless wells, profound and knowing, beyond human perception. These eyes had seen visions that were unexplainable and full of mystery, and both kind and piercing at the same time. I was afraid and yet drawn irresistibly to him.

Then I heard Gordon introducing me to Ezekiel. He looked squarely at me, and a thrill of fear and adulation ran through me. I mumbled something about his unusual home and the pleasure of making his acquaintance. Mostly I felt like an idiot for being glaringly inarticulate and hopelessly intimidated, as I imagined I must have sounded. And just for an instant, it occurred to me that if meeting a mere human, Redeemed yes but still human, was this overwhelming, what might it be like to stand before Him in His place as judge over my life?

Ezekiel was now noting my condition; that is, *not* of the Redeemed. He was kind but clearly perplexed about my presence in heaven. This was different. Frank Henderson and Dr. Kakos, and others that I would eventually meet, seemed to know why I was here, and that they had a purpose for interacting with me. Ezekiel did not know. Whether or not this distinction was of importance was a matter of consideration for some other time. Ezekiel immediately began questioning me.

A short, but intense conversation ensued. Gordon did more talking than I did. Ezekiel seemed quite concerned that my presence in heaven might be some sort of ethical violation. I hardly knew how to answer him, and I tended to agree! After all, I knew by what means I had gotten there, or least what had begun the process: the Red Hue Room, the purposeful bent toward occultic practices, the bizarre, twisted figure that had caused me (did it push me, or did I simply fall backward in fear?) to plummet through the Walpurgis Door.

Yes, Ezekiel was right. I was there for all the wrong reasons, but Gordon assured him that there was something at work here greater than my wrong-headed motive of inquiry, which I had used to justify everything I had done, no matter how iniquitous. It wasn't, however, until Ezekiel heard about my presence in the City of God and my proximity to the Throne itself that he was satisfied that I could remain. The fact that I had lived through such an experience seemed to persuade him that all was well.

"And why are you here in my home?" he asked. His voice rang through the air with a strength that demanded an answer. He wasn't challenging my presence, but an answer must be given.

"We were nearby, sir, and Gordon asked if I wanted to visit

your home." Gordon nodded in agreement, for this was perfectly true.

"What else, young Adam? What else have you come for? What provoked Gordon to ask you about coming here?"

It was striking to me how entirely intimidated I was in this setting, and I suppose who in my situation would not be. Yet I remembered countless times on Earth when I believed no one could possibly intimidate me. In my arrogance, boldness, and self-defined brilliance, I thought I was strong, intelligent, rational, and unassailable. I could overwhelm anyone if needed. Here, now, I was a lamb cowering before a wolf. Yet, it was not so. Ezekiel had no desire to destroy me, he simply wanted straight answers. And I had the feeling he would search till he found them.

"Sir, I really had no intention of coming to your home. We were walking through the island, not too far from here, and the rain and mist rolled over the land. It was so beautiful, warm, and peaceful that I got caught up in wistful memories of my childhood."

"This has happened often since you came to this land," Ezekiel said. His voice was softer but more probing.

He wasn't asking me a question. He just knew. He stated the fact of these events. How he knew was unclear to me. Gordon had called him a prophet. Was that in the past tense or was Ezekiel still a prophet?

"I have many times, sir, been overwhelmed by thoughts of my childhood, my family. I was thinking of them during that rain. It reminded me so much of golden moments of years gone by. Then I remembered a song I had learned as a little boy. A song about you, sir, from the Bible. It was about dry bones lying in a field or something, being put together somehow."

Ezekiel smiled at the mention of the song. Perhaps he did know the song or at least knew of it. Had the song been sung to him here in heaven? He seemed delighted that I had heard and sung the song about him.

"When I mentioned the song to Gordon, he knew it, of course, and immediately wanted to come and see you. He said you lived nearby the place where we were walking."

"You did not want to come, though, young Adam."

"No, sir. I admit I did not want to come to see you." *How did he know that I did not want to meet him?* Gordon looked at me with some surprise but said nothing.

He gazed at me for a while. We did not speak. His eyes were upon me. It was uncomfortable. I waited, recognizing it was not the time for me to talk. The storm still silently roared around us.

Then at last he said, "Your home was a place of goodness, peace, and joy. You want to go back to that place. Your heart breaks for those youthful years. You do not understand what went wrong. Much of what you have seen and heard in heaven has caused you to remember, and the memories are bittersweet."

"Yes, sir, that is all quite true."

Then Ezekiel said again, "You long to go back."

"Well, yes, sir, I do."

Then Ezekiel turned his head slightly as if listening to someone. I waited again. After a moment, he spoke words that frightened me yet set a deep desire within me.

"It is within the authority of my office to grant you this desire, although I do not necessarily counsel you to do this. For a brief period, if you choose to, you may go back, young Adam. I have been given leave to allow this and to assist you, yet it is for a purpose I do not understand. You may watch what you will, but you will not be seen by those on Earth. You cannot interact with any events. I do not say you should not or ought not to, but you simply cannot. Those events are part of His foreordination from eternity, which He knows at all points simultaneously. They are fixed as they were, and no one has any capacity to alter them.

"One warning. There may be danger. You will exist solely in the spiritual realm, and you will be subject to spiritual realities of which you know nothing. The human events you see are unchangeable, but the spiritual movements are happening as you are there. These have a wholly different nature and dimension. You will be under angelic protection, but be aware that there may be another presence."

Again, Ezekiel turned his head at a slight angle, hesitated, then spoke. "His purposes are served in all things, whether one wills an act for good or bad. His hand is upon you. To return to heaven, you need merely call my name."

I was quite alarmed by the prospect of "spiritual realities," "another presence," and the other darks words Ezekiel had spoken. I was not even certain what these meant, but it sounded portentous. Still, the desire to relive or even watch some tiny part of my happy youth was so powerful, the longing was so deep, and it had haunted me so greatly, that I could not deny the hope of going back, no matter how temporal. After all, I had merely to call Ezekiel's name, and I would be restored to his presence and to Gordon.

"I'll go back, sir, if I may."

"You may indeed, young Adam. My eyes will guide you. I see the day in my mind for which you are longing. Remember to call my name to return."

"Thank you, sir."

I looked into his unblinking eyes but felt nothing. Nothing changed. I just stood there waiting and wondering what to do or what would happen. It seemed a long period of time passed, and I began to think perhaps he had failed or changed his mind, or something had gone wrong. I was about to ask him if there was something I ought to do to assist the process. Just before I spoke, Ezekiel blinked, and he was gone. And all was changed.

17

Return

Instantaneously I was back in my hometown, in a little city park of maybe five acres a few blocks from my home. A small stream, no more than ten feet wide, ran along the south side of the park, and a railroad was just past the stream. The park had the usual amenities: playground, pavilion, picnic tables, lots of trees, and one very steep, large hill on the north side that led down to the park from the street. At least the hill seemed large when I was child. We loved running up and down that hill, sliding, rolling, racing, and falling.

To my amazement, there I was! My brothers were on the hill, laughing and scrambling up and down, playing some kind of game (whose name I couldn't remember) with a bouncy ball. My parents were down in the pavilion spreading out the picnic lunch. The sky was heavenly blue, as much like the real heaven as was possible on Earth. The sun was shining brightly in the noon day with an occasionally puffy white cloud trailing lazily and peacefully through the azure. This must have been a summer Saturday, perhaps in June. It did not have the wilting strength of July's heat and humidity, just a perfect summer day of happiness, serenity, and carelessness.

I knew we would play there for a while till Dad and Mom called us to eat. We would stuff the picnic food down as fast as possible and then get back to playing. Dad and Mom would clean up the table, then relax on the bench and watch us. We would play and laugh, and they would talk to each other about whatever it was that parents talked about. I didn't know what they discussed, and I didn't care either. I didn't mind the topic of their conversation, but I cared very much about them talking, being together, and enjoying each other and us.

Later on, we would all go back to our home, gather our swimsuits and towels, and head for the lake. Many Saturdays of my childhood followed this pattern, and it gave great solidity and security to my life. The joy of it flooded my mind with piercing happiness and contentment.

Then I noticed something I had never seen before. Indeed, I could never have seen it in my earthly life. Another presence was in the park—not exactly in it, not as my family was in the park, but present nonetheless and present as if on some different axis indifferent to the physics of our world.

The presence was all around. Just as the human eye adjusts in the dark to take in more light and facilitate seeing, here my eyes had begun to alter to see what must have been the spiritual realities of which Ezekiel had spoken.

They were not altogether clear. It was not at all like seeing an angel in heaven in all the crisp clarity of their presence. The shapes here were rather hazy and indistinct. I remembered that Ezekiel had said I would be under angelic protection. I wondered where my angel was. As I turned around to see if anyone was nearby, I almost stumbled into a presence directly behind me. An angel of light was standing within a foot of me, although I could tell immediately this angel had none of the warmth and inherent joy of the company of heaven. Perhaps it was just the reality of being in this earthly atmosphere.

Now, as I looked back at the park, and disappointingly the

scene there seemed to be fading a bit, I noticed that the presence consisted of seven angels. However, they did not have the feel of the goodness of angels as with the one right behind me. I grew afraid. Something was not right. The sickening awareness hit me that these were not angels, not heavenly angels.

They were advancing upon me now. The one behind me was saying or chanting something unintelligible. It seemed that its words began to produce a fog that crept into my mind, blanking out something that I was supposed to remember. What it did say (I did not understand the significance at the time) was something to the effect of, "Clean, clean, clean but not filled . . . Seven more shall enter . . . from the place of the wasteland." Had I known then what this meant, I would have been filled with terror even greater than in the Red Hue Room when that frightful specter had approached me.

I grappled with remembering what someone had told me just a short time before. Someone should have been here that I was supposed to meet. Was that it? Someone whose name I should know . . . But the fog became deeper, and my memory grew more vague. Something terrible was happening, that much I could tell, but wasn't somebody meeting me here to help me?

I was surrounded by the seven now and the one behind me. They were not ugly; they simply looked like . . . like nothing. They were gray, like a shade, with appendages, but without features, having strange flesh as though they had died and then died again.

The daylight was gone, and the sun was blocked out. I could no longer see that family that was over in that park. These who surrounded me were reaching for me—no, far worse than that, they were reaching into me with their bizarre appendages! I felt the memory of heaven fading from my mind.

That man named . . . Greg, who had led me through heaven; no wait, Greg was my brother . . . wasn't he? That man in heaven who had befriended me after the angel, Oden . . . Odega . . . why had that angel abandoned me? Why had he left me? Why had he betrayed me? I thought he cared. But who was the man in heaven? Garden . . . no, that is not a name . . . Norman . . . he was with someone . . . another name I needed to remember . . .

But a vivid thought came into my mind to forget it, forget it all, go back to the university and continue my important research, to learn, grow, and become famous with my great intellect. Yes, yes, that made sense. That was what I had intended to do before all this foolishness about heaven had interrupted my life.

Then the eight demons, for that is what they were, formed an impenetrable wall around me. I had the feeling that they had all coalesced into one. They were spinning, shaking, or vibrating. It was hard to tell where one started and another stopped. There was something horrible about this blending. Even in my stupor, I knew that something was about to happen, something heinous. Their appendages were inside of me, in my soul I suspect, and I was helpless to do anything about it. The circle drew tighter, and I knew instinctively they were all about to enter into me wholly.

Whatever state I was in—body, soul, or both—I began to gag and vomit. I was sweating profusely, and my bodily functions all gave way. My heart pounded like the throb of a locomotive reaching full speed. I violently wrenched back and forth, hoping to fend off the hideous advance of this enemy. A seizure was upon me, my eyes were rolling back in my head, and I was foaming at the mouth.

They were winning.

I could not fight this battle on my own. The thought came into my mind, *What's the use? Just give up. It is inevitable. Heaven has forgotten you.*

Suddenly, from far away in the sky, clear out on the very edge of sight, a lightning flash of blazing white-hot light burst across the heavens in a flattened circular form that instantly spread from horizon to horizon! Then, moments later, a thunderous roar screamed through the heavenly places, like that of a war formation of fighter jets, ripping apart the sky.

Angels, angry angels! Avenging angels! Angels were coming in great wrath. They tore through the gathering darkness at blinding speed, a brilliant neon blue streak of light, headed directly for the legion of demons wrapped around me. One way or another, I feared I would die. The demons would take me in death to hell, or the angels in their holy rage would annihilate me.

In mere seconds, the angel force had traversed from the horizon to the place where I was in some spiritual realm. Like the sizzling speed of a missile shot from a faster-than-sound jet, the angels bore down in a great curving cobalt arc from the sky and raced toward me in furious and visible red wrath with brutally deadly accuracy.

They slammed like a dagger into the heart of the pulsing demonic mass, tearing through it like a bullet through paper. The demonic horde was shredded into pieces. The explosion of power crushed me, flattening me like a balloon that exploded and instantly compressed. I felt as though my body had been turned inside out. The pain was intense beyond imaging with a burning inside as I suffered so long ago, rising out of that planet through the heat and fire.

I groped around, crawling on the ground, feeling my body, amazed that I was intact. The pain continued, but I was now able to see in a dim but growing light. Much to my surprise, given the incredible violence of the attack, the demons were not dead. And it struck me that perhaps they cannot die. They were stunned into conscious oblivion and in some sort of agony or pain, but none of them was dead.

An angel came to me and touched my lips, and then I remembered.

"Ezekiel!" I cried out. "Ezekiel!"

And I was gone.

When I awoke, I was alone with Gordon. I must have slept for quite some time, especially considering that we were back in heaven where sleep was seldom necessary. We were no longer in Ezekiel's dwelling place, which was perfectly fine with me. We were in some type of pavilion surrounded by the familiar woods and gardens of the island. I was lying on the ground in the pavilion but on a soft bed of wondrously fragrant and marvelously soft and comfortable bedding. Remarkably, I felt good, given the extraordinary blast of angelic power I had received.

I began to recall the events that had occurred during my return to Earth and home. I trembled at the memory of the maniacal demons, and I cried bitterly at the failure of the opportunity to revisit my young life. I had spent only moments there when things went awry. I also recalled, however, Ezekiel's warnings and his counsel to not go. Still, I had questions that I hoped Gordon could and would answer.

Meanwhile, I sat up and saw a plate of the tremendously delicious and wonderfully satisfying fruit of heaven. On the plate was heaven's version of grapes, strawberries, blueberries, and watermelon. The exquisite taste of heaven's food is beyond description, and I was hungry, a strange sensation in heaven. I ate all of the fruit, realizing as I ate that I was famished. I attributed this to being present, no matter how briefly, on Earth and to the extreme expenditure of energy I must have had due to the strange occurrence of events.

I finished and looked up from the plate, deeply satisfied and energized instantly. Gordon was standing before me, smiling, his eyes crinkled up. "Bit of an appetite, eh?"

"Gordon!" I shouted. "I am so happy to see you!"

"And I am very happy indeed to see you, Adam."

"What happened back there, I mean, back on Earth? Where was the angel who was supposed to protect me? Why were the, you know, the ..." I hesitated.

"The demons," Gordon supplied.

"Yes, the demons. How did they know I was there? Why were they after me? How did the angels know to come and save me?" I jumped up, pacing around now in my consternation, remembering the fear.

"I will tell you all that I know. It wouldn't hurt to just rest for a while, though. I know you have eaten, and quite well by the looks of it." Gordon winked at me. "But rest would be good at the moment, and it won't take long with heavenly food and rest to be ready to go again.

"As to what happened, Ezekiel was able to see the whole thing. He has those eyes, you know. It is now apparent that Lucifer, or one of his servants, has been trying to follow your movements in hopes of undoing the good of heaven in you.

They are worried about losing you. I'm not entirely sure what that means, Adam, but I fear that it could mean you are a prized servant of the enemy. That is not a good thing, not at all.

"Also, I am quite sure that the humiliation that Lucifer received in heaven over your soul—it was entirely his fault to be sure, but that means nothing to him—but his humiliation only served to infuriate him even more regarding you. He does not bear such matters well, being completely self-consumed. Long ago, very early in creation, he even stupidly challenged the Lord God for supremacy, having so thoroughly deceived himself about his greatness. And you can be sure that he was overwhelmed by the presence of Michael in the City of God. You saw Lucifer's degradation into a level of some sort of temporary insanity. I did not see this, but I heard of it through the angels. It was a very unusual thing. All the more reason he wants you back in his kingdom and away from the influence of heaven. He thinks to harm heaven by such behavior."

I interrupted Gordon at this point. "But how could they track me in heaven? I thought there was no access for the enemy there among the Redeemed."

"They can't track you at all in heaven if you are of the Redeemed. And I don't *think* they can track you in heaven even in your state. Still, they know your mind, and I suspect they have been watching any of the likely places you might show up, even places from your past.

"But that's the thing, Adam. This spiritual warfare in heavenly places is far beyond my reckoning. I know it is real, but I don't know what goes on in that dimension. I don't think I want to know. Ezekiel said that something happened to you that was similar to Daniel. The angel that was sent to Daniel was delayed due to spiritual warfare. It seems that the same thing happened to the angel that was sent to watch over you, clearly a plan of the enemy.

Ezekiel was extremely distressed over this, and we prostrated ourselves toward the Throne. He had told you angelic protection would be there, and none was there. The angel sent to guard you was blocked by the enemy. The same thing happened to Daniel. And yes, I did preach on that once!" Gordon's familiar wink and smile lightened the moment and soothed me a little.

"Did Ezekiel know this was going to happen? He warned me beforehand of potential danger."

"It does seem like he had a sense about it, although I am certain he would not have allowed it had he known the full scope of what happened or almost happened. Plus, did you notice, he was clearly listening to the voice of the Spirit as he was talking to you?"

"Yes," I answered. "I noticed something going on there besides us talking. But, if he knew or if the voice knew, why did they let it happen?" I hoped I did not sound angry, but there was some irritation within me given the horrific danger of what I had encountered.

"There was some purpose in it, we can be sure of that. And the purpose was for you, Adam, not for God. He gains nothing and loses nothing by your response. Indeed, neither you nor I, nor any human that has ever lived, can add anything to Him. He is no greater for our worship or obedience or even our existence! And He is no less for our lack of worship or disobedience. He is complete in Himself with absolutely no need for anything.

"Some have stumbled on this thinking that God needs us, was lonely without us, or some such nonsense. For God to have need or suffer loneliness, though, would mean that He is not the eternal, infinite, perfect self-existent God. And if He is not God now, then He never was God, for He cannot change. Each act of God toward humanity is from His good and for our good and is driven by His love and holiness, never out of His need. And every good, loving, and holy act is totally of grace, benefiting Him none at all! It's just all grace, Adam, pure and unbounded grace.

"So please understand that the presence of danger such as you experienced does not mean an event is not from God. The chance of failure or the opportunity for sin most certainly does not imply that a circumstance is outside of His intention. Abraham could have failed on Mount Moriah. Job could have cursed God and died. The Lord God fully knows in advance the outcome of all events, choices, circumstances, tests, yet He allows them all the same.

"To ask why an event is allowed to happen is really to ask why *any* event is allowed to happen, though we seldom want to take a question to its logical conclusion because then we must face the reality of its meaning, and that is too difficult for us. All justifications are eliminated in that context. But we ask the questions only to the point of validating our excuses. And ultimately, why did God even create *anything* if He knew every outcome in the end? For us, Adam, for us. And there we are at grace again.

"But I'm preaching, Adam! Back to your situation. The angels came to your rescue in part because of the prayers of Ezekiel and hopefully mine as well. When Ezekiel recognized something had gone wrong, he immediately began to pray fervently, and so did I. Michael himself came to the battle and set free the angel charged with your protection."

Curious about the angel, I interjected at this point. "Was it Odegeo? Was he the one who was supposed to be with me?"

"I'm not sure, Adam. There are millions of angels who serve God and serve those who are inheriting salvation. It may have been Odegeo, but I don't know for sure. Michael overcame the enemy who was delaying your angel, and he called a squadron of angels to immediate combat on your behalf. I couldn't really see what was going on, but Ezekiel said it was quite a spectacular display and a stunning defeat for the enemy."

"Spectacular isn't the word for it," I said. "Is there an adjective beyond stupendous? I've never seen anything like that. It was a little bit like jets firing missiles, but much faster and much more deadly. I was terrified of the demons, but I was also petrified of the angels as they came blazing in on me. I really thought either way, demons or angels, I was going to die. But I thought it was strange that the demons did nothing to fight back or defend themselves as the attack approached. I'm glad they didn't, believe me, but I don't understand why they didn't."

"I'm not sure I know either," Gordon answered. "But it's possible they couldn't fight because they were so fully engaged in, well, possessing you. It's also possible that in their fervor to take your soul, they didn't even know the angels were attacking. Sorry to bring that memory back to you. You look a little pale again."

"I'm okay, Gordon, but it is an awful and strange memory. If I were on Earth, it would be the stuff of nightmares for months. It was close, though, very close. What would have happened if they had succeeded?"

"I'm not sure. It may be best not even to ponder such a possibility. You escaped through the power and grace of God and the prayers of those who love you. Perhaps that is enough."

"Yes, you're right. One more question, though, if you don't mind. The demon that was behind me said something about "clean and not filled and seven more from a wasteland." That's not exactly a quote, but it was along those lines. Any idea what that is about?"

Gordon gave me an odd look, a look of concern and curiosity. He paused, pondering something, perhaps hesitant to answer.

"What is it, Gordon? What does it mean?"

"It means three things," he said. "First, it means the situation was far worse and far more dangerous than you and I imagined. Second, I am sorry to say that it means you are still in great spiritual need. Honestly, I guess I had hoped for more. And third, it means we need to keep moving."

Gordon's words shook me. How could it have been far worse and more dangerous than he and I thought initially? Was he serious? The demons had been within seconds, I am sure, of fully possessing me perhaps beyond recall. And now Gordon says it was far worse than we realized!

Despite the heavenly food and all the life pouring through me in heaven, I suddenly felt sick and lightheaded. I decided to ask no more questions about that hideous strength that had nearly overwhelmed me and swept me into unimaginable horror. I didn't feel well, but I most certainly agreed with Gordon that it was time to move on.

And then it struck me. That was His purpose in our visit to Ezekiel and the near catastrophe: *Despite all this time in heaven, my soul was still empty and in mortal danger of eternal loss.*

No lesson could have been more imperative or more clearly stated.

18

A Man Without

Eager to put the recent trial behind us, we moved on, as far as I knew, in the direction of Moses. We hiked into more of the island's magnificent woods. Soon enough, we were joyously laughing and talking as much as we had before we visited Ezekiel's home, even though the fearful and penetrating lesson was never far from my mind.

We were in a deep, dark forest area when Gordon pointed to a house, nearly invisible, hidden and without clear form in the blending of greens, browns, trees, and shade. He remarked, "There is the home of Melchizedek."

I knew few of the names from the Bible. Even the names I did know were of people that I had little or no knowledge about. This name, however, was utterly foreign to me. "I have no recollection of that name, Gordon. I assume he or she is from the Bible, and I probably should know the name, but that one is unknown to me."

"Don't know Melchizedek, eh?"

"I'm pretty sure I have never heard that name."

"He was an unusual character, unlike anyone else. He was the King of Salem, without a father, without a mother, without genealogy, having neither beginning of days nor end of life, but made like the Son of God, he remains a priest perpetually.

He is much visited by angels, more so than any other of the Redeemed, or whatever he is."

That was an odd remark: "Whatever he is." I cast a sidelong glance at Gordon, wondering what he meant by that. I was about to ask when angels came forth from an opening in the woods that looked like thick vines formed into the shape of an arch. Many of the mansions had no doors, just openings from indoors to outdoors.

Although the mansion of Melchizedek was set far off the path and veiled among the trees and foliage, it was clear that these were angels. There was no mistaking angels from the Redeemed. Not that one race was more impressive or glorious than the other, they were just intrinsically different. Along with several angels, a man of the Redeemed, I assumed Melchizedek himself came forth from his mansion.

Seven angels were with Melchizedek. All of them had a subtle reddish glow emanating from their spirits. They were all similar in size to Odegeo, about seven feet tall, and in some sense seemed to be normal, as angels seen in heaven go. That thought struck me with a degree of wonderment, that I, of all people, should see angels, in heaven of all places, and react with the sense that they looked normal, as if I were the world's leading authority on angels. Incredibly, I probably was! They had seen us and were walking directly toward Gordon and me.

As they approached us, I could see that Melchizedek did not look wholly like others of the Redeemed. He was very large, larger in fact than the angels accompanying him. He was not an angel; however, he did not appear to be quite like the other redeemed humans I had seen in heaven. Further, and much more striking than his size, of all the sentient beings I had observed in the heavenly realm, Melchizedek alone had the appearance of age. He did not appear elderly, yet there was something about his gait that lacked the energy and vivacity of everyone else (except me perhaps) in heaven.

As he drew near, I noticed that in his face there was just a trace of wear, possibly the hint of a wrinkle alongside his eyes, but hardly noticeable anywhere else. In heaven, however, having constantly seen faces full of life and newness, the sight of anything even slightly less than wholly redeemed was stark. His hair was rich and full, yet gray—something else I had not seen much of in heaven. And in his eyes, yes, more than the other features, his eyes told a story. Nowhere had I seen any of the Redeemed with a look of longing. The Redeemed were satisfied, fulfilled, and complete. Melchizedek was not. I noticed longing in his eyes. He was waiting for something.

Then he spoke. "Greetings, Gordon!"

Melchizedek did sound like others of the Redeemed; joy was in his voice like all others in heaven. And he knew Gordon.

"Greetings to you, my friend. I have not been to the island lately, and I have not seen you at the Throne."

"I have been to the Throne quite recently. But I understand that you have been occupied with leading this young man, this anomaly, through the halls of heaven." Melchizedek spoke with a deep and resonant voice, sounding kingly.

I am sure he did not mean the anomaly remark negatively, at least I hope he did not. I wasn't sure I liked the sound of being called an anomaly, although it was as accurate of a description of me as I had heard. But the more I considered this huge man standing before me, this seemingly unredeemed redeemed man, this consort with angels, the more I realized that he certainly understood the word *anomaly.*

"Yes," replied Gordon, "Adam and I have been traversing the heavenly realm. It has been a wonderful time of friendship and understanding."

I had not realized until that moment that Gordon was enjoying being with me. In some way, this surprised me. I felt an even greater warmth and affection for the man who pastored my family, and I saw him now as those he served on Earth saw him: a shepherd, a servant, a great friend, a teacher, and a man full of compassion and goodness. He would, of course, be uncomfortable with that description, but it was true.

"It's an extraordinary thing, Gordon. Where sin abounds, grace abounds all the more," Melchizedek said.

"No one understands that better than you. I am blessed that the Lord has allowed me to minister to Adam."

Melchizedek turned to me and said, "I spoke with Odegeo about you. He told me about your visit to heaven, unexpected as it was to you. You discern now, I hope, that what you and others intended for evil, God is using for good."

"Yes, sir. I do have some sense of that." His mention of Odegeo brought to mind memories of how Odegeo had found me floating in space, how he had led me up the Column and through the Eden of heaven and to the City of God, how we had talked, and how he had so patiently endured my ignorance, my emotional peaks and valleys, and my spiritual stupor. I had certainly been high maintenance, but he endured it all with grace and goodness.

I wondered if Gordon had the same thoughts toward me as Odegeo must have had. It struck me that I had never properly thanked Odegeo. We had been separated when Michael had addressed me, and then I had been directed out of the City of God to follow the river. Where Odegeo had gone I did not know. I promised myself that such an unfortunate and unfinished parting would not happen with Gordon!

It seemed, as I stood before this anomaly, that I had been brought here to speak with him (just as I had with Frank, Dr. Kakos, and Gordon and Odegeo for that matter. Accidents didn't happen here, and people like Gordon and no doubt all those in the Heavenly Realm seemed to think that there were no accidents anywhere. I did not understand that kind of thinking, and it troubled me. I thought it would be a good idea to ask Gordon about this given the chance.

Melchizedek continued. "As you have already noticed, my appearance is not like that of the others of the Redeemed."

"Well, yes, sir, I had noticed. I'm not certain . . . that is, are you of the Redeemed?"

"I alone of my people am in heaven, and I bear the curse, even here, though greatly and mercifully mitigated by His grace. You, young man, as I understand, may have seen on your journey those rebels of my ancestry who are paying the penalty for unspeakable crimes against the God of heaven and His creation, angels who did not keep their proper abode. It is ill to speak much of it.

"They sought strange flesh and relations with humanity, and I was their progeny. All of us were wicked as they were. But in my heart, I began to seek the Lord more than any other, repenting and making amends for the darkness that was brought on humanity! In sackcloth and ashes, in fasting and weeping, I sought Him day after day, and He heard me!

"In my devotion I became an example to others. I interceded with God for others. I brought them to a place of sacrifice to Him. All this was before He had established His people. And He granted me grace upon grace." Melchizedek said this with great animation and fervency. "He allowed me to serve as both priest and king and to become a foreshadow of the Son despite the evil works that led to the condition of my existence!

"You do not understand the significance of this; to serve in the offices of both priest and king is a position afforded to only the Son! (Here he had tears forming in his eyes.) You cannot possibly imagine, no matter the iniquity of your life, which is great, the rebellion from which I was born! I know as well as anyone from any age the depths to which sin can sink a being. I can identify with the sorrow and devastation of guilt no matter what depth of wickedness may have been sought, no matter the totality of the addiction, and no matter the utter blackness of the soul.

"In my repentance from such evil, He granted me the place of priest (he was choked with emotion now as he spoke), for I know the evil of the human heart as few others, perhaps none of humanity. Yet grace was lavished upon me, the chief of sinners, because I sought Him with my whole heart, soul, mind, and strength."

Melchizedek paused for a moment with open weeping. I looked at Gordon, and he had joyful tears in his eyes and somehow a look of peaceful wonder on his face. The seven angels standing by Melchizedek spontaneously began to sing a song containing the words "worthy is the Lamb" in a beautiful interweaving melody unlike anything I had ever heard. The angels did not cry, but a change came over them, a growing radiance and—could it be—a barely perceptible yet, I believe, a change in their size! They seemed to grow when they sang this song of worship!

I stood in amazement at the obvious outpouring of worship and thanksgiving. I recalled moments from ages past in my own home when my father had stood by the piano, while my mother played, and they sang religious songs out of the church songbook. They did it simply out of joy and gratitude to God. It was always quite unexpected to me, almost as if the mood had struck them impulsively to sing to God. So it was here in heaven.

When the song ended, Melchizedek went on, "And the Lord took me out of Earth one day. He said mercifully, it was finished. I have not known death because I am a chimera. My nature is not wholly like yours, so I have not yet been granted the wholeness of redemption. You asked if I am of the Redeemed. The answer is both yes and no. I am redeemed, but not yet *wholly* of the Redeemed. Centuries, in your perception, of living in the Heavenly Realm have given me excellent health and little aging, but it is not quite like having a body such as my brother Gordon.

"Surely you have noticed the effect living in heaven has had even on you, despite being lost. Understand, young man, that when this grace ends, you will soon return to the body of death.

"No one more greatly desires the day of His rising from the Throne of this realm, for in that day, I shall finally receive my whole healing. He promised me this. And He is watching over His word to perform it! Indeed, He *is the Word,* and when He performs His word, He is merely being true to Himself. For now, I say with His great servant, His grace is sufficient for me."

Some of the matters to which Melchizedek referred were, of course, foreign to me. In some matters, however, I could relate to him. He truly was an anomaly in heaven. *That* feeling I understood. In a strange way it gave me a kinship with him that I had with no one else in heaven, not even Gordon.

I also could not help having the sense that there had been something occultic about his existence at least previous to his turning to God. Little did I realize at the time how extensively his existence was tied up with what on Earth we call the occult. That was the sort of pursuit with which I could definitely sympathize. I knew all too well where it had led me. Apparently his life had been consumed in some way with the demonic world, a world I had really only acknowledged and been fully exposed to near the end—the horrible Red Hue Room.

But most of all, I saw in his life this matter of grace. This had something to do with receiving what is not earned. He said he had been involved with wickedness that I could not even imagine. That was saying something! I believe he was right about the level of evil he and his race, whoever they were, had been practiced, although I did not understand to what he could have been referring.

I also noticed he had been none too subtle about telling me I was lost! That was another memory from church, eons ago, not to mention my recent revelation resulting from the events with Ezekiel.

I remembered a guest speaker at our church, an evangelist, one Sunday evening, this was in my teen years, who seemed obsessed with screaming about being "lost, lost, lost!" It made me uncomfortable, and it was very embarrassing at that age. I recalled my parents kept looking at me during that sermon. My father frowned and nodded a lot, seemingly in an attempt to make me grasp the idea that the evangelist was speaking to me! My mother, on the other hand, glanced hopefully at me over and over again. Her raised eyebrows had been full of optimism, and her swift nods were cajoling me to go to the altar for some reason that was unclear to me. At the end, we sang a song I had heard on television and at many other church services, a song about the Lamb of God and coming to "Thee."

No one used that language in real life! *Why must these church people be so purposefully out of touch*, I had thought. Already, however, in my early teen years, I was annoyed at such undignified religious displays. The evangelist strutting around shouting, the coaxing of my parents against my will (my mother's expectant look had especially irritated me), the playing of that song on the organ repeatedly. People stumbled to the altar; some of whom always went to the altar and yet continued in their unremitting gossip, in their contempt for some other group of people, or in their indulgence of some self-destructive behavior. This was where I first learned about hypocrisy. I quite successfully managed to apply the concept only ever to others. I was most certainly not a hypocrite!

But the words of Melchizedek and of that long-ago evangelist were true. I was lost. Whatever the hypocrisy of others might have been (and, really, who was I to judge someone else's efforts to change), I had walked away from the very religion for which my parents lived. No, that was saying it too easily; I had *rejected* their faith.

Yes, I was lost.

And then another thought struck me. Melchizedek had said something about his parents being evil. Or did he? What *did* he say about his parents? He had come from something quite dark, but I did not recall that he actually mentioned parents. I ventured a question.

"Sir, if I understood correctly, you said something about your parents being wicked?"

"Not entirely did I say that. Those who gave me life were

immoral and iniquitous it is true, but to say they were my parents is inaccurate. I was formed from a union born of darkness, outside the designs of God and perilously dangerous. The torment that the guilty suffer reveals the horror of their action."

I wasn't sure how to respond to such a remarkable explanation, but I said, "Then, sir, if you don't mind, may I ask, how *were* you born? I ask because I believe it is my duty and part of the burden that Michael laid upon me to ask such questions for my own understanding. However, I mean no offense and I do not ask out of any tawdry motive."

"Your question causes no offense to me; however, as I stated previously, it is ill to speak openly of such things. Remember that I am a chimera. Beyond that, there is little that I can say of the matter."

I could not remember what the term *chimera* meant, but clearly this was not a normal union of a man and a woman. "Then let me ask in this way, sir. It seems that there was some inherent evil in your conception, is that correct? Something not normal to human conception?"

"That is true, young man. Every aspect of my origin was for evil purpose. My parents, if you will, were as unlike your parents as the night is unlike the day. I have no genealogy."

I paused and considered this statement and its implications. The light came on. I suddenly knew why this visit with Melchizedek had been ordained.

"Despite your, uh . . . origin, at some point in your existence, you began to seek God."

"Yes, Adam, I did." He paused and then added, "And you have not."

There it was.

This man was born from some evil that I could not imagine, with parents, or whatever, that were wicked beyond what I could conceive, and they apparently had no interest in their son knowing God. In fact, I now recalled that Gordon had said that Melchizedek didn't have a father or mother or even a genealogy, a statement which Melchizedek had confirmed! I didn't know what to make of that. From what Melchizedek had said, the only intent of his parents (a term which he had qualified) was for evil, and that was likewise their objective for their son or whatever he was. *Yet, he had turned to God.*

My life was the utter opposite story.

I had parents, real parents, a mother and father, flesh and blood, who had fervently sought after God, as far as I knew, all the days of their lives. They had been the very model of parenting with love, kindness, discipline, instruction, providing, protecting, and ceaseless praying. Yet I had wandered away. No, again, that was putting it too easily. I didn't wander away; I rejected, refused, and denied.

I felt a cavernous darkness in my heart. Everywhere I turned in heaven, I saw people who had sought God. Gordon had said that no one seeks after Him of their own accord, but still there is a seeking after God. I had been born into every conceivable spiritual advantage, and I had purposefully abandoned Him. *What hope could there be for me?*

Yet, in that vast harvest of despondency and unbelief, a sudden grain of optimism appeared. I was here in heaven, after all. Gordon said it was God who brought me to this place. Meeting Frank Henderson and Dr. Kakos was clearly no accident. Passing by the mansion of Melchizedek was another . . . what did Frank call it? An intersection of grace. If Melchizedek, born of such darkness and for some part of his life it seemed he had participated in wickedness, if he could have a mansion in heaven, perhaps there was hope for me!

But a new question evolved in my mind. "Sir, may I ask one more question?"

"You may, Adam. However, my friends have been called to the Throne Room. They must prepare for battle. I will go with them at least to the Throne, for I may not see them again till after their ministry on Earth."

"I understand, sir. I only want to ask, what was it that turned you from evil to seeking God?"

"It is well that you have asked that question. Your question gives me hope for your soul. I was there in the plain of Shinar. I led the way to the building of the Great Tower. But when the Lord came down upon us in His righteous judgment, I saw His power. Our plan was utterly in disobedience to His command regarding Earth, and our plan was, at its basest level, a challenge to God. 'You shall be like God.' That was the source of our plan, and is it not the source of all sin?

"Imagine, young man, at a moment in time all language is changed; your family in an instant cannot communicate with any other family. The bewilderment and confusion, the fear and sorrow cannot be explained. All of society broke down. All our cultural markers were lost. Eventually and inevitably, violence ensued. We experienced all manner of pain, and for the first time, we felt aloneness and separation.

"You might think this would lead me to further rebellion, but it did not. In fact, so astonishing was the power of God, and especially compared to the now evident unqualified weakness of man and the impotence of those spirits who were leading us, that I was determined to discover more about Him. All of the meager greatness of humanity and the spirits was pitiful and effete in the face of Almighty God, who with a mere word, brought chaos to our arrogance and rebellion.

"Adam, those who diligently seek Him *will* find Him. This was a God worth knowing. And perhaps at the beginning, my interest was less than pure, but my desire was *for* Him. In my ignorance, He passed over my motives and saw my true heart. And because of this, He honored me and gave me more light. As I walked in that light, I learned of His goodness and love and that His righteous judgment was intended to bring us out of rebellion and into repentance.

"So, I sought Him with all my heart, and He brought me to a large place of grace beyond measure and placed my name, even my name, in the book of books and honored me with a position like unto His Son. What blessing could ever be greater? Can you imagine having your name included in His Word, your name respected and honored and studied forever? Given the life I had led and where I had come from, can you see the grace immeasurable that He lavished on me?

"Yes, sir. I think I see it; I see grace. And by grace, you mean you were given something you did not deserve?"

"Yes, Adam. Grace in its simplest form is receiving something you did not earn. And mercy is like grace, but as through a mirror. Mercy in its simplest form is not receiving what you do deserve. In both cases, I was blessed beyond hope."

"But you did do good things, sir. You did try to do what was right. I mean, after you saw that judgment you mentioned. So, the good things you did must have been of some merit."

"Did you not hear? It was only by *judgment*, and in that judgment the suffering of fear, despair, confusion, and the reality of violence that I even began to see. I had no understanding, no interest even in Him outside of the judgment that He brought upon the human race!

"Adam, do you understand this? Even in judgment, there is grace! He does not wish for any to perish. Sometimes He judges with great severity in order to stop an endless parade into perdition. There is a point of darkness so deep that entire generations are recklessly beyond His call. Would He be just to continue to sit idly by and allow the halls of hell to be sated with souls? He does not choose anyone for destruction but forever calls to your soul for repentance! Why is it that you are here? It is for repentance, nothing else really.

"It was Him reaching out to me that set my repentance in motion. And as I said, Adam, even then my motives were not entirely pure, but He saw past that and covered over my darkness in calling me to Himself. Even our righteous deeds are as filthy rags."

"But you sought Him, sir. You said so yourself."

"If at any point He had withdrawn His Presence from me, I would have immediately stopped my pursuit of Him. We only seek Him because He calls us. Why should any living mortal offer complaint in view of his sins?"

I noticed that one of the seven angels standing with Melchizedek was motioning to Him. I understood it was time for them to go, and he was going with them before their departure. But Melchizedek was not quite through with me yet. One more exhortation remained.

"Adam, I must leave with my friends. Let me say this before we go. You are evil. You are far more evil than you imagine."

I reacted with a startled expression.

"You think yourself to be a decent man, able to do good deeds, better than many of the scoundrels you have known or heard about. You are better than some; therefore, you think you are somehow going to be weighed in a balance that will favor your good over your evil on some future day when you must account for yourself."

I started to defend myself.

"Do not speak, Adam! Your evaluation of yourself is the same as every man evaluates himself. Does it strike you that if every many appraises himself in the same way, then the reasonable and obvious conclusion is that they must *all be wrong!* And so they are. They are all wrong!

"You have done nothing good; you have not sought after God or His righteousness. You have never been interested in His will. You are here for one purpose only, and that is repentance. Do not forget the lessons that Mr. Henderson and Dr. Kakos taught you, nor Pastor Lachen either. And my friend Odegeo spoke to you of these matters as well.

"When our Lord stands up from His Throne to walk this land and return to claim for His own the planet where the Prince of Darkness rules the air, it will be too late, and you will be lost forever. It would be the greatest cruelty and darkest victory the enemy of your soul has ever won.

"I deeply fear your place in eternal hell would be a fearsome thing, perhaps like those of my ilk that Jude spoke of, since you have received a grace of the light of glory that is unheard of: the glory of a heavenly presence for an unredeemed man. This grace will not last forever, but the hell of your damned soul will!"

The words of Melchizedek struck like a hammer blow to the face! I stammered, unable to respond, my chest tightening in fear. A sense of horror, like a wave of nauseating heat, swept over me, starting in my head and plummeting down through my body. So shocking and painful were the words, the truths, that Melchizedek spoke that I fell down at his feet weeping as I had not wept since my early days in the Heavenly Realm with Odegeo.

The renewed sense of abject guilt and failure swept over me. I had been revealed to myself for what I was. All that Melchizedek had said was true. I had wrongly assessed myself in exactly the way he stated. I was as good as the next man, and the next man was going to eternal hell!

"Good bye, Adam. There is still grace for you, but let me be quite clear, as it is for every human, the day of grace ends. Let this not be our everlasting farewell. When our Lord arises, be sure to be among the Redeemed. He has called you to Himself, but a day is coming when the choices you have made will make you."

With that, Melchizedek turned from me along with the seven angels, leaving me starkly and abruptly in my pile of quivering tears and dread. They walked back in the direction from which we had come, heading, as I thought, for the City of God. But as I looked up through my tears, from the ground where I had fallen, to shout my gratitude and vague promises to Melchizedek, to my astonishment, he and the seven angels were nowhere to be seen. They had disappeared.

19

The Lawgiver

After a good deal of time had passed, Gordon pulled me to my feet. I stood up, trembling and frail. My cheeks were tear-stained, my eyes were puffy and reddened, and it seemed that I had been slobbering on myself, as nasal fluids were running over my lips and chin. I was a disgusting mess.

To hear the words that Melchizedek had spoken in a different setting, that of a dim and dusty old church on a cold, wintry night with the misery of an approaching day of school or work, or in the context of a hot, sweaty summer eve when there was still light to be enjoyed and games to be played, and have those words spoken by the typical balding elderly preacher preaching the message of doom that it seemed he was obligated to preach, that was one thing. But, to hear this said to me in heaven by this strange and extraordinary man who, against all odds, actually had a past in some measure like mine, this was entirely different. Among all his words, those that kept ringing in my ears were his penetrating dagger about the matter of seeking after God: "Yes, Adam, I did . . . and you have not."

"I've never met anyone like Melchizedek."

"No," answered Gordon. "And you never will again. He is a singularity. He is the only one of his kind that lives here."

"It seems like he and the angels just disappeared into thin

air. I looked up, and they were gone. I haven't seen anyone else do that. I suppose an angel might be able to disappear, but they were all just gone."

"Melchizedek may be more like an angel than a redeemed human at this point. Still, someday he will enjoy the fullness that all the Redeemed experience. But for now, we must press on. Unless I am mistaken, our next stop is at the temple, and you must see Moses."

We did press on. It was the first instance in all my time in heaven that I had a sense of hurry. I wondered at this and finally asked Gordon if there was some urgency that I did not comprehend.

"There is great urgency, Adam. Melchizedek has reminded both of us of the need for swiftness. There is urgency far beyond what you can comprehend. I suspect you may learn of this with Moses. But that urgency is different from the one I am beginning to feel. I have been too long away from the Throne. I have been too long away from the deep fellowship of those in my beloved family of heaven.

"It is true, in heaven there is no marriage. That was simply a glorious symbol of Christ and His church, a blessing and gift from our good and gracious Father, a bond of wholeness and oneness that only He could have invented. Still, though in one sense it was but a temporal beginning point, there is an undying intimacy with some from Earth that will be shared forever in the perfection of the relationship. And how could there not be an eternal intimacy that extends beyond the mere earthly life? After all, this is the place of perfection, where everything from Earth is redeemed to perfection. And although there is no sense of loss or anxiety about being apart, I do long to be with my beloved family of heaven.

"Don't fear, Adam. I do not begrudge our experiences together here in heaven, not in the least. I must say, however, that we are nearing the point of departure. We must see Moses, return to the mainland, and beyond that I do not know, except that we will be nearing the end of the Heavenly Realm."

"I know it is inevitable, Gordon," I answered him. "But I dread our parting. You'll return to all the joys you know and love and will have forever. I don't know what I'm heading for."

"Well, the end of our journey is not quite at hand. And something is going to take place with Moses and at the temple that is unclear to me, but I know we, or rather, you must go there."

With those ominous words, we walked with some fervor toward the center point of the island.

We came at last to the temple region, according to Gordon. I could see nothing of the temple from this place. I saw only the beautiful trees, the ever-present blue sky, the endless greens of the grass and all the lush, wildly colorful growth. I also saw the presence of many of the Redeemed, as everywhere in heaven, in their exquisite gladness and wholeness, greeting us with joy and gathering as always in many places for meetings full of refreshing happiness and sheer unabated uninhibited life.

Then ahead, about a few hundred yards, through the thick grove of trees, I saw some kind of climbing path. I squinted to focus on what I suddenly sensed was on outlier of the temple. Gordon, seeing my alertness to whatever was ahead, said, "Yes, that's it, or at least the beginning of the temple lands. It's a stair you must climb that leads to the temple valley."

I noted his statement, "you must climb," and I asked him if that meant he was not coming with me.

"Not this time," Gordon answered. "The temple is not the place for me. There is a better covenant in effect now. But you must go there and hear Moses. You must see the meaning of the temple."

See the meaning of the temple. I wondered what that meant, but Gordon was speaking again.

"Go, Adam. Climb the stairs ahead. The Lawgiver is waiting. I will meet you when you are finished."

Something about the way Gordon said, "when you are finished," seemed ominous and had a finality to it. The old dread began to seize me again. I did not want to climb the stairs, and I certainly did not want to leave Gordon, my friend, companion, and guide.

"You must go, Adam. This was part of the burden the Archangel laid upon you. We shall meet again. Do not fear. But understand, the temple valley is not like the rest of heaven. It is, like Melchizedek, a singularity. The Redeemed do not go there."

With a heavy heart, I said good-bye to Gordon. I felt an uneasiness in my heart. Even if our parting was only for an hour, I did not like it.

I trudged along the path to the hill. When I reached the hill itself, I began to climb, but I could not see the temple. Still many trees were lining the path up the hill. These trees resembled sycamores. There were also many tall, green, and stately bushes that reminded me very much of the hedge of yews my parents had at the back of our yard. These bushes, like those, had small red berries on them. I reached out to pluck a berry off a branch, and like our yews, it was crushed at the lightest touch on my fingers, leaving a reddish stain on my hands.

The path I was climbing had now become a stairway with

carved stairs. Though it seemed to be carved in the living rock, which was dominated by a deep black granite, many brilliant points of red, perhaps rubies, were set into the rock. It had the appearance of great drops of blood spilled onto and into the blackness. The red became more pronounced the higher I went, and by the top of the stairs, there was as much red as black. I wondered about this, for it seemed to be by design.

But as I looked up to the sky, in the space between the trees, the ever-blue sky was tinged with a golden hue. It reflected in the uppermost leaves of the trees. I did not understand this wonder until I came to the top of the stairs. Here I could at last see the temple before me. It was a vast structure built of solid gold. The gold gleamed brilliantly, sending off an intense tinge of golden light in every direction. I looked at my skin, and it had a bronze glow.

I looked out, from the top of the stairs, at the scene somewhat below me. The land here, which covered what appeared to be hundreds of acres, dropped down in a vast bowl-like shape with a flat bottom. There in the middle of this land was the temple in its shining golden glory.

The first matter that struck me was not the beauty of the temple, which was considerable, but the lack of both the Redeemed and the angels. No one was to be seen. There were small gatherings of trees here and there and a lush growth of grass but no gardens. In that sense the temple valley had, by comparison, a rather barren look to it, the first and only time I had that impression in all my time in heaven.

I was alone. The temple was before me, but I knew again the desolation of my own soul. I was lost in heaven. Lost in a place where everyone else has been found. Desolate where everyone else is full. Fearing where everyone else is at peace.

Broken where everyone else is whole and complete. I could not go backward down the stairs, though I longed to descend those steps. There was no hope in simply staying at the top of the stairs. I knew I must move forward. I had only been apart from Gordon for a short time, but already I was despondent.

I stepped from the top of the carved stairway and onto the grass of the temple valley. I began a long, gentle descent toward the temple. After several hundred yards, the ground flattened, and I was on an even level with the temple. It was a beautiful structure, golden and shining with a perfection of symmetry. There was, however, something austere and impersonal about the temple. Everywhere else in the heavenly realm had been inviting, warm, alive, and full of joy. The temple felt different even from a distance. I had a sense of foreboding growing in me.

Then I saw someone come out of the gate surrounding the temple, and I knew instinctively that this was Moses. He was approaching me, and he was already speaking. Before I could begin to understand and appreciate what Moses was saying, I was thunderstruck by his appearance. He was of the Redeemed, clearly, but the approach of Moses did not fill me with warmth, peace, or hope.

He was shining like an angel, but brighter and with a more piercing quality. He was very tall as well, much taller than any of the Redeemed I had seen. In fact, I do not know if this was accurate, but he seemed twice my size, and throughout the address that I was about to receive from him, it seemed as if he grew taller. Although, given the content of his words, perhaps it is more accurate to say that I grew smaller. And although his eyes carried the look of complete peace and that flicker of joy (but perhaps with Moses it was more a look of supreme nobility, like royalty), his eyes also had a searching look-right-through-you power, a penetrating steely gray-eyed intensity.

In spite of the striking qualities, the most notable and strange aspect of Moses was his coal-black body. I had seen varying colors of the Redeemed, none having any clear racial bearing, but no one had the utter ebony skin of Moses. I wondered at this and the other oddities of this man. It struck me that, of course, I had only seen a very small percentage of the Redeemed population, so perhaps this was not completely unique, yet I suspected that Moses was a peculiarity, as was this whole temple region.

But Moses was speaking, and I began to attend to him. To my consternation, his deep, voluminous voice was reciting moments from my life: bad moments, dark behaviors, events I thought secret, and acts I now felt were shameful. I tried to interrupt him, but though he looked directly at me (I squirmed under his glance), it was as if I were not actually there.

On and on this went. He spoke not just categories of sin but detailed accounts of sin events. I wanted to flee, but I seemed held against my will. His voice never wavered, and I had no defense against what was a list of my abject moral failure, reaching all the way back to my early childhood.

There was that occasion of stealing money from my brother's bank and even earlier in my life than that, of hitting my little brother angrily without cause. I must have been only four or five years old! He spoke of the time I lied to my mother about breaking my neighbor's garage window. He reminded me about spreading that ugly rumor that deeply hurt an outcast child at school. There were tawdry moments in the woods with the girl in high school. There was the cheating on the tests, the senseless vandalizing of a car with my friends, the thoughtless, disrespectful words toward my father, the lustful indulgence in sexual images, the arrogant attitude aimed at all authority. But time and time again, in all sorts of differing contexts and forms, which I had often exercised in the most inappropriate settings to the deep consternation of my parents, Moses kept haranguing on one thing in particular: my persistent and even angry doubt and unbelief about God in the face of the overwhelming evidence to the contrary of God's presence and love.

And Moses continued, now approaching my undergraduate college life. I could not bear to hear the darkness of my guilt. Rejection of truth, wild promiscuity, unethical behavior, arrogant anger, greed, hostility, vanity, drunkenness, disputes, dissensions, factions, envy, jealousy, blasphemy, complaining, harsh criticism . . .

I looked up at the sky. It was still the bluest of all blues, royal and fervent in its color. I turned my head, and in the distance, I could still see the lightning above the Throne flashing its proclamation of the power, greatness, and sovereignty of Him who sat upon it. That, at least, had not changed. I saw in this valley small gatherings of the beautiful trees of heaven. I saw the temple behind Moses, standing golden but austere, bright but not welcoming. The temple stood, in the midst of the living, rejoicing populace of heaven, alone. It had no marring or aging of time upon it, yet now looked ancient and out-of-date.

I looked back at Moses. He went on speaking of my sins with no sign of stopping. He recalled the beginning of my dalliance in occult practices, which I had engaged in under the self-deluded guise of educational pursuits.

As I listened, literally unable to turn away, I began to realize the amount of sick and perverse moral failure that had directly proceeded from this arena of interest. Like a single cancer cell, innocuous at first, tiny and unassuming, it begins to eat with carnivorous appetite at everything healthy, eventually spreading its foul, insidious malady, consuming every other part of the body till the death toll is paid. So were my occult appetites. And Moses seemed to know about the darkness and was bent on telling every sordid detail of my filth.

Far before he had finished reciting my litany of sins, I had given up any hope of standing on my own accord before Him who is judge of all. I had known since I entered heaven that somehow, some way, some day there was a reckoning to come. Although in my earthly life, so distant, so it seemed, from any sort of judgment that it was not a concern, despite that blathering of various preachers—yes, even Gordon. But in heaven, that vain self-consuming idea had been shattered.

I had, at times, since my first realization of a certain judgment, considered the hopeful possibility of a weighing of good deeds against bad. Sometimes my thoughts turned back to the many kind and generous acts I had done. Still, an honest evaluation revealed that even my best moments quite often were motivated by my own private gain, selfish advancement, personal reputation, or all-out greed in a variety of categories.

Whatever hope I had in that vanity was now fully gone. Had there been a cosmic scale balancing my deeds, after hearing the proclamation of Moses, which still continued, my hope was thoroughly dead. And I recalled what Gordon had said about the million points analogy when I spoke with Frank Henderson. I was irretrievably in the negative. In fact, I now realized that Gordon has massively understated the situation!

I do not know how long Moses and I stood there, outside the temple gate, fact-to-face. It was a desperately long time. By earthly standards, it may have been days. The light in heaven never changes, with no dawn or sunset. For the Redeemed, there is no sense of hunger; eating is simply a delightful pleasure, not a necessity. Neither is there a requirement of sleep. Gordon told me once that God gives to the Redeemed even as they sleep, but it is merely another way to experience His presence. The passage of time, already vague and ambivalent anyway, was not measurable.

Moses' review of my failures seemed to not have an end. It was a bit like lying in an emergency room in the hospital, awaiting care for some extreme but unidentifiable pain. Yet there did come a moment when Moses breathed his last imprecation against me. It had something to do with the Red Hue Room.

I was not even sure at this point what specific item he was talking about. I had not been able to listen cogently and had been making every effort to ignore Moses. But I most certainly noticed when he stopped speaking.

We stood silently for a moment. I did not know what to say or indeed if I was supposed to say anything.

Then, Moses spoke again.

"Proceed, Adam, to the temple. Enter the doors nearest to us, but do not go beyond the first room. Wait there."

Moses did not seem inclined to discuss why I should do this. It sounded very much like a command. The result of having all my sins, every filthy and embarrassing and humiliating one of them, spoken out loud had two effects on me regarding Moses. First, the person who knows every single secret, dark behavior of your life is a person to be obeyed. Second, the person who knows every single secret, dark behavior of your life is a person you want to get far away from as soon as possible. Heading toward the temple, though fraught with both fear and fascination, was a relief to me. I wanted nothing else to do with Moses.

20

The Temple

With great difficulty, I pushed open the massively thick, weighty, and tall golden door of the temple. It took great effort, and the struggle just getting in the door seemed to indicate that no one was welcome in the temple. I momentarily stood at the threshold and looked around me. The sky was still vibrant blue, the lightning above the Throne still visible in its piercing and thrilling glory, and the trees and grass of this valley were all surging green with life.

Heaven had not changed.

But I sensed that inside this monolithic golden hall awaited something that might change me. I suddenly felt vacant and empty. A longing came over me to be away from this place, even from heaven itself. I never felt so fully an alien, so wholly a stranger in heaven as at that moment. It was the only time in all my heavenly travels that I truly wished I was not present in this land.

A memory flashed through my mind of traveling with my younger brother through the endless, stark mountains of the western United States, on a lonely, isolated highway. The land, a continual variety of rock, sand, and dirt of browns, tans, auburns, and russets, streaked through with dark reds and scarlets, though beautiful in its desolation, was barren and harsh. The uninviting and seemingly lifeless landscape and the sky above so vast, deep, and impenetrable it made me feel extraordinarily insignificant, hollow, unnecessary, and empty. I did not like that sensation then, and for some reason, it had returned to me now.

Heaven did not want me or need me. I did not belong here. It was not the first time that thought had struck me, but it was by far the most intense moment of that sensation that I ever had.

I closed my eyes, stood, and waited. The memory of the mountains passed, and the consciousness of my aloneness very slowly faded. I opened my eyes at last and realized my fists were so tightly clenched that my fingernails were painfully piercing the palms of my hands.

I peered inside. The interior was very dark. I could make out very little of the room I was looking into, and this was with the door open and light coming in. I stood there again, waiting. I briefly pondered my choices, then realized I had none. What else was I to do? I plunged in.

The door slammed shut behind me before I could find anything with which to prop it open. There was no light, none whatsoever. I could see nothing at all. I was afraid to walk around for fear of running into something. So I simply stood in place, figuring that since I had been sent here, something was likely to happen eventually.

I did not have to wait long.

In the distance, yet within the room, I saw a small, faint reddish point of light. It did not illuminate anything, so I was not inclined to move toward it. It seemed very far off, farther than the room or the whole temple should allow. As I watched, the point of light seemed to move slightly back and forth or bob nearly imperceptibly up and down in the darkness at a leisurely pace. Why this was happening or what was causing this movement I could not yet tell.

The scene was eerie and strange, but despite being vaguely reminiscent of a spooky movie, I felt no fear. I wondered at the purpose of this, the message, for clearly nothing in heaven is an accident.

Then, again faintly, another small light appeared near the first one, but this one was white. And, like the first one, it swayed a little back and forth, up and down, often in parallel movement to the red light. Both of the lights were far in the distance, a lifetime away from me. But the very idea of time now burst into my thought, for something was occurring to me. The scene developing before me felt like . . . time. There was a sense in this room, dark and mysterious though it was, of the passing of time.

But now more white lights had been added. There was still only one red point of light. The lights weaved in and out among one another. Sometimes this appeared to be quite a random movement, but at other times showed a definite pattern, an order to the direction of the lights. Still, other than the tiny points of light, I stood in utter darkness. The slight bobbing and swaying back and forth of all the lights continued.

Then one of the lights began to move purposefully toward the red light. It became obvious that this was a collision course. I wondered what would happen when that happened. Soon enough, the two lights did hit, and at the moment of collision, a bright effusion of glittering white light exploded. It reminded me very much of the sparklers that my brothers and I would set a match to and then marvel at as children during Fourth of July celebrations. And, just like those sparklers in the dark, this glittering effulgence, against the backdrop of pitch black, lasted a few seconds, then faded into non-existence.

Two things happened at this intersection of the red and white points of light. First, it now seemed that the entire set of lights had moved slightly closer to me—still far off as it seemed—but the distance had lessened. Second, at the sparkler-like explosion, though lasting only a few seconds, I glimpsed a reflection of the light against something in which the lights were engulfed. The tantalizing hint gave the appearance that the lights were floating in what looked like a river; that is, they were being carried along in a dark river. But the instant was quickly gone, and I was left wondering. I hoped there would be another sparkler moment. Perhaps the river, if that is what it was, would become clearer. I also considered that if the lights were floating in a river, this might explain their swaying and bobbing movement.

Suddenly, another sparkler moment happened. A large white light cascaded into the path of the red light, and there was a great spattering of brilliance. This lasted rather longer than the first one, and for the first time, it looked as if the red light gained some brilliance and was brighter than it had been. The effect, however, was only temporary. The red light soon returned to its normal luminescence. And, again, there was light reflected in the surroundings, and it appeared, faintly, that all the lights were floating down a dark and perhaps even ominous-looking river.

As I watched, the white lights continued intersecting with the red light. There was always the sparkler-like display of varying intensity and length, but oddly, the red light never changed, at least not permanently. Some of the collisions resulted in a brief expansion of the red light's glow, but it always went back to where it had been. It continued to make its path down the river in seeming indifference to the efforts of the white lights.

And a river it was. Sometimes now the river was roaring as through great rocks and rapids, and all of the lights were tossed about like leaves floating helplessly along the swirls and cascades of the water. At other times, the river rolled on quite peacefully; calm and quiet pervaded the scene.

And now the whole panorama, though still pitch black, had moved closer to me.

Many of the lights floated in and out of the scene, having only a brief encounter with the red light, then disappearing. A few, however, stayed in the river, at varying distances from the red light, for long periods of time. Several of the white lights had repeated collisions with the red light. Some of these were spectacular in nature, lighting up the whole width of the river and even seeming to draw other lights closer to the red one.

The river seemed crowded with white lights, and every one eventually meeting with the red light. At times, there were almost continuous sparkles of light, one right after another. Eventually, I noticed the white lights thinning out. One by one they vanished from the scene until only a few remained. And it seemed that these had been the ones that had been there with the red light from the beginning. The collisions came almost to a complete end.

Then those last couple of white lights disappeared from view, sliding off the edge of the scene almost as if they had been tossed aside.

The red light was alone, in the dark, on the ominous river. And the scene was growing nearer to me.

Now, for the first time since the image in the dark had begun, the red light changed slightly in appearance without any intersections with other lights. It seemed to be flickering in intensity, occasionally dimming, then coming back to its original brightness. I noticed that it never got brighter than its first intensity. After a while, it dimmed and then did not come back at all. The red light stayed dim like a light bulb in a flashlight with a dying battery. It floated on alone.

I felt as if I had been standing in the temple, like a statue, motionless, for hours upon hours staring at the scene before me. Until now, this encounter in the temple seemed, if not normal, at least something that had to be done in my heavenly trek, an event I had been directed to do and accepted as somehow part of the burden Michael had laid upon me.

But now, standing still in the pitch dark, the solitary red light before me, the absence of the presence of anyone who had befriended me in heaven, the passing of time with no comprehension of what any of this meant, and the disappearance of the white lights that seemed to represent something good, all began to take a toll. The sight before me was strange, even bizarre, it's ever-advancing position nearer and nearer, and that lonely red light, still bobbing up and down and swaying back and forth.

I became afraid and took a step back, but there was nowhere to go. My back pressed against the wall. I realized I had been moving backward imperceptibly for some time, and the wall had been only inches away before my last step.

At that instant, the scene began to change. For the first time, another red light edged into the river. It slowly crept toward the first red light. Even before it reached the first one, another one appeared on the opposite side of the river and began moving purposefully toward the original red light. And, just as with the white lights, the red lights moved across the horizon of the river and finally bumped into the first red light. Unlike the white lights, however, there was no sparkle of light, only a dull reddish glare for a moment that faded.

Then more red lights began to appear on the river, each meeting the original red light in one way or another. Some moved very quickly across the river, others slowly; some of the red lights were quite dim, and others were bright in a garish and harsh way. I also noticed that the river had become quite rough, as though it were flowing through powerful and dangerous rapids. At times the entire river narrowed, as if enclosed in a narrow canyon, although I never saw any canyon walls, and it rushed forward, throwing the red lights wildly around, careening at times off each other in wild abandon.

Some of the collisions were quite violent. Others, despite the wild water, were more subtle and barely noticeable. With each intersection, the dull red glare was reflected in the river, and this gave the river a brief almost bloody and menacing appearance in the darkness of the room.

But another thing was happening too, which troubled me. Almost undetectably, the original red light was losing its brightness with every hit from the other red lights. It had already lost some of its luminosity when the white lights had disappeared altogether, but now, after many strikes with other red lights, it was barely visible.

And the scene grew still nearer to me.

I pressed my back against the wall as I realized the vista was almost on top of me. I felt water splashing on my face, chest, hands, and feet! I had thought this was merely an ominous and frightening vision, but now, was this a vision, or had this apparition taken on a physical reality? The width of the river now quickly took up my entire view. I began to shake in fear and sweat with the uncertainty of what would happen momentarily. Would I be swallowed up in the river?

My fear grew exponentially as many red lights seemed right before my eyes now, mere inches away in the murky darkness. What had begun as a distant point, farther away than the temple room would allow, now was soaking my clothing. Countless red lights raced across the scene, giving the whole room a sickening red hue. The red lights were hot. I could feel them touching my face, and despite the water pouring over me, the lights were burning me with a sulfurous stench. I tried to scream, but the water was now filling mouth, and my body was engulfed in a swirling deluge. I would soon drown!

Then, with my last moment of vision before what suddenly seemed certain death, all the lights went out in an instant. The lone red light remained. The water drained away harmlessly. And the flickering, barely visible red light began to plummet down into the void of darkness toward the floor of the temple. And it vanished into the stone I was standing on.

And I was alone in the dark, trembling.

I stood in the temple for a long time. I was terrified and uncertain, not knowing what to do and not sure I could even find my way out. The darkness was palpable. The reality of the lights and river proceedings pounded in my mind. The message of the event was not entirely clear, but a perception was forming in my mind.

A sliver of light appeared in the room. It grew slowly in a rhombus-shaped width and pierced my eyes with a brightness that hurt. I realized that it was simply the door opening, at last, and casting a long, uneven illumination across the interior. Somehow, I ended up on the far side of the room from the door. It seemed a long way off, and the figure opening it was silhouetted against the light from the outside. The figure spoke to me, calling me out of the temple. It was the voice of Moses, the Lawgiver.

I had become sickened by Moses' voice in our earlier encounter, hearing the endless repetition of my sins. Now it was a welcome sound. Anxious to get out of the temple, I hurried toward his voice.

I burst through the door that he easily held open, and I was blinded by the brightness. How long I had been in the dark, I do not know, and I never found out. The light of heaven hurt my eyes terribly, but it was so welcoming and delicious that I held my pained eyes open to drink in the beauty. Most of all, the lightning above the Throne drew my attention. Yes, all was still well. I was in heaven and had not drowned in the temple or had the red light of my life extinguished.

Somehow, a vague sense of the loss of linear time began again. Now Moses was speaking and telling me of my path out of the temple valley. I was to meet Gordon again. No words had ever been more joyous to me!

I fled along the path, out from the temple, and out from the valley where the temple rested. Up the sloping hill I ran, then over the brink of the prominence and back down the black stone steps dotted with red, and down through the greenness to the heavenly country, away from the Lawgiver, the temple, and the red lights.

Gordon was there, waiting for me, smiling, winking, laughing, and crinkling his eyes as I raced to meet him. I threw myself on him with a great hug and a shout of joy, which was very unlike me.

He gave me a curious look but laughed that infectious laugh and said, "It's good to see you too, Adam!"

"Gordon, I can't tell you how happy I am to see you and to get out of that place!"

"Really?" he said with genuine surprise.

"Yes! Yes! I felt like I was trapped in there for weeks. It was all horrible. First, Moses spoke for days on end, then I was in the temple for, I don't know, days or weeks. I thought it would never end."

"Are you certain?" Gordon answered.

"Of course I am! Absolutely! Why?"

"I watched you climb the hill and step into the valley, but it seems like you turned around and came back as soon as you were over the rim of the hill and out of view."

'Wha… what?" I stammered. "What do you mean?"

"I barely had time to turn around and here you are back again."

I stood there speechless, my mind reeling. I didn't know how such a thing could be, but certainly Gordon would not be lying.

"Gordon, I was gone for weeks, well, days for sure, but weeks possibly."

"How about that!" he said with a look of both amazement and amusement. "Well, I told you before you climbed the hill that the temple is not like the rest of heaven, but this is a new one even to me! Some sort of time displacement, I guess."

"I . . . I guess." I wondered how time could be flowing in one place, but on the other side of a hill, it wasn't passing at all. It was all hopelessly beyond me, but it did remind me of the episode I had near the Throne in the City of God, with a view toward eternity.

"I don't know what to make of the time situation, Gordon, but I do know I never want to go back there. It was awful."

He stood back and looked at me, nodding. He seemed to understand. "Not such a pleasant time in the old covenant, eh?"

As was often the case, I was not sure of the reference he was making, but I heartily agreed. "Not pleasant at all," I said. "In fact, that is the proverbial understatement of the year! But I don't think I want to talk about it, at least not yet. I just want to get back to enjoying heaven."

Then Gordon gave me something of a troubled look, or at least as much as a citizen of heaven can. This caused me some immediate alarm, but I already sensed what he was about to say.

"It's time to leave the island, Adam. Then we must proceed to where the Crystal Sea splits and this heavenly realm comes to an end. There is more to see and hear, but an end is coming. I know you want to continue enjoying heaven, but as Michael said, 'You must travel back to your world,' and as you know, this world is not your home."

We headed for the great bridge that spanned the island and the mainland. The beauty of heaven pierced my heart, and I felt a deep sadness. We talked little as we walked the miles back to the bridge. We spoke briefly with many more islanders, some of whom Gordon introduced as being "from the book of Judges," "from the book of Acts," or "from the book of Samuel," and so forth. I was intrigued by all of them, but the heaviness in my soul did not leave.

Despite my dismay about my future, as we walked toward the bridge, I had an experience that ranked among the strangest and most inexplicable of all the scenes I had witnessed in heaven. This took place in the most deeply forested area I had yet seen on the island, in a region of dark green and cavernous shadow, with trees that must have been the size of giant sequoias in height and girth. Gordon and I came across a group of angels participating in some sort of extraordinary ritual, unlike anything I have seen in heaven or on Earth. I simply stopped on the path and stared.

Before me were many angels, perhaps hundreds, who were standing, sitting, even bent over or contorted in what, humanly speaking, would have been painful twisting shapes. For the most part, they were unmoving, but some occasionally would walk around touching something that hung from the ceiling of the building they were in. At first, I thought maybe these were cosmic musical instruments, but there was no sound, at least not to human ears.

After observing this for a lengthy period (the angels appeared to be completely oblivious to our presence), I heard Gordon chuckling beside me. I had been so absorbed in the scene that I forgot he was standing next to me. I turned to look at him and realized he was watching me.

"I couldn't help but laugh at the baffled expression on your face, Adam."

"What in the world is going on here, Gordon? What are they doing?"

"We don't know for sure. (By "we" I could tell he meant the Redeemed.) This building is called the Pavilion of the Angels. I myself have asked lots of angels about this practice, but they aren't able to explain it to us. It's not that they refuse to explain it, it's just no words or concepts in our minds could help us understand what they are doing."

Now several angels moved in obvious symmetry. They walked to the objects hanging from the ceiling of the Pavilion. Upon further inspection, I noticed that what was hanging from the ceiling looked like long poles made of something like shiny reflective glass, but something about the poles seemed transient, as if they were vibrating microscopically or shifting in and out of some phase of dimension. It was quite subtle, but some aspect of these poles made it seem as though they weren't wholly present, as if they existed in multiple places at the same time, which certainly made little sense to me.

But *pole* is not the right word, for all of these were of differing lengths and widths. Some were round, some square, some flat, some were many-sided, and some went all the way from ceiling to floor. And many had varying geometrical fluctuations in size along their length. I asked Gordon if we could have a further look, closer to the Pavilion. He said yes, so we walked right up to the edge where the stone floor began.

Then I realized that the poles were not hanging from the ceiling at all. They were simply floating in space. How this was achieved I do not know and never found out. As an angel would touch a pole, I could now see a tiny spark of something like fire or electricity jump between the pole and the angel. What this meant or accomplished was unclear, and again, there was no sound.

As we stood watching, suddenly, all the angels moved at once, each going to the position and place in which another angel had been. I stood gazing in awe and curiosity. Sometimes a few angels would move about, touching various poles, and at other times, all the angels would again move into positions and places others had previously been. It seemed that some outside stimulus must have been directing them since no words were spoken; they all knew exactly when to move and where to go.

The purpose of the contorted positions was never clarified at all. I know that humans would have been in considerable pain given some of the distorted poses that were being performed, but I suppose angels, being spirit beings, can maneuver in ways that flesh and blood cannot.

Being completely perplexed by the angels in the Pavilion and not having the slightest idea what was happening, I finally concluded we might as well move on. I was about to ask Gordon if we could proceed to the bridge when one of the heavenly mists blew up from the sea and began to douse us with the sweet shivering ecstasy of the raindrops of heaven.

The misty rain, driven by winds that drove the water all over the heavenly realm, blew into the Pavilion of the Angels, drenching both the angels and the strange poles. My initial thought, from an earthly perception was, *What a shame. Everything in the Pavilion is getting soaked.* However, this proved not to be a problem but merely the catalyst to an astounding display.

Once the mist had thoroughly covered all the poles, the angels began to move out of their places and positions, each angel seeking out a pole—not the pole nearest them necessarily, for now it seemed that each angel had a specific pole. And for the first time, I realized that there were the same number of poles as angels.

Then something happened that is nearly impossible to describe, in part because I was not sure what I was seeing. The sense of some shifting phase or vibrating quality of the poles became more pronounced. Each angel standing by each pole also began to vibrate sympathetically with its respective pole. Something utterly bizarre was happening, akin to purposefully blurring one's eyesight to give everything a fuzzy, indistinct appearance. The angels and the poles became indistinguishable. I could no longer tell which was which, for the poles took on the character of the angels, and the angels seemed to metamorphose into pole-like structures. This happened while both were vibrating or during what my mind began to call a phase shift.

I became so overwhelmed by this completely bizarre, alien, and inhuman scene that I suddenly wanted to leave. It began to remind me of the melding together of the demons who had surrounded me on the Earth visit through the vision of Ezekiel. I knew that nothing evil was happening here in the Pavilion, but I was not ready for such a display no matter what the intent might have been. It was both fascinating and repulsive—and no place for me to linger any longer.

"Gordon, can we please go!" I said suddenly and with great urgency.

"Yes, we should. This is no place for you to be right now."

We quickly moved away from the Pavilion. I didn't know what happened next, and I didn't want to know. It seemed from Gordon's comment that perhaps it was best for me not to know. I wondered if my angelic friend, Odegeo, had ever participated in this rite. I never had the slightest clue what was going on in the Pavilion of the Angels, nor did Gordon, nor did any of the Redeemed. It is something peculiar and unique to angels. Perhaps it will be understood in eternity. For the present, I was more than content to put that scene behind me. I never quite felt the same toward angels after that experience. They seemed much more removed and distant from humanity than I had thought before.

We continued. The bridge was ahead. Beyond that, I knew the end of heaven was not far off, and the dread of it grew in me like the last night of a death-row inmate awaiting the morning execution.

21

Belinda

Gordon and I left the island and headed west, as it seemed to me, approaching the far end of heaven. The mountains that encircled the heavenly realm drew closer and soon were near at hand.

We were far from the City of God, although the lightning was still easily visible and powerfully present in the atmosphere above the Throne. There was no mistaking it. As if the presence of perfection in every atom of heaven were not enough, the lightning was a constant reminder of where we were, of whose land this was. Here, the gleam of heaven still washed over and permeated all things. There was no loss of the Presence in this land, even near its farthest point. And the Redeemed who inhabited this area were as holy and wholly alive as anywhere else I had been.

The land along the Sea flattened out, and the waters flowed out of the disappearing banks and onto the lowland. We began to walk through flooded marshlands. The region where the river spilled onto the land created a stunning expanse of glades with endless variations of green plants.

Tall grass-like varieties with leaves popped up from several inches to several feet above the top of the primarily motionless, watery surface. The leaves of the grasses had all manner of shapes and sizes: long and elongated, flat, cupped, curled, rounded, diamond shaped, with clustered star-shaped leaves, with pointed tips, and some with no clear pattern of form. Some smaller plants protruding from the water were not grasses at all. They were more like flower gardens that grew in the water rather than on land.

In many places of this fabulous marshland, entire acres of these water gardens flushed with the most intensely colored blossoms I had ever seen. Many were small and delicate, and others had huge blooms the size of dinner plates. Some areas were dashed with an intense rainbow of many plants with many colors, creating a dizzying array of brilliant hues that lifted the soul with the joy of just being there. Other areas were packed with a single type of blossoming plant whose radiance lit up the whole locale with the gleam of that particular flower.

We saw lakes of shocking red, ponds of vivid blue, watery lowlands of shining yellow, and massive pools of dazzling purple. Everywhere I looked, the water mirrored the surrounding colors and the virgin blue of the sky, giving the sense of walking through an artist's palette of intensely vibrant paints on a planetary scale.

Exotic trees, in unusual shapes, unlike trees I had ever seen on Earth or anywhere else in heaven, dotted the landscape. Some were low-growing trees but with massive spread. Others were tall, narrow, and palm-like in their shape. Some were full and round, and others had a billowy, feathery, and soft appearance, dense with millions of tiny, bright green leaves.

One tree looked very Earth-like, like a weeping willow: green, arching, drooping, lush, shapely, full-bodied willows that would have been objects of awe in any earthly arboretum. Thousands of them were here, all in the perfect peak of health and beauty. And between the grasses, flowers, and trees were more glade-growing plants. Many of these varied bushes and shrubs were flowering with radiant blossoms, growing right out of the water or densely packing the wet, higher ground.

Some areas were exotic and, in a sense, untended, left to create their form of perfection, while other spots had been planned around pools and ponds, manicured and maintained as though in an earthly gardener's dream or fantasy, with a symmetry and artistic stroke that was unparalleled in our world. Each of these gardens had the perfect blend of color, size, and form. At each one, I thought, *Ah, this is the perfect garden.* Then at the next garden, I would pause and consider, *No, this is the perfect garden.*

Every plant, flower, shrub, or tree was in the perfection of vigor. Water was everywhere—glorious sparkling water from the river of heaven. The brightness of the light reflected the glory of every leaf and flower in an electric shower of a rainbow essence permeating this region of heaven. The lightning of the Throne stabbed the glades with its pervasive presence, which was inescapable, omnipresent, and purposeful, reminding me of whose land this is and His claim to my soul.

Ahead of me were the mountains and the end of the Heavenly Realm.

We saw less of the Redeemed. The mansions we saw in this region had an aqua quality, with a lot of sparkling blue and luminous green. Waterfalls were abundant in, around, and falling over the mansions. Water in various designs, levels, volumes, and waves sprayed, sprinkled, and flowed. The air bristled with many facets of water sounds.

We came over a small promontory surrounded by vibrant wetlands and connected to firmer, drier ground by a green causeway. As we approached back toward the river, I saw a woman of the Redeemed approaching. She had just come out of her sand-colored mansion, which vaguely appeared like a palatial-sized oyster shell, with water coursing down the topside ridges!

Just as had happened with Frank Henderson and Dr. Kakos, a moment of recognition passed through me and, I am sure, a look of startled realization. Although she was a hundred yards or more away and looked very little like her earthly incarnation, I inexplicably recognized this woman. It was Belinda Pixton.

Her beauty was stunning. She was tall and willowy with auburn hair and, even from a distance, a smile so electric that I felt as if I were vibrating from the energy of it. Her high cheekbones accented her sparkling green eyes. Her body seemed to flow, more than walk, with elegance and grace.

On Earth, Belinda had been about thirty years older than I was. I had seen her regularly, and even as a young child had always dreaded those encounters. As a boy, I was not sure what it was about Belinda that I did not like, but at fourteen or fifteen, I became aware of the reason for my disdain for Belinda. She was a usurper, a controller, a dominator. She "wore the pants," as it were. I did not like that in my youth, and I hated it as an adult, never admitting to myself what this meant about a modern, enlightened, liberated man such as myself. However, as I child, I couldn't avoid Belinda in my earthly life. She was my aunt.

Belinda was my mother's sister. No two women could have been more opposite. Her married name was Pixton, but it would have been more honest if her husband, Vern, had taken *her* last name. In any case, she had insisted on retaining her maiden name of Mantiss, Belinda Mantiss-Pixton.

The last time I saw Belinda was probably late in my high school years, at some graduation event. Not long after that, I more or less abandoned my family. Once I was in college, the cynical disdain and intellectual snobbery that quickly took over my life led me to a place to neglect all family gatherings. Hence, my exposure to Belinda had ended. I couldn't have cared less.

It struck me that she was *in heaven*, and I didn't even know she had died! Was I so thoroughly removed from my family life that my mother's sister had died, and I did not know of it? Most likely, my parents had attempted to contact me, and I had ignored their efforts, never knowing that my mother was unquestionably grieving deeply over losing a sister.

Guilt washed over me anew. I should have been there on some level for my mother. I should have been at my aunt's funeral. It was the right thing to do, but I could not be bothered by antiquated cultural and familial encumbrances.

At the same time, as with Frank Henderson and Dr. Kakos, I was astonished to see Aunt Belinda in heaven! *How could she be here?* The question stalled in my mind. By now, however, I recognized that as Belinda was bearing down on me, I would soon hear her story. Was this an intersection of grace?

"Adam!" she called out from a distance. I am sure that for the first time in my life, Belinda was genuinely happy to see me. She smiled and radiated joy. I was overwhelmed by her beauty. On Earth, although no other woman on our planet could compare with Belinda or any other of the Redeemed women, this would have been an occasion for considerable lust, the issue of her being my aunt aside. Here, salaciousness was utterly out of the question. Remarkably, I had no illegitimate desire for any of the women of heaven. It could not exist in my heart, and that only proved how wholly different the very air of heaven is.

My first and often only response to an attractive woman on Earth was lust and craving. The game would begin, and I would ply my trade to conquer the object of my desire. And *object* was the keyword. I had dehumanized most women to be something possessed by me for my pleasure alone and then discarded when my purposes were served. The road that brought me to that point in my thinking was despicable. It had nothing to do with "art."

But Belinda was radiant. I was almost embarrassed to be in her presence. I had had little interaction beyond polite pleasantries with Redeemed women since I had entered heaven, and I now felt awkward. My lifelong treatment of women was suddenly a burden to me, in proximity to her transcendent beauty, goodness, and holiness, a word I was not yet sure of. Yet, I knew this meeting was not an accident; it was arranged. I had to respond. I knew a conversation would ensue, and I had to find the words.

"Hello, Belinda."

"Adam, it is so wonderful to see you here! In heaven!" I knew she meant it, and I was humbled at such a sincere welcome for one who had no right to be here and had treated her poorly on Earth.

I hardly knew how to respond to her. So much needed to be said, explained, and even justified as to my presence, but she put me at ease.

"I know this is not exactly the normal way to experience heaven, but I am so happy to see you!" She said this with a smile and a laugh that was so pure and real that it would have healed all the hurts of Earth.

"Thank you, Belinda. It is, uh, amazing to be here. I could try to explain it, but it would take a long time."

"We have all the time we need, Adam. I am not even sure if any time has passed since you arrived here in heaven. But don't worry about explanations. I know enough of your struggle for now."

Compassion and a sense of sympathy flowed from her heart to mine, which deeply moved me. I recognized that there was something so intrinsically feminine about her words, about the depth of her caring.

I started introducing her to Gordon, but they began talking like old friends before I had the chance.

Then Gordon turned to me and said, "Belinda and I knew each other on Earth, Adam. I met her a number of times through your mother. Quite a few times at the altar in prayer, I believe—your mother, that is, not Belinda!" As always, Gordon laughed heartily and gave his trademark mirthful wink, which made me laugh.

"Yes, I am sorry to say that for most of my life, the altar was unknown to me. But by His grace, I discovered it at last."

"You didn't seem like a woman who had much interest in religion."

"Again with the religion issue, eh Adam?" Gordon said and chuckled. He didn't seem to care much for the term *religion*, at least my use of it.

Belinda smiled her dazzling smile and a wave of affection for her flowed over me.

"I understand what you mean about religion, Adam. But often, religion becomes the purpose in itself. The very thing that was meant to carry us to Him begins to distract and take on a life of its own. It's like two roads running side by side, almost parallel, but one ever so slightly, almost unnoticeably, is veering away from the straight road. And if it is allowed to continue, eventually it finds its own path, and those who are on it are heading toward a completely different destination. On that bending road, though they can't tell that it's bending, the travelers can no longer even see the straight road, yet they believe their road is the true one because they are doing many of the things that they did on the straight road. But they begin to do those things for the wrong reasons with the wrong goal."

"I guess I understand," I answered, although it was a reach. I decided I would avoid the term *religion* from now on. It always evoked a vexed response from Gordon. He joked about it yet seemed troubled by it. I supposed this riddle might be resolved someday, but I wanted to hear Belinda's account of her presence in the Heavenly Realm.

I knew the story was coming. It was the main preoccupation of the inhabitants of heaven to relate to one another their God story. Although I was not a *real* inhabitant, this story was for my ears.

"I have heard the story of others who I have unexpectedly seen here. And I must admit that I didn't expect to see you here either. No offense, Belinda."

"None taken, Adam. Of course, my name is really no longer Belinda. I have a new name that my Lord has given me. All of the Redeemed have new names. No, I cannot speak that name to you, not yet. It is known only to my Savior and me. I know that you did not expect to see me, of all people, here in heaven! Trust me, I am the least likely person to be here in the presence of the living God and my Savior, my Redeemer, my Love. I can say with another and far greater than me, I was the chief of sinners! Oh, the depth of His love for me, Adam! How little I knew it and how greatly I abused Him!"

Such a frank outpouring of love—emotional, impassioned love—took me back a bit. Gordon read my thoughts. "Those who have been forgiven much, love much," he said.

"Yes, of course," I answered, vaguely grasping his point. Then, addressing Belinda, I broached the subject weighing on my mind since the first instant I had seen her.

"Belinda, I must apologize to you. I didn't even know you had, uh, died. I didn't attend your funeral. I gave no thought to you or my family, especially my mother's grief. I am so sorry."

Belinda's response was unexpected. "Oh, bless you, dear one!" And she began to laugh the laughter of a mother delighting over her child's innocent, pleasant play. "There is no need for that! But yes, yes, you are forgiven! A thousand times over, you are forgiven! How could I not forgive you? Do not burden yourself for another instant over that!"

"Well, thank you. I appreciate you being so kind about my selfishness and thoughtlessness."

Gordon, who seemed to be drinking in the beauty and wholeness of Belinda, turned to me with a look of surprise and an element of hope in his eyes and said, "Well, young man, perhaps there *is* something happening in your heart!"

"Perhaps there is Gordon," I answered. By this time, I was genuinely interested in hearing Belinda's story. Despite being sisters, she was as unlike my mother as any woman could have been. And although I had rejected my parent's faith, I knew, even in my days of decadence and unbelief, that if there was a God, my parents were probably the closest people to Him that I had ever known. In a way, Belinda had been like me. We had both persevered in our apostasy, actively rejecting all things representing God. I had done it in my masculinity; Belinda had done it in her femininity. It was time for me to listen.

"Belinda, please tell me your story."

"Gladly, Adam. I was a driven woman, pushed by everything that represented the masculine world. I rejected all things feminine unless there was utility in it."

Gordon and I looked at each other, smiled, and shook our heads in unison in a silent knowing agreement at the virtual impossibility of such a statement given the very definition of womanhood before us. Then ironically, Belinda brushed back her beautiful auburn hair with a gentle stroke of her soft and delicate fingers, and the entire arc and curving movement of her arm revealed an intrinsic and inescapable God-ordained womanliness as she tucked her hair behind her ear.

"You, of course, remember my father, your grandfather, Earl?"

"Yes, I remember him, although not with a lot of warmth, to be honest."

I had never liked my Grandpa Earl at all. He was mean-spirited and unkind and seemed to take particular delight in lording his adulthood over children. He was gruff, but not in a way that can be endearing in covering up a caring and gentle heart. He was rough and treated all the grandkids and me with contempt and disinterest. I suspect he treated all children who had the misfortune to come in contact with him with disdain and indifference. Children were a nuisance unless some value was to be gained from them, such as cheap labor.

"No, of course, you would not remember him with warmth, Adam. He was a dark man: angry, mean, and sometimes violent. Occasionally he would hit Mother."

Interestingly, instead of hatred and anger, a remarkable

look of compassion and indignation was on her face, but none spoke of revenge.

"He physically abused Grandma?"

"Yes, he did. And I hated him for that and many other things. Although there was always the feeling in my mind that he deserved my hatred and my secret desire for retribution. The reality is that I was no better to Vern than Father was to Mother, only a different kind of abuse, but I didn't see it that way. Such is the human heart justifying itself. And somehow, Mother always forgave him, really forgave him, which made me angrier at both of them. And I was determined to be like neither of them.

"Father, in many ways, failed in life. He was a poor father, an even worse husband, and not much of a provider. His painful personality kept him moving from job to job. We didn't have much, and we moved around a great deal, which only added to our insecurities and, for me, at least, resentment.

"Mother was too weak, I thought. She was the proverbial doormat, letting Father walk on her, intimidate her, hurt her, and keep her under his thumb. Mother was a beautiful flower, but after years of that misery, she became withdrawn and haggard looking at far too early an age. She seldom went out, and she became very introverted. Oddly, she became increasingly dependent on the very one who was crushing the life out of her!

"The effect of all that on your mother and me was the opposite. Christine sought God; she got religious, as I called it at the time. On the other hand, I rebelled against everything that stood for tradition. I would never let anyone walk on me, tell me what to do, or force me into a submissive role or, as I perceived it, a feminine position. I only acted like what I thought a woman was when it served my need to get ahead and, yes, bring others low. By that, I mean reputations, careers, and even families.

"Adam, I was a reprobate, a Jezebel. I even married Vern, not out of love or any high and noble purpose, but to dominate a man I knew could be subordinated, manipulated, and controlled. We had no intimacy or coming together as one flesh. I had no interest in such things. He would submit to me, and I would lead and control the marriage. I am sure this was nothing but a lashing out against my father. Vern was the poor soul trapped in a poisonous spider's web.

"Vern was a weak and passive man, and I knew it. My attraction to him had little or nothing to do with the design of my Lord Jesus for all the delights of love, joy, friendship, companionship, oneness, and, most of all, the completion of a man and a woman in one another. A completion that reflects the fullness of my Father, His Son, and His Spirit, as everything ultimately must. For what design and purpose can there be apart from that which reveals Him? Otherwise, it must be temporary and corrupt.

"But Vern was simply my way to dominate my surroundings, to get back at my poor suffering father, and maybe at first, at least, to appear normal and acceptable in order to advance my agenda. So, I got married."

I briefly pondered her remarks, but something bothered me about what she had just said. "Wait a minute, Belinda. You just said your father, your poor father, had suffered. That seems like an inaccurate description of him. Didn't he impose suffering and intense misery on everyone else?"

"True enough, Adam, but have you not afflicted many who were innocent of your contempt?"

"Well, yes, of course. I have been awful to my parents and many others, I guess."

"And are you not suffering the agonies of what you have inflicted on others? Have you not reaped endlessly what you have sown? Even here in heaven itself, have you not wept bitter and agonizing tears of remorse over and over? Have you not wondered about in a fog of confusion, loss, and doubt of your own making?"

"Yes, I have." She was absolutely right. *How did she know?*

"You can never inflict suffering on others without inflicting it on yourself. My father suffered horribly. His conscience afflicted him with great pain, guilt, and shame. When his conscience died, he lived the even greater horror of being hollow, a shadow of a man.

"Adam, my Father, my heavenly Father, has told me that you are near to such a day in your life. Your conscience has been temporarily quickened here in heaven, but I fear that a time will soon come when your conscience will be so seared that you too will live a hollow life, a mere existence in which the One who pursues you will no longer be able to convict your soul. At the same time, even the passing pleasure of your sins will become an empty drudgery that no longer gives any satisfaction. Then the enemy has you. You are utterly lifeless. You are an automaton. You continue the addiction of sin and darkness, but no longer is there pleasure in it. In fact, you hate the very thing that you serve. You have become your sin. I fear this for you, Adam."

Everything had become strangely quiet. Heaven seemed to pause and wait. I was alone with Belinda. I did not know where Gordon was. Belinda looked into my eyes, and it appeared her gaze penetrated deep within me. I don't know how she did this. She had nothing harsh, malicious, or duplicitous about her.

Yet, I knew her vision was more than human and was telling something about my soul—something I did not want revealed. It was very much like standing before Ezekiel. I felt naked and embarrassed. Kindness and compassion were on her face. An eager, searching look was in her eyes, that of a mother hoping to find in her child innocent after an implication of evil.

I wondered at her power. How was she able to see inside me? On some level, I fought this intrusion, but I could not escape her penetrating sight. Others I had spoken with in heaven, even the estimable Melchizedek, did not look inside me, but Belinda had some gift for discerning the inner man in a place where he could not hide. Even Moses had not looked inside of me in this way during his agonizing recounting of my sin.

It occurred to me that if Belinda, a mere mortal—redeemed, yes, but human nonetheless—could see with such perception, how much more, if and when I stood before Him, would every single secret inescapably, undeniably, ashamedly be laid utterly bare, with no hope of excuse, too late for an apology, and a complete crushing of any vain reasoning? I remember laughing with friends at the idea of having to answer to some deity. "I'll just tell Him it was my business what I did in my life!" Or, "I live by my own rules!" And, as I realized now, more gross stupidity.

Belinda spoke, interrupting my self-deprecation. "Adam, my dear, you are like a mountain. I see this in your soul. You appeared to those on Earth as strong and capable, immovable, and even rugged in a way, like a cowboy living his life on his own terms, needing no one but taking what he needs and wants from the land. You cultivated this persona to give others the feeling that you are tough, self-sufficient, independent, and intelligent. In fact, you were very much like me, Adam. I knew well and believed wholeheartedly that earthly poet who said,

> It matters not how straight the gate,
> How charged with punishments the scroll,
> I am the master of my fate;
> I am the captain of my soul.

"Such soul-scarred words, wrong though they be with the black darkness their adherents inherit, were my life's dirge. I do not say song, for these words are a dirge unto death and that place where the presence of God is utterly lost, that is the true horror of hell. That is why it is called eternal death. Yet you have embraced this dark thought as though it could bring life and purpose to your existence.

"Yes, Adam, you are like a mountain in more ways than you know, for a mountain has an appearance that belies its true character. A mountain is made from violence and heat, rock crushing against stone, lava boiling from pressure. And all of it bursting forth in random eruptions without regard to the consequences. The mountain sits uneasily on a deep foundation that moves, churns, and spills its peaks in destruction and devastation."

"Stop, stop. Please, Belinda, stop," I said, not with anger, but with pain and grief. My soul was showing, and I did not like it. Her description of me was perfect. I did not want to hear more. I had hoped to hear her story, not another recounting of my own misery, however accurate it may be.

But she answered, "It is clear why He has brought you to

me. We are alike, Adam. I see that now. My Father has revealed this to me."

"Then please," I said with some exasperation, "continue with your story. Maybe I will learn from that."

"All right, my love," she said and smiled that devastating smile.

My frustration melted away. She called me "my love," and I knew the purity and goodness from which it came. There was not an ounce of anything but kindness and redeemed pity in her love for me. I was overwhelmed by her compassion and empathy. My eyes filled with tears, and I begged her to continue with her story.

"I climbed the ladder, Adam. I became successful by every worldly definition. I had wealth and influence, and the false popularity that goes with it, but mostly power, and especially power over men. This I relished. Many men wanted me in all sorts of ways, but I was hard and cold to them, demanding and unforgiving, as I had been to my husband. And I had no further need for poor Vern, so I left him. For good measure, I left him destitute. The shame I had when my Father began to show me this was beyond bearing.

"I cast away natural inclinations, pursued vile desires, and indulged them recklessly. I sought new toys and grander appearances. I thought that more power, wealth, influence, and indulgence of whatever delighted my eyes would satisfy my soul. But it was all a lie. In my heart of hearts, I knew it was false, but I ran faster and farther from eternity in my soul than perhaps anyone who has ever lived.

"But, Adam, the day that changed my life, or perhaps began an irreversible process of change, was a vacation day I spent with my sister and her husband—your parents! Bless them, Adam! They are choice servants of my Father!" Her eyes sparkled with joy and tears. "I had not seen them in several years, time in which my life had spiraled both up and down. Up in appearances, down in the reality of my soul. You were, I believe, in your first year of college at this point. I knew my life was empty and my soul was starving, despite the façade I had built. I went to see Christine and Donald under some pretence. But I knew that my sister, Christine, most blessed of all sisters, had something that I did not.

"Here I was, empty despite all my energies to fulfill myself. Here was Christine, full despite all her efforts to give herself away. Here I was, hated by those around me who feigned interest. Here was Christine, loved by a husband who treasured her, protected her, and honored her. I am convinced that your father, Donald, would have willingly died for her. No one on Earth would have died for me, but many wished me dead.

"Here I was, rejecting my femininity and all the expressions of motherhood, thinking to unburden myself of outdated definitions, but bitter and desperate, knowing my loss might define my legacy. Here was Christine, enjoying and reveling in all the things I hated, relishing motherhood, adoring her husband. She told me more than once that he was her hero, a notion I thought nearly insane and unworthy of 'the goddess within.' She was building a posterity that would carry on far beyond her earthly life.

"And what was the difference, Adam? I was all about me. Christine was all about others. I wanted to dominate, but she willingly submitted. I had crushed people; she had lifted people up. I had used people; she had served people. I had been just plain mean, but she had been kind, generous, and sympathetic. I was eaten up with anger; she was consumed by love. And the thing that ate at me would destroy me, but the thing that consumed her made her whole, a paradox to be sure, but the more love consumed her, the more she was filled with life.

"Oh, Adam, I could tell you of endless examples of your mother's sheer goodness, as much like my Savior as anyone I have ever known. But, come, Adam, you must know of this yourself!"

I was filled with shame and embarrassment. I knew my mother was good in a religious way, but I had always thought her to be a little provincial, unsophisticated, and downright old fashioned. I even remembered an occasion in a freshman philosophy class when the professor was lecturing on existentialism, and I rather haughtily thought to myself, *My mother would never understand this*, ignoring the fact that I wasn't too clear on the concept myself. The arrogance of youth.

The caring professor had sardonically informed the class that if we didn't understand existentialism, then we had the option to continue on with our meaningless existence. I didn't understand that either.

In retrospect, however, I remembered my mother as a woman who served everyone. She never turned down a need. We were not rich, yet my parents constantly shared with those "less fortunate," a term to them that seemed endearing. Despite what often seemed to me as their obsession with giving away material things that could well have been spent on my happiness, as a family, we were never in serious need. I knew very well why, although I had denied the veracity of it.

I didn't know if Belinda's last remark had been posed as a question to me that demanded an answer, or if she was simply stating something of a slap-in-my-face fact, not that she would necessarily intend it that way. I felt I must answer in some way.

"Belinda, I know my mother was a very good woman. I see that now. On Earth I thought she was sort of obsessed with religion. I didn't think that way when I was young, but in my teen years I began to think she was overdoing being good and the religion stuff, and it embarrassed me. I'm not proud of that as I stand here and listen to you, but my selfishness, vanity, and the pressure to be like my friends were powerful.

"I always thought I was an independent thinker and a nonconformist, but now, as I look back, I see that we all thought that about ourselves, especially in college, and we all ended up being exactly alike! What does *that* say about our nonconformity!

"But how did the light finally come on for you? You said you were the opposite of my mother in just about every possible way. Obviously, you came to a point where you realized she was right, and you were wrong."

"Yes, we were as opposite as two sisters can be. My life was a house of cards built on lies. I had lied to myself, and I had also been deceived on many levels. But everything in my world—hate, anger, bitterness, rebellion, and rejection of all the good that God had created—all led back to my father. Who I became was my fault, of course, Adam. I made my own choices, but it all flowed from a river whose source was utter poison.

"But one night, as Christine and I were up late talking about our lives, she said something that absolutely crushed me! It was a true observation, but it made me furious—because it was true! My whole life came crashing down when Christine, in her typically loving and compassionate way, uttered the fateful, honest, and damning words. She said to me, 'Belinda, you have become father.'

"And she was right, my dear Adam! She was profoundly right! I fought against it for a while, and I hated her for saying that, but in the end, she was right. The man, and this is important, the man I hated most, I had become him! Adam, can you imagine the blow that was to me? How could this have happened? How could I have become him?

"I cried out to Christine that it was not true; it was not possible. The one person I would never be like was my father! But she lovingly assured me that it was indeed true. I admired her for her honesty and courage. It must have been so difficult for her to confront me with that, knowing the risk. I was hardly rational at this time in my life. Christine did not know how I would respond, yet out of love for me and for her Savior, she spoke the truth to me.

"She explained the dreadful reality of sins visited upon succeeding generations. We talked about friends we had grown up with and how this had played out in their lives. Children of alcoholics, children of abusers, children of the arrogant, and children of the violent. It was all there, plain as day, Adam. In so many cases, the children had inexplicably become their parents! The very ones they had sworn in their youth they would never be like!

"Of course, I seized upon this, in my desperation to be absolved of guilt. It wasn't my fault then, right? I couldn't be held responsible for my bad behavior, and *bad* was a monstrous understatement, Adam.

"But Christine had me right then and there. She saw it right away, of course!" Belinda again broke into her electric smile, laughing and nearly glowing with joy at the predicament in which she had been caught! Despite the trap into which she had fallen on that day, she now told the story with great relish and happiness at her own ambush.

"And in her own wonderful loving disarming way, Christine asked the question from which I could not escape. 'So, Belinda, you do admit that your behavior was bad, you do see that there is a standard of right and wrong, and you have broken that standard?'

"Yes, I saw it alright. The pain of the admission was brutal. I had been running from the guilt, justifying my actions, blaming others for *everything* that I had sensed was wrong in myself, but there was no escape now. My own sister! Adam, do you see it!" Belinda laughed freely and heartily. "The sweetest, gentlest, most loving person on Earth had hit me with a hammer that smashed every possible excuse out of my mind!

"And that brought me to the moment that Christine, most blessed sister among sisters, had been praying and hoping for through many passing years. For I fell into the love trap she had been setting; no, really my Savior had been setting, in order to rescue me from the mouth of hell! Yes, Adam, though many women of that world reject Him and the very idea of a hero, *He is the Hero of women, the Desire of women, the White Knight in shining armor!* And I was his damsel in distress! I do not apologize, for none other could have saved me in my anguish!"

I was quite fascinated by Belinda's description of her Savior. Her words would have brought ridiculing laughter, disdain, anger, even fury from many of the modern and enlightened women I knew. Yet she spoke with absolute clarity and conviction, with not the slightest concern of anyone's opinion of her admitted need or her zeal, profound admiration, and love for her Hero.

"So, what was it, Belinda? What happened next? What was the hammer that my mother struck you with?"

"Adam, everything had led to this moment. I asked the question she had been waiting for. I said to my sister, 'Christine, I don't understand. If I fell into the sin of my father and probably his father, why didn't you? Why did you escape?'

"She looked at me with compassion that would have melted the hearts of a million rebels and said, 'We shared the terrible pain of our childhood, but you turned inward to yourself; I turned to the Redeemer.'"

I was instantly struck with the burning memory of Melchizedek's words to me, "I did, and you have not." He sought God, and I did not. My mother sought God, and Belinda did not. This was certainly no coincidence that I was here with Belinda hearing her story, an intersection of grace, no doubt.

"That was it, Adam. The dam burst in my soul. The pent-up pain, anguish, unspeakable misery, blame, and shame all began to flow out from me, instead of into me as it had done for years.

"And why were Christine's words so powerful, Adam? I had heard religious instruction and pious pontification from many sources."

Belinda, ah what a beauty, burst out in laughter, shaking her head with a look on her auburn-framed face, something along the lines of amused exasperation. "But I believed my sister because *she was so much like her Savior.*

"That which is *most unlike* the darkness is that which draws it to the light. So many on Earth think otherwise, but for the foreknown who are coming near to redemption, there is a mystery and a fascination in the tenebrism of the Gospel and the shadows of your world."

I must have looked confused; indeed, I was confused.

Belinda continued. "Moths, Adam. Moths, creatures of the night, yet where do they gather? The brightest light they can find! It is a magnet for those who live their lives in the darkness.

"Christine was the most unlike me of anyone I ever knew. Yet it was Christine that most attracted me to the Light. How? Like Him, she had willingly, humbly, and gladly submitted. Although you hate the word *submit*, as most everyone in your world seems to, it is a word that reflects the life of Christ as much as any word. Those of previous generations understood the power, substance, and beauty of it! It seems lost now in worldly pursuits.

"Yes, Adam, even in the holy Trinity there is a willing humbling of the Son to the Father. He gladly submits to the One who loves Him beyond comprehension. He is not less than His Father, not in value or importance, for they are the same in substance and essence, and they share all the nature of God together. But it was the Son who made submission, the submission that Christine reveled in, a thing of beauty, worth, and great honor. Through it He became Redeemer of all who trust Him, and through it He accomplished the will of His Father and the joy set before Him. Because of it, every knee will bow to Him, and every tongue will confess His lordship. You will bow and you will confess, Adam, but the choice of willing confession or fearful obeisance is yours alone."

Belinda was no longer laughing. Her demeanor now was deadly serious, and her eyes searched me again with solemnly and sternly. I tried to look back with manly courage but failed miserably. In my earthly life, this kind of gaze from a woman would have provoked some type of ridiculous battle of the wills with the intent of intimidation. Here this was out of the question; I was hopelessly outmatched. And of course, intimidation was not Belinda's way at all. This was merely my shallow response to the convicting love that drove her.

I looked away to the royal blueness of the sky, the glory of the surrounding tropical exquisiteness, and in the distance, the ever-present lightning that now seemed to be calling out to me. At one moment, it was beckoning me to join the chorus of joy, laughter, peace, singing, meaning, purpose, and every conceivable good, jubilant, and triumphant thing. And the next moment, the character of the lightning was that of an ominous threat and a resolute warning, sounding with a clarion call from a place of unfathomable power: *You will bow*. She had said, "You will bow out of willing confession or fearful obeisance."

From this moment on, that thought was never far from my mind.

22

The End of Heaven

The interview with Belinda was over just like that.

Gordon had returned to us as soon as Belinda had completed her story. We all suddenly and quietly acknowledged it was time to move on.

In saying good-bye, she hugged me with such energy and fervent emotion that I began to weep. "I don't have words to say to you, Belinda," I said through my tears. "I can only say thank you for meeting with me. Thank you for telling me your story and for telling me things about my parents I was blind to."

"Dear Adam, I believe you will make it! I believe you are coming to life! I believe one day you will bow out of love and make a good confession. Stay with Gordon and listen to him; he is a faithful guide. 'Now to Him who is able to keep you from stumbling, and to make you stand in the presence of His glory blameless with great joy, to the only God our Savior, through Jesus Christ our Lord, be glory, majesty, dominion, and authority, before all time and now and forever. Amen.'"

I could only weep as she spoke those words. I did not yet own them in my heart, but my heart was breaking at the revelation that such splendor and sovereignty stooped down to graciously bless broken humanity in a transformation from stumbling to standing.

We waved goodbye and left Belinda standing there, radiant and breathtaking. We walked through glorious glades and magnificent flowers towards the Crystal Sea. At the last moment, I turned back for one last glance at her. She was in the distance already, surrounded by several of the Redeemed, sharing life, laughter, and the great joy that permeates all of heaven and all in heaven—except for me.

I saw many other wonders in the Heavenly Realm. I witnessed countless animals, not only those I had seen now long ago in Eden, but also throughout our travels everywhere in heaven. Far and wide were birds, mammals, and reptiles that all abounded. Some animals I recognized, but some I did not. I saw odd combinations of animals existing peaceably, those that would never have on Earth. Predators and their victims in my world lived here in sublime pleasure together.

The most startling of all, and this I saw several times on the island just as I had seen long before near the City of God, were lions and lambs lying down together. My presence imposed no fear or concern on them; likewise, I felt no anxiety in the presence of even the most dangerous of beasts. As with everything else in heaven, the animals seemed to be in the peak of health, vivacious, and happy. Most fascinating to me, however, was their obedience to all humans.

It seemed that all the geographies of Earth were represented in heaven in their perfection. I had experienced the wonders of deep forests, waters, and the often jungle-like environment, especially in some of the areas on the island. I had also been in awe-inspiring tree-draped mountainous regions on the far side of the City of God. We had walked through vast plains swathed in lush grasses and vibrantly colorful woods along the river and the sea. I had even enjoyed the fabulous glades and marshlands in the garden country where Belinda lived.

I also saw at a great distance on part of the other side of the Crystal Sea in an area that was half the size of the Heavenly Realm, what looked like a desert expanse with large areas of brown and tan. I had never set foot in this part. Gordon confirmed that although much of the "south" side of heaven was gloriously rich and green, filled with waters and woods, there was indeed a desert land, which he insisted on calling "the living desert of heaven." Apparently, it was every bit as alive and teeming with life as anywhere else in heaven.

Many rivers also surged out from the Crystal Sea, which flowed from the City of God. None were as massive as that Sea, but they appeared to flow long and far inland. When the mist came up from the great river and the Crystal Sea, these rivers also produced additional dense rain-like mists that flowed over the land, bringing an immense abundance of water. When I looked out at the farthest distance, I saw enormous mountains ringing the Heavenly Realm with unattainable heights, clothed with great green glory that included waterfalls of cosmic proportions and mountaintops that shone with dazzling purple, red and burnished bronze.

The splendor of heaven bedazzled me. Such magnificence was too great for me. The scenes of heaven, the glorious Redeemed, the singular experiences in the City of God and the temple, the strange and wonderful presence of angels, the remarkable and unexpected conversations with those I had known on Earth, as well as those who had come alive from history, had all conspired together. God had set eternity in my heart. Like a stunning sunset that burns forever its ponderous weight and glory in the mind and memory with unspeakable beauty and shouts to all flesh of its wondrous Creator, so the effects of heaven were on me. But the eternity set in my heart was careening through an oxymoronic vertigo and nearing an end.

From the time we left Belinda, it did not take long at all till we had come to the end of the realm of heaven, a full fifteen hundred miles from the Throne. Ahead, outside of heaven, on the other side of the river that flowed both north and south, out of this far end of the Crystal Sea, were the mountains Gordon had spoken about. They were not spectacular, tall, and massive like the Rockies, nor were they tree-covered, green, and inviting like the Smokey Mountains. They were rather barren and stony. They had a certain stark quality that spoke to the human heart, but this was not like the beauty of heaven.

Heaven's beauty was full, rich, abundant, and teeming with explosive life, freshness, and the pervasive joy that permeated everything down to the blades of grass in a wholeness of exquisite splendor. It was beauty without need of commentary—intrinsic, fundamental, and obvious. The draw of these mountains across the river was entirely different. Compared to the magnificence of heaven, they were empty and lifeless. The appreciation of this scenery required a past, and these mountains were outside of heaven.

Before the mountains could be crossed, however, the river had to be traversed. How this was to be accomplished was not yet clear. However, I had come to learn that the need would be met at the appropriate moment. As it had been since the moment I had entered heaven, lifetimes ago, the sky was still perfectly blue.

The hardest moment of all had arrived. Gordon could not go any farther with me. It was time for a painful parting. He had been my companion, guide, friend, and one like a father to me for what seemed like months. I was not sure what to do or what to say. I knew I would break down into tears, not only because I loved Gordon and was leaving him, but also since I could no longer delay or avoid the fear that lay ahead—the fear I had been deflecting since I had stood before Michael. I turned to Gordon with no idea about how to express my gratitude. Before I could make any stumbling attempts to thank him, Gordon began speaking.

"Adam, I haven't told you anything about the land beyond the mountains because I didn't want to unduly frighten you or lessen your experience in heaven. You asked me long ago about that land, and I delayed answering. But I must now tell you what you are about to experience. I don't know a great deal, but I will tell you what I do know."

This was the first time in all our travels together that Gordon's face carried a trace of sorrow. The glint in his eyes was gone.

"The land ahead was once a part of this Heavenly Realm and had all the beauty and goodness that this land has always had. I don't know how large the battle lands are. It could very well be smaller than the Heavenly Realm or maybe much larger. I don't know where that land ends.

"When rebellion took place in heaven, led by Lucifer in his arrogance, the Lord created this boundary, the river. No demonic power can cross the river into the Heavenly Realm. And only Lucifer himself can enter the Throne Room. He cannot pass through or over heaven; he can only come in the same way as you did. He cannot cross the river at any point. In order for him to enter the battle lands from this realm, he must go all the way around the Heavenly Realm along the mountains that surround this land. I don't think this is a difficult task for him. I don't know what is beyond the mountains around heaven. It may be the Lord's storehouses. No one of the Redeemed knows, but Lucifer is a spirit, so physical distances and barriers are of little meaning to him.

"When the Lord sealed off the battle lands from the Heavenly Realm, He did so for the Redeemed who would eventually live here with Him. In fact, as I look across the river, I can barely make out anything at all. The Redeemed cannot see the land where you are going. In this case, Adam, you can see better than I can. My eyes are blinded, or perhaps better said, my eyes are protected from seeing that land. But the angels have access to the battle lands.

"In fact, they are called the battle lands not only because that's where the rebellion took place thousands of years ago, but also because there is still a struggle in heavenly places against the powers, world forces of darkness, and the spiritual forces of wickedness. Much of the battle happens in the land ahead of you. It spills over to the air of the Earth through some nexus between the battle lands and the world of our origin. I think that is the nexus you must find in order to get back to our world."

Gordon was giving me a lot of information, but the key matter to me, at this point, was that place, that nexus he called it, where I could, maybe, get back to Earth.

"Where is this nexus?"

"I don't know, Adam. I wish I could tell you, and I'm sorry that I can't. I really wish I could give you directions or something, but I've never been there. As far as I know, neither have any of the Redeemed. I'm sure that finding that place is very much a part of what Michael said about your journey of faith. Whatever happens to you over there, whatever you go through, I'm certain it is all part of God's plan. Whether or not it makes sense to you as you go through it, it is part of His plan. It must be.

"Everyone, every believer, and I think everyone whom God is calling, goes through periods where they don't understand what is happening or why things are taking place the way they are. I am pretty sure we go through some tests and difficulties, and we never grasp clearly the purpose. God is calling you, Adam. You must trust and believe that what you face is purposeful."

Gordon's tone and words were ominous. The pleasures and joys of heaven I had experienced and relished seemed about to be balanced with a time of difficulty, fear, uncertainty, and maybe pain. As I would find out soon, it was far worse than I could have imagined.

Now, however, the worst moment had come since I had fallen through the door in the Red Hue Room. It was time to say good-bye to Gordon.

"I believe all you have told me, Gordon. But right now I don't care about that. You've been like a father to me. I can't even begin to tell you how much you mean to me and how grateful I am for all you have done. I know you have sacrificed a lot to guide me through heaven and answer my questions, which must have seemed pretty juvenile most of the time. You could have been with your heavenly friends and family, and I'm sure leading me around has kept you from the city where your heart longs to be."

"Adam," Gordon said with tenderness and compassion,

"God Himself called me to minister to you. I have been serving Him, which is always a great joy, and I have been deeply blessed to have been with you. There's no greater happiness, in heaven or on Earth, than helping someone along the road to Christ. It has been my pleasure and privilege. You know, I preached a sermon on that once," Gordon said with a wink and a chuckle.

I couldn't help laughing. One last sermon reference was an appropriate way to say good-bye. When the laughter subsided, however, we embraced, and I began sobbing with joy and bitterness, my chest heaving hard and my grip tightening in desperation. This was a parting unlike any I had ever known. As Gordon hugged me with great love and kindness, I felt strength from him pouring into my soul, the courage and hope that a father's embrace, unlike any other, gives to his son. And so it was. I was ready, enabled now to move forward in spite of fear and uncertainty.

We looked each other in the eye. Gordon, a.k.a. Pastor Lachen, my great friend and guide, said, "The Lord bless you and keep you, the Lord make His face shine on you and be gracious to you; the Lord lift up His countenance on you and give you peace. Amen."

I wiped my reddened, watery eyes and shook his hand in the manliest way I could, hoping he would be proud of me, and turned to the task at hand.

I plunged into the water. It was quite warm and refreshing. I didn't know what else to do but swim for the other side, although my heart was certainly not in it.

On Earth I had been a decent swimmer, but now I was able to swim like an Olympic champion. Having been in heaven and breathed its air, tasted its food, and walked in its light, had made my body athletic, firm, toned, and strong. Old pains had passed away, new strength had come that I had never had before.

So, I swam easily and quickly, despite the distance, but it was a grievous trek across the water. The farther I went, the colder the water became, and a deepening anxiety drifted down upon me. I dared not turn and look back on my friend, the only friend I had in the world as it now seemed. Nor could I look back to heaven! I would have sunk to my death, if that were possible, to see the living joy I was leaving behind. The meetings with Frank Henderson, Dr. Kakos, and Belinda all now were lost in the life of someone else, cast into the memory of a man who was lost in heaven and was certain he would never again taste of the heavenly gifts.

I swam on. Eventually I did reach the other side, the beginning of the battle lands. I climbed onto the shore. It felt chilly, and not simply because of the water. I knew in my heart that every atom of this land was fundamentally different than that land across the water. Sorrow was here. Pain was here. Hate was here. Anger was here. Death was here.

One final brief look at heaven . . . I had to drink it in one last time. I turned to view the scenery of the Heavenly Realm, but to my crushing realization, it was much farther away than it should have been. It seemed miles now across the river. Heaven was distant, far out on the horizon. Something of a mist or fog seemed to blur the land. The colors were dim, and even the river's water had lost its electric blue.

But then, it hit me. And left me fearfully breathless and in agonizing loneliness. For the first time since I had entered heaven, the lightning above the Throne was gone.

About the Author

GARY LIVENGOOD is an ordained minister and a former musician (mostly jazz). He is happily married to the love of his life, Carol, and is the proud father of two sons, Christopher and Joel, both of whom are married to the loves of their lives (Joy and Meghan). Gary Livengood has a Bachelors Degree in Bible/Theology and also Music, as well as a Masters Degree in Music.